Let the Wild Grasses Grow

Let the Wild Grasses Grow

A Novel

Kase Johnstun

TORREY HOUSE PRESS

Salt Lake City • Torrey

First Torrey House Press Edition, October 2021

Published by Torrey House Press
Salt Lake City, Utah
www.torreyhouse.org

International Standard Book Number: 978-1-948814-51-5
E-book ISBN: 978-1-948814-52-2
Library of Congress Control Number: 2021930393

Cover design by Kathleen Metcalf
Interior design by Rachel Buck-Cockayne
Distributed to the trade by Consortium Book Sales and Distribution

Torrey House Press offices in Salt Lake City sit on the homelands of Ute, Goshute, Shoshone, and Paiute nations. Offices in Torrey are on homelands of Southern Paiute, Ute, and Navajo nations.

To my grandma and grandpa Cordova, I miss you daily.
And to my wife and son, I love you so much.

Prologue

1927

"WHY DO THE COYOTES HOWL AT NIGHT?" I ASKED MY FATHER.

"They howl for you, mija," he said. We sat outside on a mound of wild grass and looked at the stars, listening to the cows moan and the coyotes howl.

"Why would they howl at night for me, Papa?" I asked. I wanted to believe him, but I also wanted the truth.

"Because they want you to sleep soundly knowing that you are protected," he said. To me, his story was flimsy.

"But the coyotes eat baby sheep, Papa. If the coyotes eat baby sheep, then I think they would eat a little Della for sure." I was convinced that I tasted better than sheep. I bathed and cleaned my armpits and even washed all the other places that I knew my older brother Ernesto forgot to wash because he always smelled.

"They would not eat a baby Della, mija, because I will always protect you," he said, but his story had already begun to falter. His tone changed a bit. I could feel him get a little uncomfortable with my questions. He shifted on the mound and became quiet. He hoped that I would give in and move on. I would not.

"But, Papa, you don't howl at night, except for sometimes when you and Mommy play your game in your room when you think we are asleep. So if you don't howl at night, and you will always protect me from the coyotes, and the coyotes *do* howl at night, tell me the truth, Papa, why do the coyotes howl? And, Papa, please, no me meintas." I said. I loved games, but I loved solving them more than playing them.

"Oh, mija, okay, coyotes howl at night because they call to bring their pack together and, sometimes, to warn other packs that this land is theirs. They are territorial. They want to protect what's theirs. So, it's how they talk. It's how they protect each other. Just like us," he said. "I should have known to not give you a simple answer."

My father placed his hand on the back of my neck, the soft skin between thumb and index finger cradling the ridged bones of my spine underneath my hair. The night, to me, in Colorado always felt so full but also so empty at the same time. There were so many stars, and the Milky Way looked as if God himself had taken a paintbrush and swiped white across the black, but, at the same time, the spaces between the stars felt so vast, so full of un- answered questions, so full of riddles bigger than I could solve.

"You tell me it's how they talk to each other. It's like how we talk, but different. If we knew coyote, we would know when they were going to attack our calves. We could tell them, Señor Coyote, please don't eat our calves or our baby sheep because we need them. We could know their words. We would understand their howls. We could talk them out of attacking our calves. We could win," I said, proud to have figured it out.

And then I tried it. I stood and looked up at the moon, I pointed my head to the sky, and I howled to the coyotes, "I know your language now. Stop eating our calves!" My howls cut into the night, and I heard my father muffle a laugh. I cut him a mean look to shut it, just like mother did whenever she wanted anyone in the house to shut their mouths fast. He covered his mouth, but I could still see a smile at the edges of his hands.

I howled and howled until the coyotes howled back. Then I kept howling. I howled until everyone in our family, even my mom with the baby boys in her arms, followed me out into the night. The stars shone bright in the Colorado skies on the high plains outside of Trinidad, Colorado.

Chapter One

Della
1929

I was eight years old. We still had things then. Good things. Extra things. Our fields were full as we walked through them, and I picked apples that hung low from one of the thick trees that lined up and down and up and down our land. I loved those apples.

My mom, for some reason, loved the stinky, wild grasses that grew on our property. She loved them, wouldn't stop talking about them. But I hated the smell they gave off, like rotting butthole.

"Always leave the grasses to grow free around the crops. That's how God wanted the earth to be," she would say when my dad planted his crops in the spring. "Don't take all of their home from them." My mother didn't believe in the one Christian god, always saying that having one god "seems kinda selfish, don't ya think?" and she rarely talked about her upbringing and its spiritual roots, only saying, "when my tribe was forced North, we stayed and dug into the earth," but she always brought up God when she talked about the grasses and the earth, like there was no way she could separate the two. "Let the wild grasses grow. They've always grown for some goddamned reason, so we should let them grow. You hear me, Francisco?"

And my dad did. He always let the grasses grow, for her.

I saw my father's worry grow in the long, thin lines of wrinkles on his face. I was so young, but my dad, the proud Francisco Chavez, began to worry at nights. He would sit alone in the corner after dinner and drink his homemade beer that he brewed out in one of the cattle barns.

There were always so many apples for us, but no one bought them anymore. I remembered how we couldn't grow enough of them. We used to sell them like crazy. Then that stopped.

"It's all going straight to hell, 'Cisco. It's all going straight to hell," my mom would say at dinner. She would walk around the dinner table and curse. Her little frame, not much bigger than that of a child, not quite reaching the five-foot mark, spun around the house like a late-summer tornado in a whirlwind of "shits" and "damns" and "holy hells." We learned to stay out of her direct path.

"We'll be okay, Benita. We'll make it through," he'd reply. His face, unlike my mother's whose lips and forehead twisted with each emotion she felt, stayed calm beneath his dark, pock-marked skin. I could see that he worried, and I could hear what he really meant—that he *hoped* it would be okay. He gave her a simple answer, just like he'd always given me and wished it would stop the conversation. It never did.

"Goddamnit, 'Cisco. Goddamnit," my mom would yell.

"It will be okay, Benita," he'd say. I wanted to believe him.

"Shit, mom, listen to dad," I said once, and I got a light slap across the back of the head by my brother Ernesto, Ernie for short. He did it so that my mom didn't need to, protecting me from her quick, sharp hand.

"Knock it off, Della," he'd say, covering his mouth to hide his laughter.

MANY MEN TRIED TO STEAL the harvested apples from our barn. My father and brother chased the thieves out with pitch forks and knives.

"You thieving spics don't deserve this ranch. Your dirty-blooded wife should go back to the reservation!" the men would yell with a pitchfork nearly straight up their ass.

Those men were lucky my dad and Ernie chased them off because my mom was in the bedroom loading a shotgun, one that my dad took the shells out of every time it happened so that she had to find them, load them after, and run outside. He saved her from jail, or death, by hiding those shells.

ONE DAY, MY FATHER ASKED me to pick as many apples as I could. After, he asked Ernie to take me back up to the house and come back to help him.

"But I want to help too," I yelled to him. I didn't know what Ernie was going to do, but I wanted to be a part of it.

My father reached up, held my hands in his, and said, "You did great today, Della; you have saved so many apples. You are a hero to them."

My belly felt warm with pride as I skipped into the house.

The orchard had been picked bare. The rows and rows of apple trees stood empty-handed on the earth above the rocky soil. At the edge of the orchard, the Colorado grasses ran for hundreds of miles toward Kansas, and the sun dropped pink hues on the fields. It was a beautiful end to a day of work.

My father turned away from me with that same calm but worried look and walked toward the farthest tree in the small orchid. He held a big, sharp axe in his hand. From the kitchen window, I saw him take a long swing into the tall apple tree.

I ran down the stairs and past my mom who did her best to reach out and grab me. "Della, goddamn it, stop," she called out. But I didn't. I ran as fast as I could toward the middle of the orchard. My mother's footsteps hit the dirt only a few feet back.

I stopped in front of my father's axe. He brought it back behind his ears and nearly swung it deep into my neck, but, instead, he balked and slammed the sharp metal blade into the ground in front of him shouting, "Mierda, Della, mierda. I could have killed you, mija."

He left the axe dug into the dirt and wrapped his sweaty

arms around my neck where it would have hit. Instead of sharp, slicing metal, warm skin covered my cold body.

"Papa, why do you want to kill our apple trees?" I asked him. "They are my favorite. They are the best thing we have. I love the apples, Papa," I said. I wrapped my arms around his belly and pleaded for him to come inside. "I will make you pie with them. I will make you jam with them. I will cut them up and put salt on them for you, just like you like them, Papa."

I felt his tears drop down onto my hair. They wetted the thick black hair of his arms that met my forehead. They fell on my cheek and merged with mine like two tributaries meeting at the mouth of a river.

"No, mija, no, the apples must go," he said.

My mom stood on the other side of him near the edge of the house. She dropped her head into her hands for a moment, and then reached out to me to come to her. My dad swung me around with his torso and set me free toward her. I walked into her open arms. She pulled me into her side. My tears turned from warm to cold and fell from my eyes to her thin shoulder that held my cheek. Her black hair, usually pulled back into a ponytail, fell around my shoulders and face and covered me up like a blanket of soft straw. She could be so hard, but she could be so soft too. We turned together toward the house, her arms draped over my shoulders and my stomach, twisted and achy from crying.

The sound of metal hitting wood thwapped behind us.

From the sky, a dark stormfront moved in front of the sun. Like the axe cut into the first apple tree, the dark clouds cut into the blue sky. One half of the sky was blue, the other half black.

From the small kitchen window, I saw the first tree drop to the ground and Ernie swing his axe into another. Only trunks remained where tall, strong trees stood the day before. The orchard turned from what looked like a full, warm beard on the face of the earth to wiry stubbles of wooden whiskers across our land—rough and uneven and dark.

My mom held me. She prayed. She said sorry to the gods. Everything, and I mean everything, during my childhood was religious, the mix of Catholicism and Indian prayers, even though she really believed in none of it. We cried together.

"A sacrifice so we might live. Dios mio," she said.

I watched my dad and older brother chop down trees for two days, and I hated them more and more every time they raised their weapons into the air and swung them downward into the trunk of a tree.

I told myself that I was going to watch and remember everything: every swing, every slice, every cut, and every tree that fell to the ground. And I did. I watched and watched and watched. When they came in for lunch or for dinner, I scowled at them with as mean as eyes as I could. I wanted to chop them down with my anger, the two men I loved most in my life. I wanted to slice them open because I didn't know why they did it, even though they tried to explain it to me.

I WAS MAD. I WAS "damn mad" like my mom use to say before she flew through the house and gathered me up when I said or did something stupid. Like trying to feed a chicken to a cow because, hell, I liked beef—just like my dad did—a lot more than I liked chicken, so I might as well have given the cow and me what we wanted. The cow could get a chicken. I could get more beef, so I swooped up a dead chicken that we had killed for our dinner and threw it into the field where one of our dogs seized it and ran off for his lunch.

"No cow wants to eat chicken, Della. Now you've lost the chicken. Now we have no more meat from that chicken, and I'm damn mad about it! Holy shit, girl, feeding a chicken to a cow?"

* * *

"You are a tree murderer, Papa," I said that evening before he pulled me outside toward the stumps of our orchard.

"Just let the grasses grow. Promise me that," my mother said.

My father nodded at both of us, accepting that was all he could do.

"You are a tree murderer," I said.

With that, I saw that rare anger that comes from the belly of a kind man. He grabbed me by the elbow, and we walked across the stumps of apple trees. They seemed to cry to me. I did not want to look at them. Not at all. I only wanted to kick and hit and bite my father. When we got to the end of the orchard, in a corner of the ranch that could not be seen from my furious perch in the kitchen, one apple tree stood alone.

"This is for you, my smart, mija," he said. "You are too smart for this world. Someday, you must leave this place."

He sat down onto the base of the tree where the brown earth reached up to meet the trunk. The round surface roots pushed the ground up, and the thick bark climbed up the tree behind his body. His body relaxed into the tree, his back finally rested after two days of swinging an ax, and he exhaled.

I fell down next to him.

He wrapped his arms around me.

"Mañana, we will burn this all to plant wheat," he said. "But we will protect your tree. And we will let the wild grasses grow around the farm. Then we will go into town and sell everything we have."

The night sky moved slowly over us, the storm avoiding our home. The stars followed its edge like dolphins riding the crest of a wave. The sky was full and empty all at the same time, just like my heart. The Great Depression had finally hit rural Colorado, and it hit us hard, my father's wrinkles growing and growing like weeds in the corn fields that year.

Chapter Two

John
1929

AT NIGHT, I SAT UP AND LISTENED TO MY MOTHER COOK. IT PUT me to sleep and made me feel comfortable and happy in my bed next to my brothers and sisters.

The slice of her thick, sharp knife skinned potatoes, and the smell of diced tomatoes cut the air. A slim light fell through the jaggedly thin crack between our bedroom door and the broken door jam, or, more correct, between the bedroom door and the splintered edge of the wall that shut all four of us in. Manuel was the oldest. He was older than Maria by two years, older than me by almost three years, and older than Paulo by seven years. He was my best friend. He always seemed like a man to me, long before he was one.

My mom separated the pinto beans from the pebbles that found their way into the large canvas sack that my dad, Tomas, bought from Henrique the bean seller down the road. The four of us fell asleep every night to the sound of a butter knife tapping the top of the table and sliding across the fake wood. Clap, slide, clap, slide, slide. Our loud breath in each other's ears. I loved them all.

My parents put us all to bed early on Friday nights, so they could talk and drink cold beer and laugh. When I would wake up, their talking sounded like waves, crashing and rolling up and down on the ocean's back. And the smell of food, of tamales steaming, of beans cooking, of chicharrones sizzling in a pan, and of cheeses baking in the oven, made me want to stay forever in the moment when my dad laughed and my mom cooked. When they said things like, "Those boys are going to drive me to the insane house," or, "That girl has the courage and sassy mouth of her mama, but because she's darker than you she won't have it so easy."

My mom was beautiful, a very light-skinned woman from Northeastern Mexico, where most of the indigenous population got routed out and killed leaving only a few of the old-country people there to carry on the dark skin. When she came to Colorado in the early 1900s, people didn't even think she was Mexican. Her skin was fair. She had blue eyes. She was treated good, and she got away with being white when she wanted to. Hell, her mom and dad made it to the US with no problem, just walking across the border, though the border was a different thing back then. Americans wanted Mexicans to build the railroads and dams, practically inviting them in with open arms, until it all got built, making them illegal after.

The eastern slopes of Colorado were no picnic though.

My dad was darker, not super dark like the Mayans or any of those flat-faced people that he used to talk about, but dark like Montezuma. And he was strong. So strong. He used to put his arm out for us to hang on, all four of us dangling from his biceps that were built in the mines.

I would wake up and peek through the crack between the door and the wall. My mom, with her apron roped around her, would adjust the knobs on the oven to bring the temperatures down, to keep the food warm and to keep the beans cooking through the night. As soon as those knobs were in the right place, my dad would slap my mom on the butt, pick her up with one arm, and carry her to their bedroom. I don't think they planned on having all of us kids, one right after the other.

We were real serious Catholics though. Babies came when the Lord wanted them to come. That's what my dad always said.

MY MOM, EVERY NIGHT AT 10:50 p.m., would pack up her purse, dropping her old Spanish Bible from her grandmother into it, throw on a shawl even during the hottest summer months when Trinidad baked in the night, and walk two blocks to Saint Joseph's Catholic Church. The church had been around since the century turned, so in the late 1920s when I was a boy, it had already begun to wear down. The wooden siding had darkened from bright white to dark yellow and gray. The desert winds, filled with sharp fingers of sand, stripped a lot of the paint off, and exposed the old wood that sucked in the rains and began to soften. The spire had begun to tilt.

My mom said that it tilted toward Bethlehem to honor the birth of our Lord Jesus Christ. My dad, when it came to any other matter would tease my mom about her answers, but he wouldn't dare tease her about her faith because he would get a slap from her, and he feared "getting a slap from the baby Jesus" too.

Mom left at night and performed adoration. Someone always had to keep watch on the eucharist, sitting in church and praying, so my mom did what she felt was her duty. She relieved Father Ronald every night at 11p.m. so he could go and drink some whiskey before going to bed.

"It's my duty to help Father Ronald. He deserves a drink with all the sinners out there. You two, especially," she said. She pointed at me and Maria. "You two are troublemakers." She laughed and then pointed directly at Maria, "Stop being a troublemaker. You can't get away with it."

She would take me with her sometimes. I didn't mind. I'd fall asleep on the pews, thankful for a fair and righteous God who protected us.

She'd push open the large wooden doors, all the weight of her little frame leaning into it, hang her coat on the rack next to the Holy Water, dip her middle finger in the clear liquid, perform the sign of the cross so largely that God could see her do it from heaven, walk up to the front row of the church, and kneel down—the Eucharist in perpetual adoration in a humble amber that hung on the wall behind the altar.

In a few minutes I'd be asleep.

"Get up, John. Time to go home, mijo," she'd say later. In her face, you could see the love of Jesus and her gratitude for my father's mining job and the food on our table and for her kids.

Most of the time, she had to wake up Father Ronald before we left, but this didn't bother her, "He's tired from tending his flock. He's praying in his dreams."

"He's borracho," my father once said. And he got a slap across his head.

"If he's drunk, it's because of children like yours and men like you, always judging people and talking during Mass," she said.

She went there every evening, even on Christmas and Easter. She'd throw on her shawl and walk to the church. Even when my dad finally got a car and offered to drive her in the snowy months, she said no. To her, adoration began the second she left our home. If the car engine, rumbling outside the church doors, woke Father Ronald then she would not be completing her adoration in the way the baby Jesus wanted her to do so. She loved her Lord. She adored him.

My father, however, worshipped in a different way, mainly because he feared his Lord.

"I did enough to go to hell before I turned thirteen years old," my father would say. "I need to spend the rest of my life making up for it." At Mass, when my father sang, he sang louder than any other person, belting out the lyrics of "Silent Night" and especially "Storm of Terror, Grief and Error," thinking that the Lord was speaking directly to him. If one of us broke our gaze during the ceremony of transubstantiation, my dad would flip his ring around on his hand and give us a whack on the skull. If we cried because of it, he would whack us again. He feared hell. And he didn't want to wear the sins of his children on his shoulders along with his own.

"Callete la boca," he'd say.

"I wasn't talking," I'd say.

"You're talking now, aren't you, niño, so cierralo," he'd say.

But once Mass ended on Sunday morning, my father seemed to open up his wings and fly, really relaxing for the first time all week, except for those late nights when he sat and sipped on Coors and talked to my mom in the kitchen while she prepped meal after meal.

When Mass was over, he'd throw as many of us children on his back as he could and swing us around and tickle us and play hard until he fell asleep on the couch, his head resting on the yarn-covered pillow, in the late afternoon. After he woke up, his quiet and sad demeanor woke up with him. The stress of heading back into the gold mines where he would spend the next four days in a mining camp filled his blood. He and a hundred other men from Trinidad would wake up around 4:00 a.m. on Monday morning, meet up at the train station, jump in the back of a freight box or flat car and ride the twenty-two miles to the mine. They would begin work at 5:00 a.m., work sixteen-hour days and clock out on Thursday evenings to ride the train car home. It took my dad all of Friday to gain his strength to sit in the chair on Friday night and tease my mom with a cold Coors in his hand. It took him until Sunday afternoon to gather the fortitude to play with us kids, though he always gave us plenty of love through large hugs and tosses of hair when we walked by the kitchen table.

MY FATHER HAD A GARDEN in Trinidad. He grew corn and chile peppers. The desert corn grew in the spring, and we harvested it in the early summer. It was black and red and green because it didn't have all the water in it. Colorado didn't have the water. It was the high plains. My mom would fry the corn in olive oil until it became crispy and crunchy. She mixed it with everything to add more weight to our meals. We were poor, so corn and frijoles came with every meal. They filled us up. Helped us grow.

But it was always about the chiles for my dad. He loved them as much as he loved his family, and he loved us all a lot.

My dad grew them in the summer. His chiles grew really good in the dry air, but they didn't like the sun. It's true. They'd dry up in the direct rays.

"They'll shrivel up like old ladies' boobies," he'd say to us, and then do the sign of the cross to ask for forgiveness.

Once the peppers began to sprout from the plant, my dad yelled to us kids, "Get out here now! It's time to cover them up, mijos!"

I loved hearing that. We ran as fast as we could to him.

He lay a ten-by-ten-foot blue tarp that he stole from the mines on the ground outside our house before breakfast, usually the first Sunday that it really felt like summer. That week, if the temperature hit the mid-nineties before Sunday, I knew my dad laid in his bed in the mine dormitory and thought about his chile peppers and wished that he were home to save them. I could see his smile.

"John, get out here, mijo, get out here!"

We all spread the canvas out on the ground. He stuck four thick, large pieces of dead wood into the ground at the four corners of the chile garden.

"Let's work," he said. His smile made all of us smile.

My mom hugged his shoulders. She knew. I knew. We all knew that he spent his life in the dark mine dreaming about the days he could live and work in the sun with his family.

He nodded to us all.

"Raise it up, raise it up," he said.

We all grabbed an edge of the canvas, raised up on our tippy toes to not rub the tops of the pepper plants with the blue, scratchy covering, and tied the corner of the canvas to the dead wood. The canvas covered the plants and kept them from drying up in the hot sun. The anchos and mirasol (that eventually became the guajillos), the super-hot güeros all lived in the shade until he would yell to himself in the early summer, "Let's harvest the beautiful boobies," giving the sign of the cross.

Little Paulo, my younger brother, held his end of the canvas so tight that we lifted him off the ground when we pulled it up into the air. When his grip gave out, he fell to the ground and landed on his head.

At the end of the spring, when it started to get really hot, we harvested the chiles. My father took a basket to the garden on Sunday afternoon, right after leaving church. He wore cut-off canvas shorts, ragtag from the mines. He never let us help him, at first. We wanted to. We felt like we deserved to. We spent the spring watering the chiles and rewrapping the canvas around the wooden posts after a windstorm. We felt entitled to help pick the harvest, but my father ushered us inside the house and walked out toward the chile garden, his rough, mine-wrinkled hands wrapped around the thick handle made of bent sticks.

He spent the whole afternoon in the garden picking the chiles. If he was in a hurry, he could have picked them all in ten minutes or less, but he wasn't.

He began with the guajillos and ran his fingers along the bright red skin. Before he picked them, he would touch their shiny green stems and whisper a prayer to Saint Fiacre, the patron saint of gardeners and vegetables.

"My dear guajillos," he said. "My dear guajillos."

With a slight twist of his wrist, he tore the stem from the plant and moved on to the next chile. When he finished the guajillos, he moved on to the florescent, yellow güero chiles. He said a prayer to the Virgin of Guadalupe, the patron saint of Mexico.

When he got to the anchos, he held the biggest of the three peppers in his hands, the purple and reds matching his mine-stained eyes, and prayed to Saint Joseph, the patron saint of fathers. His hands held the dark green stems like they held a baby, swaddling them with his fingers and palms.

With his basket full, he walked back toward the house and

bathed the peppers in hot water in a giant porcelain bowl for ten minutes.

"Oh, my peppers," he said. "The mine is so grey, but you are so beautiful."

"What are you all standing around for? Help me with these," he said, smiling.

We pulled the anchos, the guajillos and the güeros from the water. Each of us, except for Paulo because he might hurt himself, held a very long string, probably six feet long, with a needle tied to the end of it. My father placed all the peppers on a giant towel, wrapped them up, and did his best to drain all the water he could from their bright bodies. He divided them up among us all.

We drove our needles through the stem of the first pepper and then stuck it in fully through the next one until our strings held a long row.

He waited for me to finish up my line of chilies and hung them perpendicularly across our laundry line. When they all were attached, we clasped hands—this time with Manuel and mom included—and we said the prayer for the blessing of the harvest in complete unison.

"Almighty Lord God, You keep on giving abundance to men in the dew of heaven, and food out of the richness of the soil. We give thanks to Your most gracious majesty for the fruits of the field which we have gathered. We beg of You, in Your mercy, to bless our harvest, which we have received from Your generosity. Preserve it, and keep it from all harm. Grant, too, that all those whose desires You have filled with these good things may be happy in Your protection. May they praise Your mercies forever, and make use of the good things that do not last in such a way that they may not lose those goods that are everlasting, through Christ our Lord. Amen."

"My beautiful hanging boobies," he said. Then the sign of the cross. "You give us life."

We all went back inside the house. Then he fell asleep on the edge of his bed and rested for the long week ahead in the gold mines.

It was the best week of the year for him, for us, but the world, outside of home, ached for help. Della and her family, I knew that the Depression had begun to squeeze them hard. That's why I always walked her to the truck that took her home. You know, I wanted to make sure she was okay and smiled. She liked the stories about my chilies, so I think that helped some too.

Chapter Three

Della
1930

I USED TO BOSS THIS BOY AROUND AT SCHOOL. HE WAS QUIET like Ernie and my dad, so I liked him immediately. And he liked me, so I figured that if he was going to follow me around all over the place that I should get some use of him.

"John, go get me some water from the fountain, please and thank you," I said. I always said please and thank you. I was no damned jerk. He would grab my little canteen, run to the fountain, and pump some water out for me.

I wasn't really thirsty, but like I said, if he was going to follow me around, I might as well take full advantage of it. His older brother Manuel was in Ernie's class. They were friends too, so I figured I should be friends with John.

Sometimes, after he got me some water or carried my books to the edge of the town where a bunch of us were picked up and taken back to the ranches, I would even let him talk about his damn chile patch.

"I got a big chile patch," he said. "I start growing chilies in the early spring and when I harvest them in early summer, I ask my family to help me out to make sure we pluck them really fast. They love to help me out, but I do most of the work, Della. I work really hard at it. I'm kind of master of my chilies."

He rarely talked about anything else, so I just started talking to stop him from talking about his chilies.

"I lost all my apple trees except for one," I said. "My dad cut them down."

John stared quiet for what seemed like forever. "I'm sorry about your apple trees."

His silence made me so angry for some reason. I don't know why, so I slugged him hard on the arm and pushed him off the stump in the road.

"It's not like I cried about it or anything," I said.

"Okay," he said.

Our ride pulled up alongside us.

I jumped in the back with Ernie and the rest of the kids.

John walked away toward Trinidad where the mining kids would jump on the back of another truck that took them to their houses just outside of town.

He probably missed the truck that day to walk with me, to carry my books, and to sit and tell me about his damn chile patch again.

I think he missed his ride every day, but he never admitted it.

One day, after school, I told John to go get me some water.

"I'm thirsty, John," I said. "Can you run and get me some water?"

John looked at me and said, "No. I am too tired today. We worked all day yesterday in the garden, and I think you could go get me some water for once, Della. My whole family helped me with my chilies. They're really nice like that. My dad even put his Coors away to help me with the chilies."

"John, I think I told you to go get me some goddamned water," I said, doing my best to channel whatever it was that mother used to get us to do things. But John didn't goddamned like it. I'd seen his family at church and stuff, and I saw his brothers and sisters at school. They were quiet and kind, and I don't think John had ever heard the word goddamned before in his entire goddamned life because the look he gave me was one of terror, like Lucifer himself was going to reach up from the under the earth, grab me by my long, black ponytail, and drag me right into hell. John's eyes widened so big that I knew I had to say, "Sorry, John. Would you like me to get us both some water?"

"No thank you," John said. "I really don't mind." He walked toward the well at school and pulled up the bucket. He dripped the water into his little metal canteen and brought some over to me. Instead of walking directly back to the truck that took us home, John and I sat there and talked for two more hours.

"Can you tell me more about your chilies? You told me about how you planted them. How do you harvest them?" I asked him. Hell, I knew all of this. I was a ranchera. I knew how to harvest everything under God's sun, but the smile that came on his face grew so wide that I too became enthralled in his story about his damn chilies, like I was there with his whole family harvesting them myself.

We were so young, eight or nine years old, but I knew what it meant to touch someone. When he began to talk, I placed my hand on his, and I never bossed him around again. All he had to do—though I didn't know this before it happened—was tell me "no" and kindly forgive me.

Chapter Four

John
1930

On the Friday after we strung the chilies up in the sun, my father walked through the door, his face covered in dust and exhaustion, just like every week.

"Coors," he said. "Hand me a Coors."

My mother placed a cold beer on the table for him. He showered and threw on his cut-off shorts and an old shirt that he got during their honeymoon in Mexico City. With a wave of his arms, all of his kids sitting patiently on the couch in anticipation, he ushered us outside.

Just like he had prayed to Saint Fiacre, to the Lady of Guadalupe, to Saint Joseph, we all, together, prayed:

Bendícenos Señor, bendice estos alimentos que por tu bondad vamos a recibir, bendice las manos que los prepararon dale pan al que tiene hambre y hambre de ti al que tiene pan. Amén.

Always in Spanish. Always together.

"Let's pull them," he said. His voice rose up like a preacher talking to his congregation. "Pull them!"

Then, slowly, like we'd been taught, we reached for the edge of the strings, pulled them off the laundry lines, two of us for each string of peppers, and dropped them gracefully into woven baskets. Mama and Papa slid their hands along the strings until all the peppers fell freely on top of each other.

Mama brought a big mortar and pestle made of lava rock out onto the dirt beneath the laundry rope and placed it next to the chile baskets on the ground. We all sat on handwoven blankets, except for baby Paulo who ran around us like a bee circling a hive trying to get in. He eventually found a spot next to Manuel and plopped down on the hard dirt to watch the family work.

My father handed one guajillo and one güero to me and one to my mom.

"Flora," he said.

She took a little knife from the pocket of her apron and slit open the chilies. She placed the knife back into her apron, rubbed her thumb and index finger together and pinched the guajillo pepper between them. Using her long thin finger-nail, she dug the seeds out of the pepper by pulling her finger backward toward the palm of her hand. She repeated the same movement with the güero, and then she handed the peppers to Manuel who dropped them in the mashing bowl and ground them up. My father handed two more peppers to my mother to deseed them. She ran her nail through them and then handed that set to Maria who pulled a thin knife from her pocket and sliced the peppers into not-too-thin sections.

They did this until they made it all the way through the güeros and guajillos and we had storage bottles full of ground and not-too-thinly sliced peppers to spice and flavor our food for the next year.

When my father pulled the anchos from the basket and handed them to my mother, I knew it was time for me and Man-uel to put in some elbow grease.

"Boys, get to work," he said.

"Boys," my mom repeated.

The anchos shone bright black and purple in the sun. They had dried up just like the other two peppers, but they would soon find reprieve from their wrinkled skin. My mother took Maria into her kitchen along with the mortar and pestle. She placed two step stools next to the counter that lined the gas burner on our oven made of rusting aluminum and chipped porcelain. It sat on four thin legs under our kitchen window, the only ventila-tion for cooking that we had.

"My sweet Maria," she said. "Lista?"

She placed the anchos in a pot, drawing their dried black skin in the water, and they began to swell to life again, like God had breathed air into the shrunken and blackened lungs of a coal miner.

"Live, anchos, live," my mom said, signing the cross as she spoke.

She brought the water to a boil. The peppers floated to the top of the water and rode the bubbles from one end of the pot to the other. After twenty minutes, Maria and I were ready to do some real work. She pulled the bright purple anchos from the pot and dropped two into the mortar along with a couple spoonfuls of the water.

Maria grabbed the pestle and pressed hard down into the mortar, grinding the peppers as hard as she could against the rocky skin of the bowl. Her muscles tightened. She twisted and pushed the pestle until her arms weakened and handed it over to me. I pushed hard too, tiring quickly but not stopping until the peppers had turned to a thick, viscous paste in the mortar.

"Bueno, John, bueno," she said.

Following suit, I did the sign of the cross. Life felt perfect.

My mom spooned out the paste into the stock that had simmered in the pot and added garlic and salt and sugar. Maria and I continued to make thick chile paste. When all the peppers were pasted and added back into the pot of stock and spices, my mother heated the water again and stirred the mixture until it made a thin, rich red sauce.

That night, we would have a big meal with ancho sauce at the center of it all. We would stew chicken and pork in the sauce with bitter chocolate to make what I thought to be the best mole this side of the Mexico and US border.

"Oh, God, this is good," I said.

"Slap your brother for me, Maria," my mom said, half a smile on her face.

Maria slapped the back of my head as hard as she could.

"Don't say the Lord's name in vain, John," my dad said.

"But holy God, this is good," my dad said.

Paulo reached up and tapped the back of my father's head.

"The mine is so dark, and you all are so beautiful," my dad said. "I never want to leave you again."

Chapter Five

Della
1930

MY MOM SAID SHE STARTED WEARING A PISTOL IN A HARNESS strapped across her chest because of what she called, "Della's big mouth." I disagree with her on that. She started carrying that pistol because of the Ku Klux Klan, not me.

After we cut down our apple trees, Ernie and I drove the tractor the whole way from the ranch to Trinidad, sitting close together on the raised seat. The wind blew so cold that our faces turned bright red and caked up with drying tears.

The rest of my family crammed into the front cab of our old Chevy truck. I watched the changing leaves across the valley. The reds and oranges and yellows fell against the browning of the shallow mountains that led to the spiky peaks on the horizon. The snows had already hit the tops of the mountains and covered their rocky tips like icing on bulky cakes. I loved the fall. It spoke to me more than any other season, maybe because it's the season that I always wished would stay around the longest but always seemed to be the shortest, sometimes summer holding onto the days too long and winter deciding to come too early. Fall made me relish the days, made me ache for them to stay.

Trinidad sat in the valley of Fishers Peak, a dominating mesa that shot out of the ground, covered in scrub oak and hard dirt, a natural landmark that marked the path of the famous Santa Fe Trail that ran from Independence, Missouri, through Trinidad, a bustling railroad and mining hub of nearly fifteen thousand people. Gentle, grass and scrub covered slopes rose gently out of the town's city center that housed the stone covered Las Animas County building, the county library, and liquor stores whose signs saying "Liquor" had been covered up with bright red Xs over the letters. An old train line that had been converted into a small trolly ran down main street. The main train station, built up in its small-town grandiosity sat just outside of town. The county courthouse, at the center of town, rose up out of the flat ground just like Fishers Peak, but instead of rock shooting straight up, pillars of stone that rivaled the Romans' created a grand entrance. Our little truck and tractor rolled into town like a snail entering a small mound of boulders.

A large white sign that read "Confederate Reunion Rodeo and Parade, 1930" hung from the Opera House on one side of the street to the Trinidad Hotel on the other side of the street. It flapped in the slight breeze, and crowds could be heard cheering from only hundreds of feet away.

My dad got out of the truck, helped us down from the tractor and hugged us, and led us to the cab of the truck and left the thing running so the heat from the engine would warm our skin.

"God bless Larry," my mom said. She looked up at the sky as if in prayer, but, instead, she pointed at the sign that hung across the road. "But let's get the goddamned hell out of here as soon as we can. Crazy is in the air. A whole lot of crazy. And this type of crazy doesn't like us."

LARRY WAS THE REASON WE had the car in the first place. He owned a hardware store in Denver for a couple decades and had a nice life until his wife died during childbirth, leaving him completely alone in the city. He bought a piece of land, a nice farm truck. He bought some cattle. He bought a tractor. And he planted his first season of corn and wheat. He was a true gabacho. But my family loved him.

When Larry got lonely, he drove his fancy truck over to our house and scared the sheep and mules halfway to hell when he did. It didn't much bother the cows and the bulls, but it sure scared the hell out of the mules. They would honk and moan as soon as his truck came over the hill on the stage tracks. We knew he was coming long before he pulled up next to our old fence. He joined us for dinner two or three times a week when the harvest was good, before we had to burn down the apple trees.

Sometimes he drank too much of my father's homemade beer and whiskey and cried because of his wife. My father would lean over the table and place his hand on his arm to comfort him. Larry would place his own hand on my dad's, prop his forehead on both their hands, and sob.

"There's no room for this crying from grown men," my mom yelled.

"I'm sorry," Larry said.

"Stop goddamned crying," my mom said.

She stood up from the table, grabbed a wooden spoon and smacked Larry across the top of the head and then smacked my dad, leaving bright red marks on the skin of their balding heads.

"My boys don't need to see you cry like this. Stop crying now," she said, and as if he were one of us throwing a fit, she mimicked Larry's whine, "If you don't stop crying, I'll give you something to cry about, and you, Francisco, if you don't stop holding his hand, your friend can't come over for supper anymore."

"Goodbye, all," Larry said. He felt embarrassed. "Thank you for dinner. It was lovely. I'm sorry for my drunkenness."

"It's not that you're borracho," my mom said. "It's your damn baby tears. I'm sorry you lost your family. I truly am, but if my father were here and saw you crying in front of his grandchildren, he would beat your ass. You know that, right? And you, Francisco," she turned to my dad, "You should beat yourself for holding this man's hand all night long. What? What? Do you want your boys to grow up to be jotos? Pull yourself together, Francisco."

"I think it's okay if they cry," I said to my mom. "I think it's okay if they hold hands, too."

My mother picked up her wooden spoon, pulled me up from my seat at the table, and whacked me across the ass with the damn thing.

"No, no, Della, it's not okay. You don't have to run this farm when you grow up. You don't have to work like your brothers do. They can't see this. They can't live in a house where men cry and hold hands. They have to have families of their own someday, and they have to teach their boys to be tougher to survive in this country, this country where every white man, except for crybaby Larry here, wants to shoot us. They wear their hoods. They burn their crosses. The goddamned governor of Colorado is a grandmaster. A goddamned grandmaster, Della. He hates you because you're Indian. He hates you because you're dark. He hates your father because he owns land. He hates us all because we're Cattolica. He wants to kill us. Him and every other man like him. You see, Della," she whacked me again, this time across the back of legs, "you see. Your brothers can't watch this cry baby and think that all white men are like him. The governor is a goddamned elected Klansman."

"Don't be a nina, Larry, okay," I told him.

The next morning, in the middle of winter, Larry drove back to Denver where he would shoot himself in the head with a .22 rifle and survive, only to be shipped off to some mental hospital to live the rest of his days eating pudding and shitting in a diaper. At least that's how my mom described it. My father said it more gently, "Our friend will have to have others care for his needs from now on."

"Thank God he left his goddamned truck as a gift," my mom said. Then she caught the cruelty in what she said. To her, she didn't mean to be uncaring. She only cared so much about the family in front of her that she sometimes failed to care about anything else. "God bless his soul. I know that if I lost you all, I'd probably shoot myself in the head too, and I got the gun to do it."

* * *

In town that day, my mom's eyes moved from us to the parade coming down the road. She quickly changed from the reverent, "God bless Larry," to, "Goddamnit! Holy shit, goddamnit. This is why Larry was a bad damned influence."

"Kids, let's go. Get in the truck," my dad said. "Get in the truck now."

A parade approached us from the end of main street in Trinidad. Boy Scouts rode on horses and waved Confederate flags in the air. Their uniforms were perfectly pressed, and they smiled like they had no bigger smiles to give. Their scout leaders rode next to them in Confederate uniforms, the Denver Hotel and the American Diner shading their eyes from the sun that had begun to drop in the west.

Men in white capes and white pointy hoods walked toward us. Children ran alongside them, and horses pulled other men in a cart behind them—men with patches on their chest and their eyes poking out from the large holes cut into their silly, pointy hoods that, to me, looked like bad clown costumes that weren't quite finished or ready for the party.

"Let's go," my mom said. Before we could gather all of our things and place them into the back of our Chevy, the KKK was upon us.

"Keep your mouth shut, Della," my mom said.

"Me? Why me? What's wrong with my mouth? Everyone else has mouths. Why do I have to keep my mouth shut?" I asked.

"Callete la boca, Della, quiet," my dad said. He placed his hand on my shoulder and scooped up one of my little brothers. Ernie scooped up the other.

Since there were no African Americans living in Southern Colorado, the KKK had to hate someone, so they hated us. They actually called it their mission to rid this part of the United States of America of all us. They didn't care if you were Spanish or Mexican or Indian or a mix of them, which I am. They only cared that you *weren't* them.

"Hurry, mijos, get all that stuff in the back," my dad said. "Get it all in. We need to go. We need to go now."

"Why are those people wearing those hats?" I asked. "I think they look like stupid idiots."

Children of the Klansman ran up and down the lines of men. Their little legs carried them in and around their fathers and uncles and brothers and grandfathers, weaving like birds around tree branches. It must have been the way the men walked or carried themselves, but all the children knew who their family members were, even though they were covered in those stupid clown outfits. They would run up to them and hold their hands as if they were in some kind of Thanksgiving parade.

The women, too. They walked with their men. They carried pies like it was Easter. They wore their Sunday best. It was a family event. They smiled like they were going to have a cake walk afterward.

It looked kind of fun, just like any other parade, really.

They smiled and waved and held banners that said KEEP THIS COUNTRY PURE. KEEP THE SPICS OUT. KEEP AMERICA CLEAN. MAKE AMERICA GREAT. Children's faces were smeared with chocolates, and the women were smiling with pride. The men were young and old. The size of their midsections told this truth. The ropes around the waists of the young men tightened against flat stomachs, and the excess rope fell down nearly to their knees. The ropes of the older men stretched out along their frumpy waists and got caught up between the bottom of their bellies and the top of their thighs. They dangled only a few inches down from the curl of the round knot that clung to them like a barnacle doing its best to not lose the side of a boat when it swayed over a portly wave.

"Look, the fat ones look like marshmallow treats," I said loudly.

"Della, callete," my dad whispered. "Shut it, Mija."

There was laughing and singing. The tossing of candy. Dogs

running around. The sheriff of the town sat on a step outside his office. He too, somehow in the Depression, had to spread his legs in order for his belly to find room to hang down when he sat there. He reminded me of a mom giving birth, his belly the baby and the stairs below him, the stirrups. He just smiled and watched the parade go by. Bygones be bygones, I could imagine him saying in his mind, the butts of rifles sitting in the arms of some of the men like babies in the arms of their mothers. It was a goddamned family picnic.

They smiled until they saw my small family hurriedly packing our things in the back of the truck.

"Why are they staring at us?" I asked.

Two men at the front of the parade pointed toward us. Three other men walked in unison toward my family. Two wore jeans and work boots. The third wore slick, black slacks and shiny, black dress shoes. That's all that showed, except for the popping veins in their white hands and the thick black hair on the backs of their wrists.

My father put all of us behind him with one sweep of his arm.

One man put a wheat bag from the back of the truck onto his shoulders and then threw it at Ernesto, hard enough to knock him back but not hard enough to force him to the ground. This pissed the man off. He picked up a shovel that had been lain on the ground to take home with us and swung it at Ernesto's face. Ernie ducked, and the shovel hit one of his companions instead.

That gave Ernesto his chance. My older brother ran back toward us, ducking another punch that had been thrown at him, and stood next to my father. Within a minute, five of the men who were left standing, the sixth still bleeding on the hot blacktop on main street, circled our family.

And I saw it. Fear.

Their eyes peered out from behind the eyeholes in their hoods. We scared them, somehow. Somehow, the six of us, even the littlest of our family, scared these men.

The sheriff at this point had gotten up off his step and moved toward us.

I saw him coming out of the corner of my eye. He placed his hand on the butt of his gun that sat in its holster around his waist.

Like we had become celebrities, the crowd gathered around us.

I lifted my fist up to the first man whose eyes I could see.

I unraveled my middle finger from the middle of my folded knuckles, "Chingate."

The man's eyes changed from fear to anger.

He raised his hand to slap me down.

My father's arm swung out in front of my face to block the man's open-faced hand. Then his friend, seeing the opening, hit my father's arm, the one extended out in front of me, with the butt of his gun.

I heard, simultaneously, the break of a forearm and the deafening echo of the sheriff's gun that had flung a bullet into the sky.

Chapter Six

John
1930

My dad was proud of his car. He was really proud. He loved his car almost as much as his chilies.

Nobody who worked in the mines and who had dark skin had a car. But he saved up for it, not telling my mom what he was doing, and drove it home one Friday afternoon.

He pulled it around the garden and right up to the front door and parked it in front of the tiny kitchen window to make sure my mother saw it. When Manuel realized who it was, he flung open the front door, sprinted to the car, and silently, in pious admiration, ran his fingers along the long, smooth curve of the fender, hovered over the front tire, and swooped his hand down the side toward the back tire.

"I worked out a deal with my foreman. I slipped el jefe two dollars a week for years to buy it, Flora. It's ours," dad said. "I only had to smell myself all the way home," he laughed.

He waved his hands over the Auburn 5 Passenger Brougham.

"We don't need a car," my mom said. "Jesus didn't have a car. He had a mule. All we need is a mule. I think this is too much. It's greedy."

"In Trinchera's history," he said, "I am the first Mexican miner to own a car. Hell, I am the first Mexican to own a car, I think. And I don't care! It feels wonderful. Does anyone need anything from town? I can drive us there."

"This smells like pride to me, honey," my mom said. "You smell like pride. Pride never leads to anything good."

"I worked hard, Flora. This was not a gift. This was not luck.

I worked hard to earn it. I have pride in my hard work, thank you, Jesus," my dad said.

He leaned across the front seat and opened the passenger-side door, nearly hitting Manuel in the head, and then leaned back and opened the driver's side door. I jumped in. Manuel, within a second, squeezed next to me on the back bench seat, leaving room for Maria to slide in next to him and shut the door behind her. The three of us sat snuggled up behind my father whose hands draped over the very large steering wheel, still caked in the thick layer of earth that he lived under for four days a week.

"Get in, Flora, and bring the baby boy. Let's go to town," he said.

He waited patiently while my mom threw off her apron and grabbed Paulo by the hand. He wiggled in her grasp, but she shoved him into the front seat next to my dad, placing a hand over his whining mouth to quiet him.

She smiled.

Once the door was shut, my dad pushed his foot down hard on the spatula-sized clutch, wrapped his hand around the black stick shift, and crammed the Auburn into gear. The transmission ground into movement. And my family, for the first time in my life, rode in a car together. Feeling the machine move around us, its thin tires kicking up the dust of the clay earth into the low sky, felt powerful, like we were in control of our world, like we—one of the poor families on the edge of a gold mining town—were a part of something new, no longer the riffraff on the outside.

About twenty minutes later, we pulled into Trinidad. My dad stopped at an intersection when a flying bottle flew toward the car and broke on the side the thick metal.

"Get out of here, spics!" a man in a white mask yelled toward us. A parade of white masked and hooded men walked through the streets of our town. The parade seemed to consume the whole street like white caps on the edge of a river, bursting and bobbing and ready to slam into anything it could.

A giant chicken head slammed bloody against our front windshield.

My father slammed on the gas, spinning out his tires on the gravel road.

"Pride, you see, Tomas, pride put us here!" my mom said.

"Wait, Papa!" I yelled. After a wave of men passed us and the blood from the chicken thinned as the head slid down the glass, I saw Della. Men in white hoods surrounded her family. I wanted to cry out, but Manuel beat me to it.

"Papa. It's Ernie and Della's family!" Manuel yelled. "We have to help them."

Paulo cried in my mother's arms, and Maria opened the car door to run to them. She was always brave without thinking about it.

"Stop her," my father yelled. "Stop your sister."

Manuel pulled her back and slammed the heavy metal door behind her.

A group of men in hoods walked toward the Chavez family. The sheriff got up off his step. One of the men threw Ernie backward, but he did not fall.

"Chingate!" Della yelled. I could hear my friend's voice across the expanse of the dirt road.

One of the men swung down toward her, but her father blocked the blow with his arm.

"Tomas!" my mom yelled.

"Okay," he said.

The sheriff's gun went off.

"I got an idea," my father said.

Again, he slammed on the gas. This time he pointed the car directly in Della's direction like he planned to hit her entire family.

"Tomas," my mother yelled.

He drove the car closer and closer at a speed that made me sweat. At the last moment, before slamming into Della's truck and her family, he yanked the wheel and then skidded to a stop. He placed the car between the KKK and Della's family. The Chavezes did not hesitate. They jumped in their truck, leaving their tractor behind, the kids crowding in the empty truck bed. They too spun out on the gravel and drove toward home, spitting up hundreds of tiny rocks in the masks of the men on the road.

We followed, a dead and bloody chicken head on the front of my father's new car, staining it permanently.

Chapter Seven

Della
1930

WE HAD ONLY BEEN HOME A COUPLE MINUTES WHEN JOHN AND his family knocked on the door of our home after the showdown with those stupid, hooded assholes. My mom acted weird. She stood with her arms wide open and greeted each one of them with a hug. She began with Flora, then Tomas, then Manuel, Maria, and then my friend John. When the littlest of them all came in, she scooped him up and hugged him tightly.

I'd never seen her do this with anyone before. It was like she had been taken over by some crazy white lady.

"Della, take John outside. Ernie, you and Manuel, go and light the fire in the pit. The rest of you, sit here," she said. Then she reached toward Maria and gave her another hug, "Aren't you beautiful?"

My dad shook Señor Garcia's hand.

"Can you help me with this?" he asked. He pointed to his broken arm that had fallen limp below the elbow.

"Of course," Señor Garcia said.

John didn't say anything. He was probably thinking about his chilies.

"I've seen this a lot," Tomas said. "People break things in the mines every day. We fix them up until they can see a doctor."

"Go outside, kids," my mom said, this time ushering every child outside the front door.

"I think I'll stay," I said. "I want to see."

"Della, get the hell out of my kitchen before I toss you out," my mom said. She smiled at Señora Garcia, a glance that said, "Kids, they never listen, especially this daughter of mine."

"Della, go outside, mija," my dad said.

"No, I think I'll stay," I said. I knew that my mom would control her temper with our guests there, the ones she hugged too tightly. I could probably say "shit" and "damn it all to hell" and "shit the bed" and survive without a smack to my head.

But I felt a tiny squeeze above my elbow. John had wrapped his hand around the bottom of my triceps and whispered, "I'd like to see your apple tree, Della. Can you show it to me?"

My dad looked at us both and smiled.

"Take your friend to see your tree, Della. I'll be here when you're done," he said.

I led John outside and then poked my head back in through the kitchen window to watch.

"Stay here, Ernie and Manuel. I'm going to need you to grab that bottle of whiskey and hold Francisco's legs and body," Mr. Garcia said.

"I can hold something," I said though the window. "I can hold something good. I can hold that son-of-a-bitchin' arm."

My mom shot up from her chair and walked toward me.

John moved his body between us just like his father had moved the car between us and the KKK, the same slow, non-aggressive slide of a foreign body between us.

"Let's go, Della," he said. "Show me the tree."

"Fine, goddamn it!" I yelled.

Señora Garcia looked at me. Her chin dropped down to her neck and her brows hung heavy over her thin eyes. I had used the Lord's name in vain and crossed a line.

This time, I grabbed John's arm and led him to the tree without looking back at my mother. Maria had corralled her little brother and my little brothers near the pigs. They fed them scraps of food that had fallen away from the edges of the fields. The little boys laughed hard when the piglets rolled over each other to get the food.

John and I stood under the apple tree when I heard my

father scream out in pain. His cry rang across the ranch and had to have scared the coyotes away.

I turned to run back to the house, but John grabbed my arm, this time with a bit more force.

"Let go, chile boy, let go," I said.

John never talked back to me. He always did what I said.

"No," he said. "If you go in there, your mom is going to slap you silly. I don't want that. Sit with me here under the tree."

The fire inside of me, the one that roared through me when I heard my dad cry out, had somehow been softened by my friend.

We sat for another ten or fifteen minutes to make sure there were no more cries until my mom yelled out to us, "Get your asses, I mean, butts back in here and start cooking the corn. Della, grab some apples to cut up for dessert."

John and I gathered up apples and ran toward the house with our arms full.

He beat me. He was fast. It really made me angry, so I threw an apple at his feet to trip him, and boy, did it work. His foot rolled over the apple and his body flew forward. His head crashed against the hard, dry earth, and blood shot out from his lip.

I felt bad for hurting him but also proud of my aim.

"Sorry, John," I yelled. "I didn't mean to hurt you."

I reached down to pick him up.

"It's okay," he said. "That was a good throw. I am fast though. That's how I can carry your backpack to the truck after school and then make it to the truck that picks us up every day to take us home. I bet you thought I missed it for you every day, didn't ya? I like you, but I'm not gonna miss the truck home for you."

He smiled and then sprinted to the house and through the front door.

Chapter Eight

John
1930

I RAN TOWARD DELLA'S FRONT DOOR AFTER FALLING OVER THE apple she threw in front of me. I thought it was funny, but I could see that she felt bad. I'd tripped on a million things in my life. My friend throwing an apple at me did not hurt my feelings one bit. It's exactly what my sister, Maria, would have done if I tried to beat her to the house.

I opened the door, the first of all the kids to come back in, and saw Señor Chavez on the ground. Ernie lifted the bottle of whiskey to his lips. My dad wrapped a piece of cloth around his arm from shoulder to wrist, a sling to hold the broken bone in place. Della's dad squinted, and Manuel stood next to Señora Chavez and helped her lift her seasoned cast-iron pot up onto the stove. She didn't even look over at her husband, just dumped lard into the pan and asked my brother Manuel to help her light the wood in the stove.

"John," Señor Chavez said, announcing my arrival in a quiet, kind way, "Did you fall? You got dirt on your knees and elbows."

"Della threw an apple at my feet to trip me," I said.

"Della Benita Chavez!" Her mom announced her arrival in a loud, shrill voice.

"He didn't care, mom. Look, he's okay. He's not a wimp. See, look at him," Della said.

She smiled at me, a little grin that she hoped she could hide from her mom.

A wooden spoon flew from the kitchen to the doorway. "Trip on that, Della," Señora Chavez said. She laughed. I laughed. We all laughed.

LET THE WILD GRASSES GROW

"He's clumsy," Manuel said. "You could have thrown a tiny pebble within ten feet of him, and he would have found a way to trip on it."

"Get in here and get cooking, Della," her mom said. "Start the corn. Start the pork fat. Heat up the beans."

The men hoisted Della's dad up, placed the whiskey in the crook of his arm, and then sat him down on the sofa. The men found their way to seats, leaving me, the only boy left in the house, standing next to Della.

"Can I help you cook?" I asked her.

"You can do it all if you'd like. I think I'll just have a seat and relax," she said. She wedged her body between her father and Ernie.

"Della Benita Chavez, get up off of that godforsaken chair and help," Señora Chavez said.

My mom winced. I could see the strain in her. She raised her hand up to her chest and squeezed her crucifix and did a small sign of the cross that no one noticed except for me. Using the Lord's name in vain was one of the worst commandments to break. It was right up there with murder to my mom. Then, after the tiny sign of the cross, she said, "Can I help too?"

"Holy hell, absolutely not, Flora," Señora Chavez said. "Absolutely not."

"Can I?" I asked.

"Sure, John, sure," she said. "You can help Della cook and keep her mouth shut."

Señora Chavez walked to the counter in the kitchen and began to slice the apples. Della and I stood with wooden spoons over two hot cast iron pans.

Della played with the food more than I have ever seen anyone play with food before. She sectioned off squares of corn, about ten in all. She made them all exactly the same size in less than a few seconds.

"See, they make a pattern," she said. "If you section it all off

41

in sixteenths, you get a lot more crispy edges. It's like a game to me. I hate cooking, so I try to figure out exactly where the hottest section of the pan is and make sure every piece of stupid corn touches it. It's the only way I can handle cooking while ERNIE sits on his butt over there."

I smiled. "Do you have more salt?" I asked.

Della pointed to a sack above the oven on a shelf.

"Butter?"

"We have lard?"

"Okay."

"Why would you need extra?"

"Because it tastes better."

"Chilies?"

"No, John, we don't have any goddamned chilies," Della said.

The whole room went silent for a long second. Señora Chavez somehow reached back from cutting all the apples with what seemed like a third hand and smacked Della across the back of the head, and everyone laughed while my mom did the sign of the cross and held on to her crucifix, letting go of the slightest smile.

I dropped some more salt and lard into the corn, stirred it, and then let Della section it off to make sure every piece of corn touched the hottest spot and tasted exactly the same. It's like she had figured out a formula that I had never thought of.

Within twenty minutes, we all sat down at the dinner table. My mom led the prayer, though no one asked her to, but, at the same time, no one complained.

"And to hell with the damned Klan," Señora Chavez said.

"To hell with them," my dad said.

"To hell with them!" Della said.

And then, to everyone's surprise, my mom piped in, "Dear Jesus, to hell with those goddamned Klan. In the name of the Father, and of the Son, and of the Holy Spirit, Amen."

We all ate.

Della squeezed my hand underneath the table, and somehow, it became one of my favorite days in my life. Right then. Life felt good.

My parents laughed over a few beers. Della's dad slowly drank whiskey in his sling and moved up to the table to join us. Ernie and Manuel left the table early and went out to the deck. Maria took care of the three little boys, cradling them in her arms, letting the adults talk. And Della and I walked again out to her apple tree to sit and watch the stars flow across the sky.

The grit from the mines couldn't find us. The KKK didn't exist. The dry, dying earth sat beneath us like a cradle, and our parents' voices and laughter fell out of the window of the tiny ranch house under the Colorado sky.

I imagined that this could be our life forever. We were friends. All of us, friends.

Della talked and talked and talked. She talked about puzzles and the land and how she was going to break away some day and live somewhere else.

And this broke my little heart.

I wanted nothing to change, ever.

Chapter Nine

Della
1933

ONE MORNING, THAT WINTER, MY MOM LET US ALL SLEEP IN, even my father, who moaned when he turned from side to side in his bed. She did what she always did. She made coffee. She fried eggs from our chickens. She made tortillas and placed them in a warming towel to keep them fresh for all of us.

The ravaging dust of dead, drifting soil rolled across the country, and all the ranchers in southern Colorado could see it sweeping its wide brush of destruction a year before it hit them. It devastated Oklahoma and then Kansas, Colorado's neighbor to the east. The dry winds and smell of the deepest drought could be tasted on the shifting winds of the Gunnison River Valley.

My parents were scared. My father began to drink a little bit more. The Depression had hit hard, but prohibition had lifted in the early thirties, so money was scarce, and food was scarce, but liquor was now available everywhere.

"They won't feed you, but they'll give you booze," my mom said. "The last ten years, the government said, no, let's not let those people drink. But now, when times are shitty as hell, they let us drink. Drink, drink, drink away! Plenty of food, no alcohol. No food, what the hell? Let them get drunk with their empty stomachs. Let them drink when they are hungry and wondering if they will eat that night. And then let's tax it!"

"It's getting worse," my dad said. "The soil is getting worse. Every day, every week, every month."

"Keep the wild grasses growing, Francisco," my mom said.

My father started drinking and pacing. He would work all day in the barn and in the fields, and then he would come in for

a simple dinner of tortillas, beans, and sometimes fried corn—
that's all we ate for years, along with a few apples from my apple
tree. Then he'd pour a little bit of whiskey, slosh it around in a
glass like he was continually making sure that it was still there,
and pace, back and forth and back and forth until the wooden
path had worn so smooth that I avoided it when I wore socks in
the house to not slip.

He paced and grimaced. His mind sat on the fields and
yields they might bring. There were five years of this before the
Dust Bowl began to strip the land of middle America. It was the
only thing anyone ever talked about.

At school, the teacher just talked about the dry-ass land.
Kids, that's all they talked about too, because that's all their parents talked about.

John? Well John never really talked.

"What do you think about the land, John," I asked him one
day while he carried my backpack from school to the truck that
took us home.

"It doesn't really hurt the chilies," he said. "The dryer the
better for the chilies."

"You and your chilies, John," I said. "You're going to turn
into a damned chile."

The layer of dust had eaten up fields from Missouri to Colorado, from Oklahoma to New Mexico, and from Kentucky to
Wyoming. The farmers killed it. They planted too much. They
sold too much. They did it to feed their families.

We had two fields and a whole lot of Texas Longhorns that
many men had tried to steal in the night. They snuck in, they
rattled around in the field, and they cut our fences, but my parents didn't sleep during those years. Within minutes of hearing
sounds in the quiet night, my dad ran outside with a shotgun
in his hand, and my mom followed shooting her long-barreled
shots into the air like she was Benita the Kid.

To my parents, if the world had been doomed, us being

children wouldn't protect us from damnation, so my dad paced back and forth and back and forth, sloshing his whiskey in his glass first, and then four or five drinks in, sloshing his whiskey in his belly.

"I'm gonna go walk around the barn and fields," my dad said.

"Can I come with you?" I asked him.

"Sure, Della, venga," he said.

"No, she is not walking around with you, Francisco, unless you want me to strap this gun of mine around her waist. Do you want that, Cisco?" my mom asked.

"No," he said. "Della, stay here. Ernie, come with me."

They went on patrol every night for two years.

We only lost two steers and one cow throughout those years. After the first five or six failed attempts, men stopped trying, but my parents had already stopped sleeping. They worried more about the Dust Bowl than any stupid men trying to steal their cattle. They could shoot those men, but they couldn't shoot the black storms of dust that started to roll violently toward us.

At one point, I think we ate corn for three months straight. My mom did her best to vary the taste. She would make corn fritters, which were my favorite because I made apple sauce from my apples and spread it across the tops of them, sharing the sauce with my whole family and feeling like I had done something special. She would make corn tortillas, of course, though all of us would rather have flour tortillas because of the taste. We were flour tortilla types of people. She would fry corn, crispy and black on the outside and sweet on the inside, in a big cast iron skillet and sprinkle it with salt and pepper and just a little bit of cheese from the cows. We would have done anything for a big batch of ancho chiles, but we had none, so we ate corn for every meal for months at a time.

Drunken, one night, my dad got mad. He paced back and forth and back and forth and cursed God for betraying his family.

"What do you want me to do, God?" he screamed into the

air. "I pray to you. I protect my wife and family like you tell me to. I work hard all day long, and all you give me is corn and dust. I'm not ready to return to dust. From dust to dust. Dust kills. Dust does not give life, but I will give blood. Will blood feed my family? Will blood dampen the soil? Will blood make the ground rich? Will blood make my little girl grow?"

And then he stopped pacing, walked outside and into the fields with his shotgun, and loaded it with two shells, one for each barrel. He looked old in the moonlight. Wrinkles found his eyes and hugged them tightly. The last few years had been hard on him. He did not want us to know how hard, but mom talked about everything in front of us. It would make my father a little uncomfortable. He would look down at the ground when she talked about how we had so little money and how all the kids would have to stop going to school to help out around the ranch.

"It will never end. We will never live without all the worry again. We will always eat corn," she'd say. "I'm so goddamned sick of all the corn—I got corn coming out of my ears and asshole."

Outside, he looked down to the ground like he was to blame for the Great Depression, the oh-so-cheap cost of the wheat and corn and beans and milk and cattle, like he was to blame for the dust that rolled across the plains toward them.

"We are the early birds, but we never get the worms, we never even see the worms. Hell, I'd eat worms if we saw them. The ground is too damned dry. They have crawled to the center of the earth where there is something to eat besides goddamned corn." My mom ranted as she watched my father walk outside with the shotgun in his hand.

She knew that the Great Depression wasn't my father's fault and that the erosion of the farming soil from Kentucky to Colorado wasn't his fault either, but she had to talk, she had to complain, she had to bitch and moan. Bitching and moaning made her feel better. It was like air to her, like meditation.

"Should I go with dad? Can I, I mean, can I go to him?" I asked.

"Stay right the hell here, Della, and shut your mouth so I can talk. This man out there walking around drunk with a shotgun and this girl of his wants to go out and talk to him," she said to me.

"He won't hurt me," I said,

"Not on purpose, he won't," she said, shouting out the now open window. "But he's borracho and stupid right now, and he has a shotgun, understand, Della? You're so smart, but sometimes you think too much, and sometimes you think you can solve every damned riddle. You can't."

"Dad just feels bad that he can't feed us anything but corn, beans, and bread, on special occasions," I said.

That night, drunker than I've ever seen him, he looked older under the light of the moon. His shoulders had fallen a bit. He slumped. I had never seen him slump.

We all gathered around the kitchen window and looked out at the man who had slung the shotgun over his shoulder and walked over to the fence next to our cattle, our lifeblood, our last bit of anything worth anything. He pulled the gun down from over his shoulder. At first, he held it in front of him.

My mom gasped. I knew what she was thinking. We all knew. The man from Denver shot himself. During that time, men killed themselves everywhere. They didn't care if children found their bodies. They didn't care at all. There has never been suicide in the country like there was then.

TWO DAYS BEFORE MY DAD walked out of the house and toward the cows, we all stood in a line in downtown Trinidad and waited for things like salt and pepper and toilet paper, all the stuff we could have easily bought before. We had also taken one of our steers into sell. They had become our only real source of money between the time we planted the crops and the time we harvested them, a whole farming year. We sold milk from our cows too, but it wasn't enough, so my dad took one of his best, fattest cows and sold it for dimes on the dollar.

The trains rolled through town less and less. They had nothing to carry from us to Denver or from Denver to us, but they still came once or twice a week. The train station sat right in downtown, and we could all hear it roll toward us out of the mountains.

It chugged along and began to slow down before the train station. And then the screams came. I left the line, although my mom told me not to, and I got five or six lashes from her wooden spoon that night for doing so, but I ran toward the screams. When I got to the women who cried out into the hot day, I looked down.

Two men had waited for the trains to come. They lay and waited on the tracks. The train screeched toward them, the conductor yanked on the brake, and smoke spit off the tracks.

The last thing the men did was lift their heads just slightly to greet the train. When the train stopped, their bodies had been split in quarters. Some of them remained trapped under the steel, bloodied the wheels, but the other parts had been tossed forty or fifty feet away from the tracks, staining the fields around them.

OUT THERE, THAT NIGHT, DAD lifted his shotgun in the air and pulled the trigger twice. The deafening sound of gunfire sent me to my knees and Ernie out into the night after my dad. When I stood up again, I saw my father put his hand out toward Ernie to make him stop, and then he loaded two more shells into the gun, climbed over the fence and into the pasture, and stopped again, raising the gun barrel upward one more time.

MY FATHER WALKED OVER TO one of the biggest cows that we had left and shot it in the head. It dropped hard, scattering dust for twenty feet around it, and then he walked over to another cow and dropped it too. Two dead cows at the end of my father's drunken shotgun.

He waved Ernie over. They grabbed the mules in the middle of the night, threw straps around their thick bodies, and dragged the dead cows into the barn. They didn't come in that night, not at all except to grab whiskey, Ernie out there drinking with my father and cutting up cows for the butcher. Meat sold well, but once it was gone, it was gone. It took another couple years to grow a big calf to a big cow, and we only had a few cows left to breed, so I don't know what the hell my dad was thinking, but I knew he shouldn't have shot those cows. We were down to less than ten at that point, and my mom was hell set on the fact that we were at the end of times and that the tide would never change. To her, we were in hell with no way out, and my dad just shot two of our last few cows.

She went on a rant before heading to bed, not only with her words but also with her little body. Her hands dug so far into her hips that I was scared she just might squeeze her guts right out of her butt. I just stood there and placed my hands on my hips too and tried to scrunch my face, doing my best to show her that I wasn't with her or against her—mainly to show her I sure as hell wasn't against her.

"Great, now we won't have milk to sell because of El Borracho. That man, in our entire marriage has been the best man I've ever met, but he has some loco in him too: cries with friends at the dinner table, shoots las vacas in the middle of the night, and loves his daughter more than his boys. Lo siento, Della, but that's weird," she said. It didn't bother me. I took it as a compliment.

"And I love him more than I love you, mama," I said.

She smiled and said, "I know, Della, I know."

She never did say anything to him about it though. I knew she understood his loco and that she would take my dad's kind of crazy over other men's kind of crazy, the beating-their-wife or lying-down-on-the-train-tracks kind of crazy. He didn't like other women, and he never paid for sex outside of the home, and, hell, he made his favorite daughter work in the fields just like he made his boys because he needed the help and because I asked him if I could. The fields, to me, were like giant puzzles that I couldn't complete without really thinking about it, like working with tall thin dominoes, pulling corn and completing the game. My mom loved his kind of crazy, I think.

THE NEXT DAY, MY DAD and Ernie were gone before I got out of bed. They must have left long before dawn, never sleeping until they were done cleaning and sectioning out the cows the best they could before handing them over to the butcher.

I spent the day picking corn from the stocks, hauling the blackened and yellow and orange corn in a basket back to the house. I shucked the ears, dug my nails deep into the husks and yanked them off in one downward shred with my hands. I watched the sun drop down behind the tall peaks of the Rockies, my nails digging into the meat of the corn cobs and shedding the rich corn into a large metal bowl, enough corn to feed that family for days.

I waited for my dad and brother to come home, and when they did, I could smell pigs before I could see them.

They rode in the back of the truck that bounced along the road toward the ranch, and when Ernesto and my father stopped the truck, the smell overcame me. Pigs. I *hated* pigs.

I wanted to give the men hugs, but I couldn't. I could tell that they had been wrestling with those filthy beasts to get them into the carriage.

"Come here, Della," my dad yelled. I did, with hesitation. I didn't want to touch those pigs. I walked over to them. In the back, there were at least ten piglets running around. I admit, they were cute, but they stunk. At the back of the carriage, huge sacks were filled with beef. He had killed two cows, sold one, had the other one butchered and brought home for us. He used the money from the first cow to buy the pigs. Pigs were cheap. Cows were not. Pigs would eat anything. Cows needed fresh alfalfa. I got it. I just didn't like it, but I did like carrying the beef to the barn and salting it down, curing it to keep it as long as we could. I did like ramming the sticks into the ground with Ernie. We strung up barbed wire from stick to stick and laughed about how stinky the pigs were but also about how cute they were.

"I'm naming that pig Desayuno," Ernie said.

"I'm naming that one Cena," I said.

We'd had pork before. When we had a little money before the Great Depression, we used to eat bacon at the cafe in Trinidad when we'd go shopping for supplies. I liked bacon, but I was positive we wouldn't be eating much of it. My dad would use every ounce of the pig to make chorizo. The mixing of the fat and the meat and the brains and the stomach and the organs would make a lot more meals than just slicing up small parts of the pig. He could mix all that stuff together, and we would have a lot more to eat. That's okay. I loved the stuff.

"I'm naming that one Chorizo," I said.

When we got the fence area made, we released the pigs into it. They squealed and yelped, and we fed them corn, corn husks, and any mushy alfalfa that had sat too long and had been turned down by the cows. By that time, a layer of dry earth and dust had already begun to cover the land. Things weren't growing as good as they should. It was like people from Mars had come down and started secretly changing our planet to theirs. It was colder than usual, but the layers of dust that clung to the barn and our home made it seem like we were living close to the edge of the Sahara, like we would round the bend and see the pyramids of Giza or the Sphinx. But just like a frog being slowly boiled, we got used to it, day by day, the new normal of wearing handkerchiefs around our mouths when we worked outside and of cleaning dust off our clean dishes before we ate dinner. The black blizzards of dust and the dry lands had shrunken our crops and suffocated some of our chickens, but we moved on and lived in it and called our new pigs Chorizo, Dinner, and Breakfast.

That night, after my father had spent the day curing the beef, he came into the house late. He had grown so old since the dust began to come and since the money had begun to go away. His eyes had wrinkled even more with the booze, and his hair began to fade back along his scalp like he had become some caricature of my father, an old and tired man in the shell of my dad. It's crazy what three or four years can do to a person. Stress, stress is a real son of a bitch. Work is different from stress. My father always worked hard but smiled through it because he could see something come of it. He could see the money being placed in hands.

We never really had "money" money, but we always had enough, more than most along the ranch-filled land of southeastern Colorado. The miners did pretty well, but they all died young. I'd rather be poorer than die with black lungs, but they didn't have a choice either. They too had to live the life they had been given.

THAT NIGHT, WHEN HE CAME into the house, he looked worn, but he smiled. He smiled until my mom tapped him hard across the back of the head.

He dropped three huge ribeye cuts from the cow onto the table. It was enough to feed us for days. We could cut them up and put them in stews or let them soak into soups. We could slice them thin and place them into tortillas with fried corn and lard. We could even batter them in corn meal to thicken them up. Three large ribeye cuts. They lay on the table between my father and mother. Would this decision be the end of my parents? The look in my mother's eyes told me that it would.

"Let's cook them up, Benita. Just once, por favor" he said. "Me and Ernesto could share the big one. You and Della could share the next big one, and the two boys could share the little one. I will make a sauce to dip them in. You don't have to cook at all. Della will cook the corn, and Ernie can fry some tomatoes from his garden."

Ernie and I shook our heads up and down. We were like two damn lost dogs begging for scraps. Hell, I had already shucked the corn while I waited for them to get home, and I was loading up the frying pan with grease when my mother protested again by kicking me in the ass with the back of her foot.

"Benita, please. I don't think this dust will ever lift. This might be our life forever. Can't we just enjoy one day this year?" I'd never seen my father plead like that. Yes, he was kind, but he was no beggar, not even to his wife. He raised up both his arms to the sky like he was praying to the wife gods to show mercy.

Sheepish. The steaks on the table had made my father sheepish. The pigs in the barn had made him smart, but the cow on the table had made him vulnerable. Hungry. He was hungry for red meat, hungry for something besides fried corn, hungry for what all those years of work had earned him, a big, red steak, cooked just enough to stop the blood from leaking out of it.

"Please, Benita," my father said.

She looked at him with his arms in the air, with the steaks on the table, and with me and Ernie watching to see what would happen, and said, "Stop whining, Francisco, I'll cook up your meat for you."

She grabbed the steaks, laid them out on the counter, pounded them thin with our kitchen mallet, stuffed the wood stove, lit it on fire, and then turned to us and told us to do what my father had promised her that we would.

Ernie ran to his garden and pulled out some big, ripe tomatoes, and since I had already shucked the corn, I gathered it up in a big bowl and waited for my turn with the fry pan.

My mom threw lard in the pan, and when it began to sizzle, she grabbed the flattened steaks, tossed them in corn meal and spices, and then fried them up until their skins sizzled golden brown. She dropped them on a towel and let them sit. They were not just the chunks of meat that my father had begged for; they were fried steaks in lard with an outside layer of crunchy skin that he loved more than anything else on this earth. She cooked a meal for him that he could not have enjoyed more. She bitched about it the whole damn time, with little whispers of "borracho" and "estupido" under her breath, but when the steaks came out of the pan, she smiled.

I used the same lard and fat and grease-soaked pan to fry my corn, and the bright yellows and purples and greens all turned to a dark black skin that had been flavored by chicken-fried steak and lard. When I finished, Ernie dropped his tomatoes in, only for a few seconds on each side so that he wouldn't lose the flavor of his favorite red fruit, and then pulled them out and placed them in the middle of the table for us to stare at until my mom filled our plates with thin, hot, juicy steaks and fried corn.

My dad did nothing that night except sit there and drink whiskey and smile. He watched us cook, something he rarely did, always jumping in to move a pan so we didn't burn ourselves or wipe up grease splatters from the wall or oven. That night, however, he just sat there and drank whisky and listened to my mom call him borracho, a drunkard.

We sat and ate together. The little ones barely finished their little steak, but we let them sit there and work on it for more than an hour. It was theirs, and they too had earned it for being a part of this world for the last few years when the earth and money had all dried itself up. My mom and I split the middle steak. It was heavenly. Son of bitch, I can still taste that steak on my lips and on my tongue. Outside the ground had become like the skin of an old man who had never used lotion in his entire goddamned life, but that steak felt like the rich, moist earth after a heavy rain from only a few years back in our memories.

My dad and Ernesto shared the big steak. They didn't speak

at all, my brother already becoming the spitting image of my dad. They finished the first half of it quickly, not able to hold themselves back from what had seemed like they had been waiting for all their lives. Then, however, when half of each of their portions disappeared from their plates, they slowed down. I think they knew then what I know now, and wished I knew then. There would never be another steak like this in their lives.

My dad had become so visibly drunk that each time he put a piece of steak in his mouth, he couldn't chew and keep his eyes open at the same time, his muscles so weakened by liquor that they could not use all of them at once. When he finished his steak, he lifted his body from his seat, and, like he had been lifted by the hand of God, he floated to the floor of the living room and laid down and fell asleep.

The next morning, he woke up in the same clothes he'd slept in and walked out into the fields and did his daily work. He never touched another sip of alcohol in his life.

Chapter Ten

John
1933

Since that day with the KKK, our family joined Della's family once a month for dinner. It was always the same. Either they came to our house and had chiles or we went to theirs and had corn. I looked forward to the next meal the second we left their house from the last, looking back to see the Chavez house disappear behind the dust cloud that the Auburn kicked up.

At her house, Della and I played outside by the apple tree until she was called in to cook, and I would help her. She set up scavenger hunts for me before I got there. She left little clues everywhere that led me from one treasure to another—little things she found around the ranch—and got upset when I couldn't figure things out.

"Dammnit, John, are you dull?" she'd ask when I'd try to decipher a code she had put on a piece of paper. She would replace letters with numbers or vice versa and expect me to know which of the other they represented. When it took me more than a few minutes, she would rip the clue out of my hand and lead me through it like a teacher schooling a child.

"In this case, 23 equals W, so when you see a 23, it's a W. If you see a 23 and 1/2, it's a lowercase w. Understand, John? If you see a zero, that's an O. The clues are simple. Here you see, 23 and 1/2 00 d. What does that mean, John?"

I stared at it for a bit, "Wood."

"Yep, and where do we find wood?"

"In the woodshed!" I yelled.

We ran toward the woodshed, opened it up, and found her dog waiting there for us to rescue him.

"Della, get in here, time to cook," Señora Chavez yelled from the kitchen window.

When we got to be about twelve years old, we stopped playing games and started harassing Ernie and Manuel who had begun to sneak off behind the barn and smoke cigarettes that they rolled between their fingers and shared, waving the smoke away from their mouths.

Della had the idea once to drop water on them from above, so we climbed up through the barn with a bucket of water and dumped the whole thing on their heads. Within minutes, Ernie held Della out over the edge of the second story of the barn and Manuel wrestled me to the ground in the hay.

"Knock it off, Della," Ernie told her, "or I'll drop you."

"No, you won't. That's just a weak threat," she said. "And if you drop me, I'll tell dad you're smoking. He hates that shit and you know it."

Manuel slugged me hard in the arm and then in the quad. Both muscles went completely numb. He and Ernie were fifteen years old, and I was a long way from catching him in strength. I wiggled to try and get out of his grasp, but it didn't work.

"Come cook!" Della's mom yelled.

When she yelled, we all listened. It didn't matter how strong our older brothers had gotten. Señora Chavez was no one to be messed with.

THE NEXT MONTH, THE CHAVEZES came to our house for dinner. We filled them with chile rellenos, stuffed peppers from the big peppers in our garden. I made a lot of it with my mom, but Della never helped me cook like I helped her. Instead, she moved between my dad and hers while they took apart the Auburn and put it back together. It had become a ritual, pulling pieces out of it, cleaning them, and then reassembling the engine.

Della brought a pencil and paper out and started inventorying the pieces that came out after the first time they did it and when they put it back together, two pieces remained on the ground. Somehow it still ran when my dad said, "Aww, no neces-sitatamos." Della made it her business to make sure every piece that came out not only went back in but also went back in the right place.

After dinner, my mom left to go to adoration and the rest of us stayed.

My dad and Francisco sat on the deck and talked about the fields and about the mines and about the drought. Frank didn't drink anymore, but it didn't bother him when my dad put back his Sunday afternoon Coors. They'd become close friends, just like the rest of us, and at twelve years old, I'd begun to see Della in a way that I didn't over the previous four years.

I began to have an urge to reach out and touch her face, to hug her when there was no need to. I even had to close my eyes as hard as I could at night to push the images of kissing her out of my brain like squeezing a sponge dry.

It became a nagging image that didn't go away. I thought about it in school. I thought about it when I plucked chiles at home. I thought about it in the shower. I thought about it so much that I could barely look at her anymore.

THE DAY AFTER WE DUMPED water on Ernie and Manuel, I walked Della to the truck that would take her home after school, just like always. I carried her backpack. We talked. She mostly talked. She had begun to talk about leaving the ranch and Trini-dad, to talk about going to places she had read about in books—California or New York or Chicago or some place called Miami for some reason.

This shot a mixture of fear and anger through me that I didn't know existed. But it was different than when I got mad at Manuel for slugging me or taking the last tortilla from the batch. Or cross at Maria for always doing exactly what she was supposed to do or being my father's favorite child. Or frustrated with Paulo for crying in the middle of the night. The anger came from what I could only call my heart.

"Why would you want to leave?" I asked her.

To me, I planned to be a miner. I thought she could be a miner's wife. I had imagined this for so long in a childish way. I imagined her being my wife because we got along so well, but that day everything changed. I didn't want her to leave because of something different, and I got angry when she started to talk about it.

"Here's your bag," I said prematurely, an easy ten minutes before I needed to. "I gotta go."

"What?" Della asked. "Why are you being such an idiot o?"

"I'm not. I just got to go is all," I said. I turned away from her and began to run, but she caught my hand. A rush ran from her finger tips to my skull, like I'd stuck my hand in a fire. When I turned to her, she gave me a look that said *Don't go, John. Stay with me.*

I stopped dead in my tracks.

She squeezed my hand a bit, let it go, and then she—the Della who never shied away from anything—turned away from me, blushing at the tops of her caramel-colored cheeks.

"The world is a puzzle that I want to solve," she said. "Trinidad is just so…so tiny."

I heard her talk, but I wasn't listening. The blood rose up toward my skin, and I could barely feel my lips, and then they became the only thing I could think about. My lips. Her lips. Our hands touching.

"Chilis," I said. "I have to tend to the chiles."

"What the goddamned hell is wrong with you, John?" she said, loudly enough for every one of our classmates who headed out to the ranch too could hear.

I had used up all my words.

I sprinted away from her with enough adrenaline in my legs

to skip the truck that carried us home—I ran all the way home, my legs fumbling beneath me by the end of the sprint.

"Go on a walk with me, joto," Della said that following Sunday at our house.

"Nope, I think I'll just hang out with Ernie and Manuel," I said. "I think it's time for me to just hang out with the boys."

I followed them to the field to do whatever they did in the field after dinner. Manuel was my brother and my best friend, but when we went to the Chavezes, or when they came to our house, he only wanted to hang out with Ernie. Ernie did the same thing to Della.

The truth was that I think they both knew that me and Della wanted to be together too, at first as friends and then, now, as whatever this awkward thing was that we were since the moment she grabbed my hand earlier that month.

"I'm going to go to the field with them," I said.

I started to run away from her, and then I felt a foot hook me at my ankle and the ground slam into my face.

Chapter Eleven

Della
1933

YES, I TRIPPED THAT DUMBASS. HE STARTED RUNNING TO THE barn like we hadn't been friends for nearly five years. He was acting so weird. I knew why, of course, but I didn't want to let him know I knew. This gave me the upper hand on the feelings I'd begun to feel for that niño more than a year ago. My mom always said girls mature so much faster than estúpido boys. I had been looking at John like he looked at me the day I grabbed his hand long before he noticed me that way. But *I* didn't have that stupid "I don't know what the hell is going on and I'm going to run away now look" splashed across my face. I could control it all.

He could not.

So I tripped him.

He fell harder to the ground than I thought he would. He didn't expect it at all. His hands and wrists failed to brace him. He ate the ground hard, harder than I had seen any boy or man who hadn't been drinking all day fall to the ground, and even when they fell, they wobbled to the ground like they fell through a big layer of jello.

"Ouch!" he yelled out.

No one but us were there to see him hit the ground. I ran over to him and turned his body over. He bled from his cheek, his mouth, and his palms and elbows.

"I didn't mean to trip you," I said.

"Yes you did, Della," he said. Blood began to pull up next to the edge of his lips.

"Well, okay, I didn't mean for you to fall that hard," I said, which was true. I thought he might just stumble, brace himself, and then get the idea that he was being a stupid idiot and come back and go on a walk with me.

"It hurts," he said.

"Don't be such a joto, John," I said.

I helped him to his feet.

"Want to walk now?" I asked.

"Yes, I can't go into the barn now without them asking questions, can I?" he said, not really as a question.

"Nope, let's walk. Show me the chile garden again, joto," I said, but I said it in a really sweet voice that sounded so awkward coming out my mouth, like a pussy cat's meow coming from the mouth of a lion.

"Okay," he said.

All I ever had to say was "chiles" and John would perk up. Strange, strange boy.

We walked through the chile garden and into a few rows of corn stalks that reached up to the sky, taller than any Chavez or Garcia heads.

I grabbed his hand.

"Thank you," I said with that same meow from before.

"For what?" he asked.

"For falling on the ground like the clumsiest dumbass I have ever met in my entire life," I said. Just like before, I said it with sweetness.

And then that rare smile of his popped out in the form of two fattening and bloody lips.

"No problem," John said. "I can fall again."

He flopped to the ground. He actually made a joke.

I knocked him on the top of his head.

"Get up," I said.

I grabbed both of his hands and pulled him up. We were nearly thirteen, and neither of us had ever even come close to kissing someone, so when he stood so close to me, I felt like my knees melted.

I knew then why he ran away from me, why he disappeared that day by the truck and ran so fast that I could barely see him go.

This feeling was really weird, and I didn't know what to do with it. We just held hands. Like magnets, we leaned in toward each other to touch lips.

And that's when my father grabbed John from behind, pulled hard on his shoulders, and threw him hard to the ground.

"You two will remain in my sight for the rest of the day—for the rest of your lives," my father said. "Mierda!"

He dragged John by his shirt out of the rows of corn. I followed them.

"Get up," my dad said to John. "Follow me. You too, Della."

He walked fast toward the house, through the front door, and into the kitchen.

"I found these two in the cornstalks," he said.

Señora Garcia had come back from church, and she stood with my mom in the kitchen, cleaning.

"They were this close to making niños," he said.

Señora Garcia's face looked like it was going to slide off. Her mouth dropped open. She said nothing. She made a sign of the cross so big that she nearly touched her toes with the bottom of the cross.

"Were they naked, Francisco?" my mom asked.

"No, but they were about to kiss," my father said.

"Could you see his chorizo?" my mom asked.

Señora Garcia made another huge sign of the cross.

"Well, no," he said.

"Then they weren't gonna make any niños out there, Frank," she said. "Now let go of that boy and shut the hell up."

"Sit down," Señora Garcia said. "Both of you."

We both sat at the table.

"You are not allowed to be alone together anymore, okay?

It's that time of life, and you are too young to be fornicating. It's a sin," she said.

John was always so quiet. He loved and respected his mom and dad, and I had never seen him talk back to them, ever. They were so kind that he never really needed to, not like my mom who would tell you she loved you in one sentence and tell you to get the hell out of her face in the other.

But that day, he talked back.

"I love her," he said. "I love Della."

Within a second, Señora Garcia stood up, grabbed her son's ear, pulled him out of the house, yelled to the other children and her husband to get into the Auburn, and drove off.

John fell hard three times that day.

I fell really goddamned hard too.

Chapter Twelve

John
1933

"Aren't we going to the Chaveze's today?" Maria asked my dad from the back seat of the Auburn.

"No, I think we're just going to have a family day, today," my mom said. She held her crucifix necklace in her hand, raised it to her mouth, and kissed it.

"Está bien," Maria said. "But I will miss the little boys. I look forward to seeing them every week."

"And John will really miss Della," Manuel said. He smiled at me and blinked his eyes seductively.

"No I won't," I said. "I won't miss her at all."

We rolled up our car windows. All of us did. We shut out the high winds on the edge of New Mexico. We lived, for ten minutes while heading into town, in our own capsule of time and space, separated from the heavy dust in the air that hovered over the cracking earth of the high plains.

We bumped along the dirt road and into town where my dad pulled into the only gas station. We all stayed in the car. Even though the interior air had begun to heat up and we all sweated next to each other in our seats, we left the windows closed, encapsulated together in the modern world. Victor Galvez, a dark man like us, who had retired from the mines and worked the pumps at the station, walked around the car and peeked in the windows, touching his hands to the glass to wave at us kids and our mom.

Victor filled the tank. It cost a lot money to fill it for sure. But my father dug into his pocket and pulled out $1.65, which included Victor's tip for filling us up. Victor gave the seven-cent tip back to my dad and patted him on the shoulder, nudging my father toward the driver's side door. The old man tapped on the back window and waved at Maria, Manuel, and me. We waved back.

Paulo climbed over the front seat and onto Maria's lap, pressing his nose and mouth against the window. Mr. Galvez placed his hand on the window in the face of my little brother, and Paulo let out a howling laugh.

The Sangre De Cristo, the closest mountain range, lay ahead of us like it had been framed perfectly to fit in the edges of the windshield. Snow sat on the high peaks, but green had begun to sprout at the edge of the tree line.

I could have sat in the back seat of the Auburn for the rest of the day and thought about Della. She covered my thoughts. I wanted to jump in the front seat, grab the wheel, and turn it back toward Della's house. I didn't care. I loved her. I had found the girl I wanted to marry. She swam in my mind. I touched one hand to the other and pretended it was hers.

My dad drove out toward the mountains. The sun had moved across the eastern plains and settled on the face of the mountains. We parked at the base of the hills that gradually moved in waves up toward the rocky cliffs.

"Everyone out," my father said.

The smell of sage brush and pine swam around us. A breeze streamed down from the summit between the canyon's walls.

From the back of the Auburn, my dad pulled out two baskets of food and handed them to me and Manuel.

I peeked under the lid of the basket and immediately smelled fresh pastries. He must have picked them up from Rosa's Bakery in downtown Trinidad. We ate there once a year after Easter Mass. That was it. We sat on two fallen trees next to the creek. Deer ran above us through the patches in the trees—huge mule deer with small tails and horns that had fuzz on them.

We sat near the desert pines and ate our pastries. The only thing that was missing was Della.

My father's parents had passed away very young, his mom dying of untreatable breast cancer in the early 1900s and his father dying of a heart attack at fifty years old, just a few years before Manuel was born.

They lived in Trinchera, moving from central Mexico in their teens with the railroads. My dad used to talk about them after he had a few drinks on Sunday afternoons. He missed them que horrible, he would tell us. It was his father who taught him how to work the chiles in the garden and his mother who taught him how to cook them. She, too, taught my mother how to cook them when my parents were just dating, inviting my mom into her kitchen to walk her through the process of preparing a large meal for a large family.

My mother's parents, however, were still alive and lived in Reno, Nevada. I really knew nothing about them, except they left for Reno the year my mother married my father, two days after the wedding.

"They didn't like my color," my dad said. "I was too dark for them. They wanted your mom to marry a white man. They said she should because she could pass and that she deserved a white man and not a dark Mexican who couldn't do anything in this world." He scoffed and slammed his hand onto his knee every time he told us that. "And the mines won't take a white man's wife and leave her alone with all their children the rest of her life, used up like a dish rag or cotton diaper." He had to stop himself before rage took him. He did that by shoving a beer bottle to his lips and muttering into the brown glass.

AT THE FOOT OF THE canyon that afternoon, my dad didn't say another word about my maternal grandparents. Manuel, who had just turned fifteen, had already begun to act like a young man, walking off into the trees and coming back with firewood without being asked to do so. Maria sat next to my mom and held her hand while Paulo chased after Manuel and carried sticks back, the sticks in his arms nearly as wide as his bones. Manuel patted the boy's head. He was seven years old and still followed his oldest brother around like a pet.

The early spring rains came so fast that day. They came like God had turned them on to wash us out of the world. They came on like the rains of Noah's flood. They came on like rage from the darkest clouds I had ever seen in the sky, before then and since. They came on and drenched us and our food and our hair.

The sound of water rushing in the stream echoed through the canyon, and the large slap of rain hit the rocky canyon walls and rustled the pines.

The winds followed the rains. They rushed down over the summit. They pushed the trees like a man shoving children who got in his way. The winds blew hard and mad.

We ran to the Auburn. We jumped in. We pulled off any wet clothing that we could. The bare chests of children filled the back seat and steam covered the windows. My mom threw food our way, and we ate until the dark covered us, the rain and wind still pounding the Auburn when my father finally gave up on the weather subsiding.

The Auburn barely made it out of the canyon. The hard dirt on the road had softened. It seemed to reach up and grab the tires of our new car, but my father twisted the steering wheel back and forth and eased his foot slowly back and forth on the gas pedal until we wiggled out onto the road that led back to Trinidad.

We sang songs together, our voices low against the pounding of the rain outside and our breath beginning to conjure steam on the windows, while my dad slowly followed the lighted path in front of the car. The heavy rains made the road in front of him blurry through the windshield, and the winds pushed us back and forth on the road, the broad-sided Auburn catching the winds like a sail. We had many, many miles to go to get home when the front tire popped. Its unevenness pulled us onto the small shoulder of the highway. The wind and rains remained angry and pounded and pounded on the car.

My dad told everyone to stay in the dry cab, even Manuel who said he wanted to help change the tire. My father told him 'no' in a harsh, gruff voice that planted Manuel into the bench seat.

Within minutes, my dad had removed the spare on the back of the car, hoisted up the front of the frame, and began to undo the thick and lumbering nuts that held the tire onto the wheel.

He worked on the tire for ten minutes. The crackle and crank of the metal crow bar against the lug nuts and metal rim shook the car beneath us. When he was done, he stood up and walked back toward the car in the rain. He started to jiggle that handle as quickly as he could, frantically trying to get the door open, but it had stuck. The cold rain had made the metal stick to the frame.

Headlights flared behind us.

They filled the back window.

He finally got the door open and tried to jump inside, but the big truck that barreled down the highway smacked his body and flung him and the door fifty feet into the road.

From within the winds, from the heart of the rain, I heard a solid thud and then my father's body roll against the earth.

In our headlights, he lay in the road, motionless.

My mother's scream deafened me.

Manuel opened his door to run out, but my mother slammed him back into his seat with one arm. She made the sign of the cross and then opened the car door and ran out into the blurry, wet scene on the other side of the glass.

We watched her run out to my father. We heard her scream, "Mi amor! Mi Amor!"

More lights came on the other side of the road, and as the next car crested over the hill, it swerved to avoid the stopped truck that had hit my father. Its back end slid, pushing its front end toward my mother.

I wanted to somehow stop it, to reach out and stop the movement of time and the world and the heavy and road-splitting metal truck that slid toward my parents.

"Dios mio!" Maria yelled out.

Paulo cried.

I could not open my mouth, but my heart leapt to my throat.

The lights hit the dark outline of my mother who had knelt down to drag my father out of the road. Her shadow reached down to pull my father toward the car. His body was just a broken pile of flesh in her arms. The second car hit them both.

Her shadow flew into the sage brush and tall grasses, followed only by the roll of my father's body into the gully on the side of the road.

The wind and rain stayed angry.

Maria and Paulo cried and gasped like the wind and rains. Manuel ran to my father. There, he found his head nearly crushed by the blow of the car. I ran to my mom. She looked like she always looked, beautiful, but when I tried to pick her up, her body folded over.

"He's dead," Manuel yelled out. He cried into the night.

I held my mother. I did not cry out into the night. I did not say a word, but in my head I screamed, "Lord Jesus, why have you killed my mother? She loved you!"

Chapter Thirteen

Della
1933

I HAD DEVISED A REALLY GOOD PLAN, AND IT INVOLVED GET-ting John to grab his cajones and kiss me at school. Or behind the school. Or on the way to where the truck met us to take all us rancher kids home. We all had bags to carry our books. I would treat mine like a mistle toe, but instead of holding it up above our heads, I would hold it out in front of me, grab him by the arm, and kiss him.

We had almost kissed in the corn, and I really wanted to, but more than just completing that kiss—I hate when things are in-complete; it drives me crazy—I wanted to get it over with so that he would stop running away from me, so I wouldn't have to trip him, and so that he would wipe that stupid, awkward expression off his face.

I got to school early that day. It had been eight days since we stood in the corn fields. John had walked me to the stop every day the last week, but he stood five feet away from me. And, of course, he ran away when I reached for him to help me up into the back of the truck. I didn't need his help, but goddamnit, it would have been nice to touch again. I had fallen so hard for him that in the back of my mind I cursed myself for it.

"I am not the type to fall for a stupid boy, especially el stupi-do like John Garcia, seriously, Della?" I said to myself every day before school the whole week after the almost kiss. But every time I saw him, I just wanted to hug him and, yes, kiss him. I'd never kissed anyone besides my mom and dad—rarely my mom who hated affection—and the tops of the heads of little brothers, and after John and I had gotten so close, I wanted to finish what we started. I ached to finish it.

I was so mad at my dad for ruining things, and even angrier at Señor and Señora Chavez for not coming over the next Sunday.

"What the hell?" I yelled into the air on my way to school.

"What's wrong with you, Della?" Ernie asked.

"Nothing Ernie, callete, okay?" I said. "Shut it."

We didn't have a phone. There were no lines that went out into the prairies. If we did, I would have called John and told him to grab his cajones because we were going to finish that kiss today.

At school that morning, I stood and waited for John, Maria, and Manuel to come clogging up the road toward the schoolhouse, Maria always leading the charge. She was smarter than her brothers, and I loved her. We rarely talked, but she always—very naturally—took care of my little brothers when they came to our house, so I didn't have to. That's a legitimate reason to love someone. Beyond that, she was probably the kindest person I had ever met. There was no cattiness to her, only a soft, loving, and warm glow. She was always happy. White boys at school would tease her because she was so dark like her dad, saying things like, "Your dad must have been covered in mining soot when he screwed your mom because you came out almost black." She never listened to them. She only smiled and headed into school and sat at the front of the classroom and opened up her books and smiled at the teacher when she began to speak. The teacher had no choice but to smile back at Maria.

The whole group of miner kids rambled up the road toward the school house, but the Garcias were not with them. By the time the last kid walked past me, I was infuriated with John, his parents, and his family.

I grabbed the last boy's arm and yelled at him, "Where the goddamned hell are the Garcias, Peter?"

"I don't know, Della, now let go of me," he said. He tried to act tough, but I knew I scared him.

The bell rang for school, and I had to walk in without finishing my kiss.

"It must be some stupid religious holiday or something like that and Señora Garcia is keeping everyone home to pray," I said out loud. She'd been known to do that for the feast of whatever the hell saint is was, especially for any feast that involved Mother Mary, and John would always come to school the next day talking about all of the ways they put chiles into their dinner.

I walked into school, my hands tucked beneath my armpits and with a heavy scowl, and watched the door the entire day. The ugly clock ticked above the teacher's head. Ernie nodded off at the exact moment the warm sunlight shone on him through the thin window glass, and I had, without knowing it, dug a long, thin canyon into my wooden seat with my fingernail. I just wanted to see John come through the door that day, that very specific damned day, but the Garcias never showed up.

After we had been in school for three periods and three of Ernie's nod offs, a knock came on the schoolhouse door. Without waiting for my teacher to walk to the back of the room, my mom flung herself into the classroom.

"Mija, let's go," she said. "Let's go now."

I didn't even think to grab anything. My mom's face said, "Venga, ahora," so I ran toward her.

"It's John, mama, isn't it," I said. "Isn't it?"

"Si, Della, si," she said. "Don't be so goddamned smart in life. It will only bring you trouble. The world doesn't like smart girls or smart women."

"Della," Ernie began.

"Callete, Ernie, callete," my mom shut him up.

My dad sat in the front seat of the truck. My mom hated the truck.

"It has death on it from Larry," she'd always say.

"He didn't die here, Benita," my father would say.

"Yeah, it has death thoughts on it, and that's worse. Those are contagious," she would answer.

I jumped into the truck, the four of us squeezing onto the bench seat in front. My father pulled me over to him and squeezed me with a hug.

"Della, we have to go the Garcia's. Something has happened," he said.

"It is John? Is John okay?" I yelled.

"Don't be so selfish, mija," my mother said in my ear. "John is okay."

To me, if John was okay, I was okay. But I would find out within minutes that they lied to me. John was not okay. Nobody was okay.

We pulled slowly up to their house. There were no lights on, and Father Ronald's car sat in the driveway, an old, old Ford that one of the parishioners had gifted him years ago so that he could give communion to the elderly and check on the sick people way out on the plains and near the mines.

"Stay here, Della," my mom said. "Let us go in first."

"No," I said. "No, I'm going in. What happened?"

"Goddamnit, stay here, Della, and shut your mouth," she said.

My dad placed his hand on my knee to anchor me into the seat, and they both got out of the car at the same time, leaving me and Ernie there to wonder what in the hell was going on and why in the hell they brought us if we were going to sit there in the car.

They walked through the front door, and a minute or so later, John and Manuel walked out instead of my parents. Through the window, I watched my mom wrap her arms around Maria and Paulo, Paulo snug against Maria's body and both of them within my mom's tiny grasp.

Ernie got out of the car and met Manuel halfway with his

palms raised in the air, silently asking him, "What happened?" Manuel told him something, and then his knees buckled a bit, and my older brother caught him in his arms and held him up.

I sat melted in the seat, just like my father left me, and watched John walk with his head down toward me. When he reached the door, I opened it for him, and he climbed in. He threw his body up onto the woven bench seat like he were a sack of beans being tossed into a bed of a truck, a lump of something inanimate.

He raised his dry eyes up to me. But when they met mine, tears flew from them. He had been holding them in. I could tell.

I saw the same look I saw in Larry's face when I brought him food and booze. He had lost everything he loved. I quickly scanned the windows, hoping to see Señora and Señor Chavez in the living room of their tiny home, but I only saw my father standing and talking to Father Ronald. John's parents were gone.

John leaned into me. His body had given way. We had never been so close before. Our bodies had never touched like that. The rush of young love had been replaced by a need to console him. I was the only one he wanted to see that day, the only one he wanted to cry to.

I hugged him into me.

I looked up, with John's head on my shoulder and his face covered in my fallen, black hair. I expected to see my mother rush out of the house with a cleaver to separate the two of us. I did see her. She did not hold a cleaver in her hand. Instead, she raised her hand in the air to me and nodded. John lay in my arms for another five minutes before he spoke. When he did, his words were slurred like a borracho, and the only ones I could make out were, "Muerto."

A knock on the driver's side door woke us to the rest of the world. Ernie opened it up and said, "Bring John back inside."

Chapter Fourteen

John
1933

"I DON'T THINK YOU SHOULD TAKE THEM WITH YOU," FATHER Ronald said. "I've met Señor Cordova, Flora's father, and he said that he was on his way to pick them up, and I think it's best if they are here, at the house, when he arrives. I do think it's best. He's a strict, stern man."

"I don't give a shit what you think, forgive me, Father, but I don't. I'm taking these children to our home until their abuelo gets here. They won't need to go to school. They can stay at our home during the day, but I am not leaving them here another godforsaken night, Father," Señora Chavez said. She raised her little finger in Father Ronald's face, and he nodded.

"Francisco, take them all out to the truck and throw them all in the back, except Maria and Paulo. They can squeeze between us in the front. Della, John, Ernie, Manuel, get going. Della, help John get some stuff. Ernie, help Manuel. I will gather Maria and the nino's things."

That night, Della laid out sheets on the floor of the Chavez' living room. Ernie and me and Manuel and Paulo lay together and fell asleep in the light of the moon and stars. Maria and Della slept in the bedroom. I missed my mother and father so much that I wanted to cry out, but I didn't want to wake the house. But there, in their home, I felt loved too, and if I couldn't be home, I wanted to be there, only a sliver of a wall away from Della. There was no way Señor Chavez would let us sleep next to each other, but we were close enough, and in a moment when my parents didn't cover my mind, I smiled and fell asleep.

The next day everyone stayed home from school. Maria and

Señora Chavez took turns comforting Paulo who, at seven years old, cried out for our mom and dad to come back. He still didn't believe it. He asked us to go pick them up off the road.

Maria helped cook. She had already slid into our mother's role. She did not cry anymore. She only walked around and fed people and did the sign of the cross and pointed up to Jesus and said, "Jesus, pray for us."

Manuel and Ernie went to the barn and drank beers that they weren't supposed to have, and Della and I walked through the corn stalks together.

"It's all going to shit, you know?" she said.

"What is?" I asked.

"The goddamned crops and dirt. It's all dying and drying up," she said.

"That's what the teacher said," I said.

"Well, I'm not the teacher, John, but I'm the one who sees it every damned day. The soil is dying."

"Do you still want to leave?" I asked her.

"Of course, John, of course. Don't be dumb. Why would I want to stay?" she said.

"Family? Me?" I asked. I felt brave to ask. It felt brave to tell her that I loved her in this way.

"You're leaving, John," she said. "Father Ronald said your abuelo was going to take you to Nevada. That's not close, John."

"When he gets here, I want to ask him if we can just stay," I said. "Maybe he will see that we are alright with your family, and we can just stay."

The night before when I lay on the ground, I imagined it. Manuel and me could sign up to work in the mines like my father did. We could bring home money, and we could stay in our home.

"I don't think he's going to say yes, John. You're naive," Della said. She said it with kindness though and dropped her hand into mine and slid her fingers between mine too.

She turned to kiss me. I could feel it. Her body swung around slowly, and she leaned in with her eyes closed. When her lips got so close to mine, a large piece of corn hit her on the head.

"Ut, ut, ut, no!" Señor Chavez yelled from the edge of the corn. Then he disappeared into his work. They had sympathy for us, but they were still watching me and Della. "No babies!" Her father yelled. We were thirteen years old. I really had no idea why he thought about babies, but he still frightened me enough to back away and smile.

Walking with Della out in their corn, I somehow believed the universe and Chavez' love for us would convince my grandfather to let us stay there with them. I made the sign of the cross over and over again until my eyes got tired—and I prayed.

Chapter Fifteen

Della
1933

THERE WAS SOMETHING ABOUT THAT QUIET KID WHO SLEPT IN the living room that kept me up that night after we had gotten caught, again, in the corn trying to kiss. I think if I would have just been a little quicker, we could have gotten away with it, but he had to start talking about asking his grandfather if he and his brothers and Maria could stay.

I thought this was dumb. First, I don't think my mom would have let them stay even if John was able to convince his grandfather. She was kind, but her kindness had its limits. She knew she could keep us all there for a few days, but I could not see my mom agreeing to having all of them live with us.

"We're not the goddamned grandparents," I imagined her saying. "Family is family is pinche family." Her cursing of the idea already had become real in my mind.

But deep down, I wished they could stay. I wished their grandfather would never come. Who knew, maybe he wouldn't. Maybe my mom wouldn't have anything to say about it at all, and we would have to keep them because there was no way she would let them be taken to a home ran by all of the honkies in town. She'd rather die than have that happen.

"What would they eat, porridge? Corn bread? Ew. That stuff is so dry it makes the milk in my tetas dry up just thinking about it," she'd say. I imagined her telling Father Ronald that since John's grandfather never showed up, the only option was for the children to stay with them and for, "the church to kick in to show that it really is a house of God. Nothing extra, I'm an honest woman, but the church could show some mercy."

For a moment, I thought about us spending the next five or six years together before I left for a university. At that point, I think I would probably have fallen out of love with him—I imagined—and would be ready to move on, but those five years would be wonderful. No one, except for my father, liked to listen to me talk as much as John did, and I liked it when he listened.

I lay there for a little while longer. The snores from the boys rattled together against the thin wall and beneath the door and into our room. I thought about the chance that maybe his grandfather would never come, and when I finally fell asleep after lingering in that in-between place where dreams and reality merge together, I believed it had already happened.

Chapter Sixteen

John
1933

HEADLIGHTS STOPPED ON THE DIRT ROAD IN FRONT THE HOUSE. They were square and lit up the front window of the Chavez home. The bright light screamed in where there were no curtains, and soft light made the curtained windows glow. The light seemed so foreign, like aliens themselves had come for our frijoles.

Paulo was asleep beside me, but Manuel and Ernie and I shot up and looked out the window together. The three of us huddled together in the kitchen, somehow knowing that life was going to change, and not for the better.

"Mama, Papa," Ernie yelled out. Before he finished screaming, Señor and Señora Chavez had already come out of their bedroom, the pistol hanging from around Señora Chavez' waist, clinging to a belt that encircled her cotton nightgown. She was ready to shoot anyone in her path. She placed her hand on the butt of the pistol and pulled us behind her.

From the car, a body emerged and stood in the headlights. The man raised his hands in the air to show that he wasn't there to rob them, not of their food or clothes or valuables, that is.

He obviously saw all of our silhouettes standing in the windows watching him because he yelled out, "I am Mr. Cordova. I'm here for my grandchildren." He didn't say Señor Cordova. He didn't say mi nietos. He said "Mr." and "grandchildren," and it felt really weird to me.

He walked toward the front door with his hands falling down toward his hips, walked up the front steps, and then through the front door without the slightest hint of knocking, treating the Chavez home like it were his own.

He was light skinned and had a top hat balanced on his head and a cane in his hand like the rich men who owned the mining company. The cold night sucked the warm air out of the house and into the darkness behind him.

He stood for a moment and looked directly at all the children and then found Paulo asleep on the floor in the living room. He was never too far from the rest of us. We thought that if we let him out of our sight, somehow a car would find him and fling him into the desert too.

"Let's go," the man said. "Which ones of you are my grand-children?"

Señor Chavez stepped forward toward him and stuck out his hand.

"Buenas noches, Señor Cordova, would you like to talk over some coffee?"

The tall man just shook his head, not even extending his hand to Señor Chavez.

"We don't have time. I have business on Thursday in Reno that I cannot miss. Children, whichever ones are mine, get your stuff to the car and let's go," Señor Cordova said.

"Well, that's some rude-ass shit," Della said under her breath. Maria came from the edge of the bedroom and merged next to her.

"At least have some coffee and stay for a moment."

"I will not stay in a home with a child who has no respect like this young lady," Señor Cordova said. He pointed at Della and shook his head. "Uneducated ranchers and miners. This is why we left here twenty years ago."

"She is really smart, the smartest girl I know," I said to my grandfather, frustrated at the way he looked at Della.

He was not a stranger in the real sense of the word. He was my mother's father. But he was a stranger to us.

He walked up to me, asked me my name, and when I told him, he backhanded me.

"You will learn quickly to not talk back to me, Johnny," he said. My parents never called me Johnny. He did it to make me feel little.

Señor Chavez shook his head. He closed his eyes and dropped his head. I expected Señora Chavez to do something, but she didn't. With her gun on her hip, she just shook her head, gathered us all up, gave us hug, and whispered in our ears, "You're always welcome back here."

I looked at her, begging her with my eyes to stop him, but she only said, "He is family. There is nothing we can do, John. I am so sorry."

And that was it.

A howl of a lone coyote cut between the rumble of the engine and Paulo's budding cries in Manuel's arms after he picked him up off the soft makeshift bed we had made for him out my parents' clothing that smelled like them.

"Move, or I'll move you with this," my grandfather said. He waved his cane in the air.

I looked back at Della. I wanted to stay with her. At that moment, it wasn't because I loved her like my dad loved my mom, but because she was safe. She was not Reno. She had become my home.

She ran to me, quickly, and hugged me, kissing me on the cheek.

That's when I felt the first swift swat of my grandfather's cane against my back. He stood in the doorway, his eyes squeezed at the bridge of his nose. His brows followed them to form a deep 'V' in the center of his forehead, and his nostrils flared above a very thin, black, and manicured mustache that ran above his top lip.

He raised his cane in the air.

"Get in the car," he said. "Now."

He did not yell. He only raised his deep voice.

The four of us stood still. It was less an act of defiance and more a state of paralyzation.

Paulo broke the silence again with a howl into the fleshy nook of his older brother's shoulder.

The man's cane swung down fast toward the littlest of us all, the tiny boy who had just lost his mom and dad and who couldn't understand why they weren't coming home.

Manuel swung his left side toward the falling cane to shield Paulo from its blow, but the loud thwack of the wood against bone did not hit him. The cane landed square against Maria's dark, dark forearm. She had jumped in front of us to take the blow just like Mr. Chavez had done to protect Della, and the cane broke the skin and bone of her thin but strong forearm on its way toward Paulo's body.

She fell to the ground, holding her bloodied arm and holding back tears. She would not let him see her cry, even if her wrist fell limp at the point of impact.

"Out. Now," my grandfather said.

He placed his top hat back on his head and then he growled a little when we didn't immediately move. Within a second, he snatched little Paulo and carried him off into the night. We had no choice but to follow him.

"Adios," the Chavezes said together behind us. And I swear I heard Della cry.

TWO DAYS EARLIER, I HAD gathered things. Somewhere inside me, even so young, I knew we couldn't stay home. Someone would come to take us from the house we grew up in; the place where we ran around my mother, fighting and slapping and pinching each other; the place where my father would eventually catch us and pull us over his knee and spank us for bumping my mom and spilling hot corn and bean soup all over her bare skin. Someone would take us away, eventually.

I dug through my mom and dad's closet. Before they died, we had no business in there.

"You have this whole house and all of the countryside to play in. There's no need for you to be in our closet," my father would say when one of us would hide there during hide and go seek or one of us would just get nosey and start snooping through their things on a long, hot summer day when the lazy, wandering scorpions and snakes owned the desert landscape, hiding in my father's chile plants and sunbathing on the front step of the house. "This closet is mine and your mother's."

It was the smell that hit me first. My father's leather shoes. The ones he only wore to church. My mother's floral perfume. The scent she only wore to church too. I dug through their folded clothes and the blankets my mom had knitted. I didn't know what I was searching for. But I dug through it all, my hands swimming through old socks and shirts that my father saved for planting the chiles, all of them stained with oil or dirt. The smells consumed me. My parents lived in those clothes, they sweated in them, and no matter how many times my mom scrubbed them and dragged them back and forth over her favorite washboard, she couldn't wring out her sweet sweat and my father's musky and rich odor mixed with the sand carried by the dry wind of the badlands of New Mexico.

I fell into the clothes and cried. My body rolled back and forth, smacking the bottom shelf. I yelled out to the heavens, cursing God.

And then I found what I had been looking for, or, more truly, it found me. From the top shelf of the closet, a photo drifted down through the air and landed on my chest. I watched it float down. As if it were being held by an angel and slowly pulled down through the air, it took a couple seconds to reach me.

I held it in my hands. An old picture of my parents when they were young and without kids.

My father had to have been about seventeen years old in

the black and white photo. His skin was so dark that he nearly blended into the giant boulder that he leaned against. His hair, as thick as wool, climbed down his forehead, nearly touching his thick, black eyebrows. His pants, held against his body with a very thin belt, were hiked up about six inches above his very thick, hard waist. His young skin, so taught and smooth, only looked rough because he stood next to my mother. He leaned in to stare at her eyes. She looked away from him, a shy gaze into the mountains.

Her light skin contrasted gravely against his like the two colors of a magpie clashing against each other on the belly of the earth. Her hair looked nearly blonde, and though I couldn't see the color of her eyes, I imagined the grey and blue tint that circled in the white around them. Her dress fell around her. She had none of the weight she had gained from carrying and bearing four children, and her shy smile and open gaze transfixed me. For a moment, I didn't think about her as my mother but more as just a young girl whose life would end a short fifteen years later.

It was all there, of course. Their young, yet-to-be-tortured faces. Their shared love for each other. My dad's eternal need to make my mother smile by whatever means possible, whispering something in her ear as she turned away from him to control her blushing. The truth that I wanted to see, that they were made for each other. It lived in black and white and the shades of gray that swam across the slick photo. And, of course, scattered across their faces were hints of my brothers and sister; Maria's dark skin a copy of my father's; Manuel and Paulo's light skin that reflected the sun like my mother's; and mine, of course, a shade or two lighter than my father's and Maria's and a shade or two darker than Manuel's and Paulo's. It was all there. The truth that they were perfect for each other.

I found my father's chile knife and shoved it in my pocket too.

* * *

I STUDIED THE PHOTO IN my grandfather's car on the way out of Colorado. I ran my fingers across their faces even though I couldn't see them in the dark night, the house of our childhood disappearing into the cold.

Besides the rumbling of the thin tires over the dusty, rocky road that would lead us to the Highway that stretched across the country from Atlantic City to San Francisco, the quiet of the night put us to sleep in the back seat of my grandfather's new car. Our bodies fell over onto each other. What would have started a war of pinching and hitting in our shared bed at home gave us comfort, like our shoulders and arms and legs and laps were the only part of home that we brought with us. My grandfather had sold the house and everything in it before he even came to see us.

In the quiet night, my grandfather looked back on us through the rearview mirror, his white eyes reflecting back at us.

"Where's Maria," he asked. "She back there? Because I can't even see her. She's so dammed dark like your father that she blends into the night. I can see the rest of you, John fades out a bit, but you two, Manuel or Paulo, I can see just fine."

Maria sat up, bleary.

"I'm here, Señor," she said. "I was sleeping."

"I still can't see you, you little darky," he said. "I'm guessing all those little black boys whose fathers worked with your father in the mines really like you, don't they?" He laughed as if he had just made a joke. We were used to laughter in our house, but this laughter sounded different, filled with meanness instead of the happiness we got when my dad chased us around the house and tickled us until our stomachs hurt.

"Well, maybe we can scrub some of that skin off you. You could just be dirty," he said.

My sister Maria was the cleanest person I knew, and when I looked at her, I saw my father. I wanted to grab my grandfather's eyes, dig my fingers into his sockets, and tug. I wanted to feel his blood on my fingers and hear him yell in pain.

Manuel shook next to me. He too felt that rage. But Maria quelled it.

"How long until we get home?" she asked.

My grandfather's eyes darted forward toward the long-outstretched road. Then his eyes shot back at us again.

"Ten hours," he said. "Now, go back to sleep. From now on, you are no longer Mexican or Indian. You are proud Cordovas from Spain. Do you understand me?"

"Yes," we all mumbled.

Under the man's breath, carried in the warm air of the heater that sat on his shoulders first and then drifted back toward us, he whispered, "The dirty brown one will spoil it all."

We fell back into each other and sleep came again. Together in silence, with each other, we knew that we may never have that piece of home again.

Chapter Seventeen

Della
1933

I DID CRY.

When I saw John leave with that asshole of a man, I did cry. I wanted to chase after that stupid kid who could have kissed me ten times if he wasn't so damned shy and dumb.

Like looking through a telescope and seeing the blurry blinks of night come into focus to form patterns across the black sky of Western Colorado, I saw John's life so clearly. His grandfather was a mean bastard, the likes I had rarely seen outside of the racist KKK in my life. He was cold. Cold men were sometimes crueler than hateful men. Hateful men have passions. Their passions can be turned to caring if you get into their heart, but cold men are just cold. They are cut off from the world. They have walls. There is always a sliver into the heart of hateful man. Cold men seal everything up with walls of ice.

John left with a cold hateful man, and I wanted to chase after him, but my mom held me against her.

"How can we just let them leave with that man?" I screamed into the crook between her chest and arm. "How can we be so weak? We're Chavezes!"

I tried to pull away from her and yell into her face, but her sinewed arms held me close. She whispered over my cries.

"Family is family, Della. We have no right to keep them here. If we tried to fight them, we would lose. We would lose them eventually. Family is family, mija," she said.

The little boys had woken up and wandered into the kitchen with their eyes covered in sleep. Ernie fell to the ground and leaned against the wall. He dropped his head into his hands. He too had lost a close friend. He too had lost a Garcia.

"Let's all get to bed," my father said. "Let's all sleep and we can talk more in the morning."

He made the rounds, gathering the boys and me in his arms and pulling us through the house toward our room. Like he did when we were little, he tucked us all in together beneath the sheets, kissed each of our heads—even Ernie's—he said goodnight, and he closed the door behind him, the light disappearing with him.

"I could have shot that son of a bitch," I heard my mother say.

"I know, Benita, I know. Me too," my father said. "But you are right. Family is family. Blood is blood. And we couldn't afford to raise eight children, not today, not this year. The dust has come. The land has dried."

I did cry.

Chapter Eighteen

John
1934

COMING FROM OUR HOME AT THE EDGE OF THE DESERT AND entering theirs felt like moving from the warmth of the edge of fire to the dry, cold surface of the ice that covered Lake Tahoe. The land felt barren. We had just moved from where the land had died because of the dust, but I remembered the green and fertile fields from before the earth had died around us. Where my grandpa took us, however, had not died in the dust but seemed to live until we hit the edges of the Truckee River whose waters sprouted greens more green than I had ever seen, and the water itself flowed so wide and strong that all I wanted to do was jump into it and float away home to Colorado.

Beyond moving from the low desert to the high desert among the mountains, we'd come from a place where hugs and kisses were shared between our parents and given out to us like children tossing candy from a float in a parade. We landed in a home where physical affection seemed to be banned—somewhere in the house a book of old rules lay, I imagined, and the first rule was to keep all forms of outward affection to thyself. This gospel was so foreign to us that we got in trouble for hugging, told by our grandfather that that kind of stuff was not for us and that we should keep our damned hands to ourselves because this wasn't kissy Mexico.

My grandma had a niceness to her that my grandfather did not, but she held it very close to her—except with baby Paulo. We, as my grandfather liked to rant, were given to him so that Christ could test him. He believed his grandchildren had been dropped in his home to be the burden that Jesus spoke about in the Bible, something we all had to carry, a testament of faith, to get past Peter's Golden Gates. And he wanted his new burden, his four freeloaders, to keep the house as clean and as quiet as it had been before we got there.

We were to be seen very little and not heard at all.

We did what our grandfather told us to do, but all for different reasons. We stopped speaking Spanish, first off. It wasn't spoken in the home, and if we got caught speaking it, Grandpa would whip us with his belt. I remember his eyes the most. If you could capture steel and rust and round them out, shining them up to make a glossy glow on a little ball, and put them into my grandfather's deep eye sockets, you could see what I saw. They seemed so confident behind the belt, so full of the outright righteousness that came with every slap of leather across our bare skin. He believed what he was doing was right, and you can't fight with or change a man like that. We learned quickly to do everything he said to avoid the beatings.

Once, one day at dinner during those first few months, Manuel asked if he could have some more bread without it being offered. My grandpa backhanded him so hard that one of Manuel's teeth cracked. Instead of saying anything about the tooth, Manuel swallowed it, not willing to give my grandpa the satisfaction of breaking part of him. Manuel was quiet and stubborn and tough, just like our parents, and I loved him for it. Maria and I never said a word at the table after that, and I know Manuel was glad it all happened that way so that we could avoid making the same mistake. He was always such a damned martyr.

They only allowed Paulo to go to school. And my grandmother brought Paulo into her arms like he was her own. He alone escaped all the whippings and lashings and the silvery and rusty glare of my grandfather.

The boy slept with my grandma in her bed for the first year after we were thrown in their home, the other three of us huddling together in a twin bed in the cold corner of the ranch house. For us—Manuel, Maria, and me—seeing Paolo, our littlest, avoid the belt and the beatings and the shovel and spend his days wrapped in my grandmother's love or in the wooden seat of the local school, made our work worth it. We loved him, and we knew that we couldn't bear it if he had to live the life we lived, so we didn't say a word about it, fearful that my grandfather would turn on our young brother out of spite, to punish us for our words. We hugged him and played with him when we could, comforted in the fact that his smile was real.

When we went out in public, before any of us could leave the house, my grandfather made sure that we all looked as European as possible. He went to extremes to kill the Mexican parts of us. For Manuel and me who looked somewhat Mestizo, he dressed us in slacks and collared shirts, slicked back our hair, and made us wear hats, tapping our cheeks and saying, "That stuff sure works. You're getting back to your real color every day." He was talking about the stuff he made in his basement to cover our skin. He rubbed it over our skin and smeared it across our arms. He was pretty proud of his concoction, though I don't know what he put in it. It smelled like rubber.

The darkness of my father's skin began to fade in us, to shed like the skin of a snake, and, looking in the mirror after a full winter and a summer of having had our skin covered in slime, we looked lighter, very close to my grandmother and grandfather's shade, more olive than brown, and this corresponded with less whipping.

When the language had been eradicated like a swarming bug and our skin had become closer to my grandfather's hue— when he looked across the table at us two boys and saw younger versions of himself—the man stopped hitting us as much. But only us.

Chapter Nineteen

Della
1934

I'D BEGUN TO LIVE IN THE TRINIDAD LIBRARY. IT WAS BIG, AND I could disappear in it. I'd find myself lost in the stacks, and, yes, damnit, I used to smell the must of the books and lick my fingers when I got paper cuts from the magazines so that I didn't have to get up to go to the bathroom to wash the blood off. And my curiosity, though I tried to read fiction or poetry, always pulled me toward science. Once I had devoured all the old science in the old books, I went straight for the periodicals section to see what was new.

"POPULAR SCIENCE MONTHLY translates the wonders of science into terms that apply personally to the average man... THE average man's biggest task is to rule himself before he can learn to control the elements...THE average man has an average body. It may be likened to an automobile engine that must see him to the end of his journey. But any engine, to operate success-fully, must have a car...MOST men today have automobiles, or hope to have them. With car ownership come problems...THE average man has a home and family, or expects to have them. He wants to know how to make new and useful things at home. He wants to know how to lighten the daily labor in his household.

"IN SCIENCE there is imagination. And for the average man, the curious man, the imaginative man, POPULAR SCI-ENCE MONTHLY is like a magic carpet. Hundreds of articles and pictures in each issue can transport him to places where men are doing new and amazing things and thinking significant thoughts."

I put down the library's copy of *Popular Science Monthly*.

The average man? What about me? I thought to myself. That was bullshit. I scanned the pages of the magazine looking for a mention of a woman scientist or a woman professor or a woman scholar. I stopped briefly and read the article "Checking Up on Einstein's Theories," which was good because it looked at Einstein's theory that time and light bend in space and said that a new telescope, taking a look at the sun, proved that to be true, but, hell, I'd already taken Einstein's word for it. I'd read the theory in *The Scientific Journal* when I was around eleven years old, and it made a whole lot of sense to me. It almost pissed me off to so see that some jackass thought that he needed to check up on Einstein.

I scanned and scanned and then I found a picture of a woman with the abbreviation "Dr." before her name, and I almost tore that goddamned page out of the magazine when I saw her in a hat with flowers on top of it, her thick, round, and sagging face beneath. She looked smart. Dr. Katherine B. Davis. She was the only woman mentioned in the magazine, so instead of reading the brief caption below her photo, I read the captions of Dr. C.W. Kanolt and Dr. O.E. Hovey whose photos shared the page with hers. She had landed on a page of men who had achieved scientific breakthroughs.

Dr. Kanolt worked with liquid and solid nitrogen and had led the way in element transformation—I liked that, taking one thing and stabilizing it as another. Dr. Kanolt, in his picture, stared at a giant tube with nitrogen frozen in it, his thick goatee hanging down in unison with the tube. Dr. Hovey held a tiny microscope up to his eye and looked a small example of a petrified thunderbolt. It was black and white and small, so I couldn't get a good look at it, but I imagined how beautiful the glass would look up close.

After reading about their achievements, I scanned over Dr. Davis' photo, excited for the grand finale, excited to see what the one woman in the magazine had accomplished.

"Dr. Katherine B. Davis, Director the New York Bureau of Hygiene. Discussing answers to questionnaires recently sent to 1,000 married women, most of them college graduates, she says: 'We are certain that in the future scientists will place at the disposal of humanity something that will help solve the serious problems of sex relationships.'"

What? Sex relationships?

"One of the most hopeful bits of evidence about American social life is that 872 of 1000 women answered, without qualification, 'Yes' as to the happiness of their married life."

"This is bullshit," I said out loud.

The librarian, a woman who had come to know my outbursts, whispered loudly, "Della, shhh." Then she smiled at me.

Women are happy in their married life? That's the whole goddamned study? That's not science. That's feeding manure to the cow, telling men who read *Popular Science* that all is good in the world, and a woman doctor is here to prove it. These women must not live on los ranchos or with husbands who come home from the mine. They must not live with men who get drunk and beat them. They must not have to haul shit out of a barn or take care of their kids alone when something happens in the bottom of a mine and their husbands never come home.

This is it? That's all we get. Pinche bullshit, is what that is.

I flipped to the back of the magazine. On the second to last page, there were two puzzles. On the top of the page, it read: Interactive Animal Stroop Effect Experiment.

Below the title there were instructions: Have someone count out time in seconds. As soon as you see the pictures, identify the animals as fast as you can and write them on a piece of paper in order. When you have finished, say finish to the person counting time. The time it took you to name the animals will be your initial time. Then move on to the second set of animals and repeat. When finished with the second set of animals, subtract the first time from the second to create a difference. This is your final score. Flip to the next page to see how you compared to other men who have taken the test.

Below the instructions, the first test had pictures of twenty animals with the name of the animal printed on top of the picture. A penguin picture had the word "penguin" written on it. A bear picture had the word "bear" written on it. A cat had "cat" on it. Twenty animals in four rows of five.

I didn't have anyone with me to count the seconds it took me to do it, so I imagined a place in the corner of my brain that would do the counting while I named the animals, a little room in my brain that felt separate from the other part of my brain that would read the text. Then I began.

Penguin. Cow. Pig. Bear. Turtle…Giraffe. Pig. Spider. Horse. Bee. Part of my brain counted while the other wrote down the names of the animals. It was easy. It was supposed to be, though I don't think many people could count at the same time while playing the game. I had started doing that when I was four years old. I would talk to my dad in the rows of apple trees, help him pick them from the branches, and count how many we were picking.

"Nine hundred seventy-eight apples today, dad," I told him when we gathered them up into the baskets and threw them in the cart.

"I didn't hear you count them," he said, "but I believe you."

He smiled and kissed my forehead and tossed me a sweet apple from the top of the pile.

"Nine hundred seventy-seven now," he said.

"Yep," I said.

He always said he believed me, and I know he did, but one night after dinner, I heard my dad rustling around outside. He was thumbing through the baskets of apples. About twenty minutes later, he came back in, walked into my room, sat on the bed and said, "How do you that?"

"Do what?" I asked.

"How do you count, pick, and jabber your mouth all day, all at the same time?" he asked.

"I just find a little room in my head for the counting and it counts for me," I said.

"Nine hundred seventy-seven," he said.

"I know, dad," I said.

He tucked me into bed and walked out of the room shaking his head.

It took me eight seconds to write down the names on the piece of paper. Of course, I got them all correct. A baby could do that.

The second test was the one that really tested this supposed Stroop Effect, supposedly. There were twenty animals in five rows, but instead of their actual name printed on them, a different animal name was printed over each animal. A cow picture had the name "spider" printed on it. A bear had "bee." A pig had "dog."

I started the time in my head again and began.

Nine seconds. It only took me nine seconds, the timer in my head going off when I finished. I checked to see if I got any wrong. I didn't.

It's easy to subtract eight seconds from nine seconds. There was a one second difference between the first test and the second test. I was kind of disappointed they weren't the same and that my time had slowed.

Jesus, Della, what are you? Some kind of idiota or something?

I flipped the page over to read what the average man had scored.

It read: most men need to take the second text on average of three times before they are one hundred percent accurate. When they are one hundred percent accurate, the average difference between times is eleven seconds.

"Hah!" I yelled out into the quiet library around me. "The average man is a pinche burro!"

The librarian shushed me.

"Pinche burros!"

"Quiet, Della," she said.

I giggled inside.

Then I flipped to the last page of the magazine. It was full of very tiny listings. Job listings and services offered. Two little lines stuck out to me.

Universities in Pennsylvania and New York looking for smart girls. Scholarships available for the most needy.

And then there was an address to write for more information.

My heart exploded. I knew I was getting away from the ranch since my dad had told me a hundred times that I would never work it when I grew up, that it would be Ernie's to run and that I was too smart to be a ranchero, but I had never known how to get there.

Now I had found the map.

IT CAME SEVEN MONTHS AFTER John and his brothers and sisters had been torn from our house in the middle of the night. It was grey and yellow, and the handwriting on the outside looked synthetic, like it had been stamped on. If it wasn't for the slight smear from the rain that dropped on it between the mail carrier's bag and the mailbox, I would have thought it was stamped.

To:
Della Chavez
Trinidad, Colorado

From:
John Cordova
Reno, Nevada

I didn't know who in the hell John Cordova was, but it only took a second to put my twos and twos together and figure it out. The old man had changed their names to Cordova. "A proud Spanish name," I could see the old bastard mouth with his lips emphasizing the "S" in Spanish.

I didn't tear the letter open, though I wanted to. I ran inside, grabbed a knife, and slid it through the folded seam at the top, doing my best to not tear the edges. I could feel John in it. Since he left, he had grown even more important to me. Those walks to the truck after school had become so lonely. Ernie and I walked together, of course, but Ernie was a lot like John. He was so quiet and rarely said anything back. Ernie, unlike John, didn't say a lot back because he wasn't listening. John listened. I could feel him, his neck turned toward me with the honest intent to grab everything I said and keep it inside him. I learned once he left that he was the only one that I wanted to hear what I had to say.

I had just turned fourteen years old when I got the first letter. And holy shit, I never thought that that boy who followed me around, said so little, and never said a word in school could express himself so well. His writing. Holy shit. He was smart.

Dear Della,

The last few months have come and gone like both a bucking bronco and the slow movement of water through a creek without a current. It moves quick because my grandpa makes Manuel and me and Maria work the ranch all day and go directly to bed after dinner. We have no family time like we used to except for when we climb under the covers together and look up at the ceiling and out the window and talk about our escape back to Colorado.

We won't come though because mis abuelos have really cared for little Paulo. We have to stay and look after him. I fear that my grandfather will turn on him someday, and I could not live with it if he hurt him.

Maria takes the worst of all of this. My grandfather hates her because she has dark skin like my dad. He whips us. He backhands us whenever we speak at the table.

I miss you. I think about those times together in the fields on Sundays, and I dream about them. I put myself in those memories when I fall asleep at night. I can smell your apple tree in my dreams, and I miss your laughter.

All my love,
John

I read the letter and then I imagined John next to me on all of those long walks from school to the truck and our treks through the hay fields and our talks by the apple tree that my father had saved for me. He was so quiet, but his brain was thinking these beautiful things. His heart was talking about love and the smell of the apple tree.

I put the letter down, grabbed a piece of paper from my school's supplies, and started to write him back, but everything I wrote seemed so goddamned infantile compared to the way he put his feelings down on paper. I could solve puzzles and do algebra without a hint of effort, but, it turns out, I could not write about my feelings or love. Damnit. Because I wanted to.

Dear John,

I hope to see you soon. I like the apple tree, too. I am lonely on my walks. I hate your grandfather. What an asshole.

If I could be in the fields with you, I would do it today.

Ugh. That's awful. I had never felt so stupid in my entire life, like an idiota responding to Shakespeare. I tried to write three more letters, each one worse than the previous one.

When I finally sealed up the letter, wrote John's address on the outside, and licked the sealer, the letter read:

Dear John,

I miss you, and I think I love you.

Always,

Della

And then I put it in the mailbox and sat on our porch until the mailman picked it up and took it away to Reno.

Chapter Twenty

John
1934

RENO WAS HARD FOR ALL OF US, BUT IT WAS HARDEST ON MARIA. Her skin would not lighten. Her face would not change. No matter how much gunk my grandfather slathered across her face, no matter how hard he tried to rub it in, she had the rich, dark Garcia blood from my father that, to me, looked so beautiful on her, like the surface of the richest soil of the earth where my father's chiles grew bright crimson and purple.

At times, at church, my grandfather deserted my sister, very tactfully, because he would never want to be seen as cruel by his fellow church members. Many times, he would ask Maria to do a special chore before Mass, warming up to her for a couple hours before church, playing on her desire to be loved by him, a young girl who had lost her father and craved the attention. The chore would take all morning of her devoted efforts to get it done. Meanwhile, the rest of the family would get ready, climb in the Cadillac, and go to Mass where my grandfather would shake everyone's hands, wish them peace, smile a charming smile, piously drop twenty dollars in the floating tithing basket, and return home just while Maria finished up washing all the baseboards in the house or letting out all of my grandpa's waistlines or, even, doing something fun like adding trim to hers and her grandmother's dresses to fancy them up—letting her do something she liked so it didn't seem as though she was only there to be a Cinderella-like slave. She loved Mass like my mom did and wanted to do adoration too, but he wouldn't let her because she would have to sign in, and everyone would know the dark girl was his granddaughter.

When he ran out of things for her to do, we all walked into church together and he would find a pew that only had room for five people. He systematically ushered five us in and left Maria standing in the aisle. My grandfather waved Maria away, not even looking at her. She found a spot in the back corner of the church, alone, her face full of sadness.

I once tried to join her. I jumped up and began to shuffle my body over the bent knees of my family. And I got a solid whack against the back of my neck. My grandfather's knuckles stained my skin purple and black for days. Manuel had tried once too, the oldest of us doing his best to protect his sister, but so very quickly, my grandfather quietly led him out of the church, ripped off his belt, and gave Manuel a solid beating to the back of his calves, showing all of us that even our oldest brother could not defy him. It only made Maria sadder, knowing that we had both suffered for trying to be with her.

She began to get up very early, do her chores, and go to Mass on her own, returning before we had all finished breakfast on Sunday morning with light in her eyes.

My grandfather did his best to extinguish the light. He yelled at her. He told her that she could not use the family name when she was out of the house. He whipped her for not being there in the morning when he woke up. He called her names. He did everything he could to break her, but once she had gone to Mass on Sunday, the light would not go out. She had found a place away from him, where he could not hurt her, for one hour a week, and that was all she needed.

AT FIFTEEN, AFTER A YEAR of his abuse, Maria left.

On those Sunday mornings when my grandfather made her sit away from the family, she wouldn't come home right after Mass. At first, she would stay at church for an extra hour, praying and saying the rosary. My grandfather stopped caring. He didn't like her around. As the weeks went on, she stayed longer at the church, not coming home until dinnertime. She'd told me she had begun to help clean the church for Father Bill, a young priest, and that he was paying her under the table to do so. I was just glad to see her come home with a smile because the rest of the week she would have to deal with my grandfather's cruelty.

And she did smile when she came home from church, a smile big enough and steady enough to walk past my grandfather as he scolded her on her way into the house, saying she didn't deserve God the way her whiter brothers did. He'd known that the church was all she had, and, with his cruel words, he did his best to try to strip her of that happiness too.

ONE SUNDAY, ALMOST TWO YEARS after my parents died, in the dusty heat of late July, a car pulled into our driveway after we had gotten home from Mass. I sat on the front steps and shucked corn, my fingernails full of the thin hair of the inner, white husks. Manuel cleaned the barn. Paulo lay inside beneath the fan and played Rummy with my grandmother. My grandfather walked out from behind the house and met the car in the middle of the freshly laid blacktop that he had become so proud of; his house was the only one in the neighborhood with a smooth, black driveway. Like a game of chicken, he walked toward the car, both him and the car stopping only feet before colliding.

The sun reflected against the windshield, making it difficult to see who sat behind the wheel, the glare like a bright white curtain that lay diagonal across the glass. The light breeze that had kept me just cool enough to bear the heat, the threads of corn husk weaving through my fingers, had suddenly stopped when Maria popped out of the passenger side door.

She tried to walk past my grandfather in a straight line toward me, but he caught her by the arm and yanked her back toward him so hard that I feared her arm might break again. I stood up. I ran to them both. I held my finger in the air, and I shouted.

"Leave her alone, abuelo!"

With his other hand, the man slugged me in the face so hard that my cheek split open, and the sound of my jaw breaking echoed across the dry earth. At fourteen years old, I had no chance against the strong, fifty-year-old man.

He held my sister so tightly, his lighter skin pressing fleshy caverns into her brown arm. Then he hit her hard, holding her up from falling only to smack her again.

My eyes burned. I couldn't talk. The bones in my mouth rattled with each shot of sharp air that I pulled in.

The driver's side door of the car opened and Father Bill stepped out of the car. His white face reddened in the sunlight. Red patches of anger mixed with quickly pinkening skin.

Blood seeped into my eye. The liquid burned. My grandfather held me down on the ground with his foot, his knee bent above me, Maria gripped in his hands. He slapped my sister again, right in front of Father Bill.

The young priest did not move. Instead, he just rubbed his white collar with his left hand and patted the sweat off his forehead with a cloth with the other hand as if my grandfather didn't hold his granddaughter in the air and his grandson on the ground.

I thought of scorpions and snakes roaming beyond me, smelling my blood and inching closer to me.

Father Bill took a few steps toward my grandfather.

The sun hung above us at midday.

"Paul," Father Bill said. My grandfather's birth name was Paulo, and if you wanted an ass whoopin' you would call him by his given name. Father Bill, knowing the man who stood his ground in front of the priest's car, called my grandfather Paul.

"You're a good Catholic man. This violence doesn't suit you.

Now does it?" the priest tried to be confident, to persuade my grandfather to listen to him, but his voice gave him away. What should have been a statement came out as a quivering question, "Now does it?"

My grandfather remained silent.

The priest walked up to him. He set one foot down in front of the other with purpose. Like he was climbing the pulpit, the Bible at the top, already opened for him to read and his flock out in front of him waiting for him to speak, he walked with confidence. His black shirt tugged at the edges of his rounding belly. He stood in front of my grandfather, his head held high like he himself were the same Word of God that he was in Mass, standing on the blacktop with the same bravado and divine authority.

My grandfather backhanded Father Bill's bright, red face. His big knuckles cracked the man's nose.

The priest fell to the ground. He looked across the dirt and into my eyes. We lay level with each other. A trickle of blood fell from his nostrils, and I could see it in his face, the shock of never having been hit before in his life. The widening of his eye lids. Then the squint when the pain came on. And then, yes, tears from the man who stood in front of the pulpit every Sunday and warned against God's wrath.

His fingers scraped the newly paved driveway. His forearms pushed him up off the ground. He came to his feet. I wanted him to fight back, to at least throw a punch. He didn't. He walked slowly back behind the driver's side door of his car.

The pain in my jaw became thick like lava, hot and viscous and flowing in and out from my skull to my toes. Maria swung in his arms. She tried to smack my grandfather. She tried to hurt him.

And Father Bill stood behind the car door, the reflecting sun retreating to the west and the shadows of the giant spruce in the yard merging with the already bruising—black and blue and purple—skin that circled his eye and nose and cheek bone.

"Paul," Father Bill said.

"Not another word, Father," my grandfather said. His eyes twitched when the word "Father" came out of his mouth. "Get back in your car, leave now; this is not your church."

Maria swung a fist toward my grandfather. He dodged it and gave her another slap across the face.

Pain struck Father Bill's face. It wasn't empathy for one of his parishioners. It wasn't the church that hurt.

In me, I knew. And though I lay there, pressed into the hot blackness of driveway, I knew what was going on. It became clear in Father Bill's wince when my grandfather hit my sister. Father Bill wasn't there to talk to my grandfather about God. Not at all.

"Maria?" I said. "Father Bill?"

And with that, my grandfather let me up off the ground. Somehow he knew I was no longer against him, not completely at least.

At that point, my grandma came out of the house with Paolo beside her. The ten-year-old boy ran toward Maria. His tears wetted the blacktop for a moment and then dried away.

"Let her go," my grandmother said, following her husband with her eyes.

And he did.

Maria gave little Paulo a hug. And then me.

The pain in my broken jaw ran out of me for a moment, the thickness thinning while I watched Maria climb into Father Bill's car. They drove away, a long way away. He would leave the church. They would get married and move to Elko, Nevada.

In the moment in the driveway when I saw my older sister drive away, I felt the first real sense of relief that the world had ever given me since my parents died.

Chapter Twenty-One

Della
1934

I WANTED TO FIX IT ALL. EVEN AT SUCH A YOUNG AGE, I WANTED to fix all the problems that had been unfairly laid on my parents' shoulders, so I started reading—a lot—about farming. My father would watch me read. He'd never learned to read himself. He would glance from me reading to our small fields of alfalfa that covered the earth outside the window. If the alfalfa died, the cattle and pigs and sheep would die too.

The little boys weren't old enough to go to school in 1934 when I started grabbing the *Farmer's Almanac* from the library and taking it home with me to study. The newspapers did a good job showing how the whole middle of the country had been swamped by dust and dead crops.

My dad lingered over my shoulder while I read the almanac, wondering what in the hell a fourteen-year-old girl wanted with it.

"Maybe you could teach me to read it, mija?" he asked once.

"Yes, yes, I could, papa," I said.

He milled around, rubbed his hands through his thinning hair, and muttered, "Nah, you can't teach an old perro new tricks, darling Della."

Then he went outside with a glass of milk from Ernie's cow and watched the dust blow by. He was sad, but he wasn't drinking, and this had softened my mother to him. She would join him on the porch, place her hand on his knee. They wore handkerchiefs across their faces to filter out the dusty breeze.

The dust was ugly, but it made for the most beautiful sunsets. It layered the sun in oranges and yellows and sometimes greens, dark reds, and browns swirling together across the horizon.

Exactly four months before the Dust Bowl would give Colorado its biggest blow, when the winter had yet to leave, I sat down at the table with a piece of paper and tried to fix things for everyone. Of all the things I read in those almanacs, I learned that how you place your crops and how you rotate them can make them stronger, more durable, and give them more endurance against the dry climate. I learned it made a difference in what you grew too. Some crops are weak. Some crops are strong. And my mom was right about the wild grass. As a natural weed, it dug its roots deep into the earth and kept the soil from floating away.

"Keep the grass where it goddamn belongs," she always said, so I kept that in mind the whole time.

I began to draw. I started with two large rectangles that mirrored the crop fields outside the kitchen window and a large circle to the west of them that outlined a perfectly proportioned image of the grazing fields. Then I began to divide the rectangles up, first converting the two rectangles to four squares and the four squares into eight rectangles. And I didn't stop with them. I divided the grazing fields up too, tracing rectangles along the edge of the outer fence and drawing stick figures to represent the cattle in the middle of the triangles. At the edges, I colored in wild grass as a border.

When my father came inside from work each night, he found me sitting there drawing. He always did his best to not let me see the worry on his face, to wipe it away with the cloth that cleaned his face.

"What're you drawing?" he'd ask me each time.

"My crops," I told him.

"Not your crops, Della, my crops," he said. "They'll never be your crops, Della. They'll be Ernie's crops."

This used to piss me off for the longest time. What the hell? They could be my crops. I could work them. I could work them strong. But I didn't say anything, just let it go as old machismo bullshit that ran through his old Mexican blood.

"Can I have a look?" he'd ask.

"Nope, these crops on this piece of paper are my crops, so since they're not your crops or Ernie's crops, I'll keep my crops to myself," I'd say.

I could see that he wanted to get angry with me, to tell me to watch my mouth, but I knew he didn't have the energy for it, so he just kissed my head, the smell of sweat and dirt and soap falling off him.

Truth was that I am, and I always have been a perfectionist, and I didn't want my dad seeing my crops until I had figured out exactly how to fix it all. I studied the almanacs, I drew, I crumpled up my school papers that I used the backs of to do my drawings. There wasn't any spare paper laying around those days, and paper was not highest on my parents' shopping list for sure.

I drew a proportionately perfect rendering of their entire property, parceling it out in plot after plot, and marking each plot with numbers from one to twenty-two. This seemed like the way to start, to draw exactly what we had and what was still growing. Over the last few years, we had lost a lot of land to the dust. It had eaten the edges of what was once rich soil and slowly eroded away, the wind carrying the topsoil away to the west, so I didn't start with what we once had but what we had now.

Then I lined out a chart. On the top row, I wrote in the names of crops and the cattle. Down the left-hand column, I filled in the numbers, twenty-two in all. In the intersecting cells, I scribbled in the next three years of upcoming crops 1934, 1935, or 1936 next to the crops of Alfalfa, Corn, Beans—beans, a crop they hadn't grown in years because it didn't sell at a high enough yield to grow compared to corn or alfalfa—and livestock which had been divided into three cells at the top of the chart, fenced in by a horizontal slash and then vertical slashes through it. I left the pigs in the barn. They could survive on any leftovers, but the cattle needed to be fenced in or they'd wander off in search of food and either get killed or die in the mountains, starving because they were too stupid to stay put.

I crumpled the paper up, threw it in the garbage, grabbed another, and started over. My hands shook as they rushed over the drawing, the pencil gliding across the paper's yellowish surface. Teeth bit my lower lip, eyes dry from barely blinking as I drew out the plots again, shifting the sizes of the area of the plots and then drawing the chart again, matching the crop with the plot with the year, a shuffling of growth. It had become one of those moments when I knew I was close to cracking it, to figuring it out, to finding the answer—to fixing the problem that lay in front of us and to saving our farm. Blood trickled from my lip and onto the paper.

When my father came out of his room and saw the bubbles of red on my chin, and my red eyes, he tried to tell me to stop, using his stern voice that didn't really seem too believable.

"Della, stop, you're hurting yourself," he said.

"No, Papa," I said. "Not yet."

Again, I tossed the goddamned paper in the garbage. This time, however, before starting again, I ran out into the fields. I ran as fast as I could, the quick burst from the table scaring the living shit out of my dad who dribbled hot coffee on his chin and said "Della, que pasa?" as the door shut behind me.

In the alfalfa field, I stopped at seven different spots, dug my hand into the soil, and siphoned the dirt through my fingers. I did the same thing in the middle of the corn and in the middle of the beans. There was a difference. Huge differences.

I dug my fingers into the soil that surrounded our cattle. This time, instead of pulling the soil up, I pushed all of my fingers straight down into the rich earth.

"We've got all of this," I said. "It's rich. It's been turned over by those stupid cows."

I stood among the longhorns. They roamed around me.

Some, in the darkening of the day, lay down on the earth. Manure covered the ground in brown and green splotches. The cattle had lived there for years, eating and shitting and roaming and copulating. They'd had no need to move them—the soil on the top of the world, more than six thousand feet above sea level and in a valley that had never really been harvested over the millions of years of its life. The smell of manure. The ripeness of the earth. The sun setting over the Rockies.

"Goddamnit, that's it," I said. "Holy hell. I got it."

I stood and breathed in. Then I looked east out over the plains at the dust clouds of the earth.

The kitchen, the warmth of the world in one little room, had been filled with my mom and brothers and dad by the time I came back in.

"Corn," my mom said. "Time for the corn." She had become impatient with me. The corn should have been made twenty minutes before while I stood with my fingers in the dirt. I reached for my pencil and paper, but my mom shot me a glare that said, "Nope. Nope. Not if you want to keep your fingers, mija, adelante."

I heated a large cast iron skillet over the open burner, the one freed up from the beans that had been transferred to a bowl to be passed around the wooden table. I dropped a teaspoon of lard into the pan. The sizzle sounded so lovely against the laughs and chatter of the kitchen. My father, standing next to me, watched the lard sizzle over my shoulder and then placed his hand on my head and kissed my sweating brow. We always shared this. The lard became a thick, full liquid that spread out across the pan. It lacquered the base and I dropped in the corn.

The cold corn danced across the cast iron base, the yellow and orange against a black canvas and the beauty of a year's worth of work. I loved watching it every time I cooked it. The corn cooked so fast—so effortlessly, so durably. I reached out my hand, and my dad placed a bowl of crispy, moist pork bits scraped from the edges of the pork pan into them. I dropped the pork into the corn, pushing the corn to the edges of pan, continuing to sear the corn's skin. Then I saw it, right there before I stirred the corn into the frying pork, right there in the pan that I had always used to cook.

The rich juices from the meaty chunks at the pan's center had already begun to seep out from the center and hydrate the corn with its fat and flavor, decreasing the heat and friction between the yellow and orange kernels and the sizzling hot cast iron pan. The rich, fatty juices from the chorizo melted into the dry, crispy corn. The corn sucked it all in and became moist again, at first, losing its water in the pan but then replacing it with the richer, greasier fluid that would give it so much flavor.

I quickly stirred the pork together with the corn to finish my job, to serve the family, and get back to my pencil and paper. When the skin of the corn had gotten crispy and the interior warm and soft, I pulled it from the burner and dumped it into the same bowl my dad had used to transfer the pork.

My family sat, ate, and talked. I remained quiet. My mind turned over. The thought of the soil outside circled through it again and again.

When dinner had been eaten, when the dishes had been washed in the bucket, and when the family sat at the table, my brothers reading and my mom knitting, I pulled another piece of school paper from my bag and began to draw again.

I quickly plotted all of our land and filled in the chart. The alfalfa—the strongest and most durable crop of them all—would shift along the edges of the cattle and around the beans and corn in the now twenty-three different plots in their field over the next few years, beginning with the planting in early 1934. My father knew about shifting crops. He was a good rancher, but I, at fourteen years old, knew more. He could not read the farmer's almanac.

I moved the weaker crops to the center where they would be

protected from the waves of dust that rolled across the oceans of the plain states. I loved it. Like the corn pulling the juices from the meat.

I finally had what I needed to let my dad in. I pulled the piece of paper off the table, moved his book out of the way.

"We're going to make it through dad, but we gotta plant beans too, and we got to shift all the alfalfa to the edges. It's the toughest crop. It will hold the burn back, and the rich beans and corn will feed it from the centers just like the pork in the pan— it'll feed the corn and the mierda will feed the alfalfa and the beans will feed us all, including the earth," I said.

I handed him my drawing and chart.

He lifted his coffee mug to his lips. He smiled a real smile. I could see that I had given him hope, too. Not just hope, belief.

He hung the piece of paper on the wall next to my photo and nodded his head.

Then he turned to me and said, "You will be something that I can never imagine, and someday you will tell me what you have done in this life, and it will be spectacular, and I will believe every word of it. And, from now on, you will never work in the fields again, basta."

He gave me a big hug and told me that he loved me.

"You will only read, study, and write from now on. Your younger brothers have been cradled too long. They can take your place in the fields. This ranch will never be yours. I will strip you of your love for your hands in the dirt. Lo siento, Della."

I cried.

He patted my head.

He put on his boots, and in the middle of the evening, he headed out to the fields to begin the shifting of the earth.

Chapter Twenty-Two

John
1934

MANUEL AND I HID IN OUR CHILE PATCH.

After Maria left, we found a patch of dirt, hidden near a tree along the Truckee river, about half of a mile from my grandpa's house.

My jaw healed. It took a long while, but it healed, and my grandfather never hit me again. Manuel rarely talked. He just worked hard, keeping the ranch clean, keeping his head down, and nodding a "yes" to my grandpa whenever he got asked to do something. He ate. He worked. He slept next to me in bed. He remained so quiet, only smiling when little Paulo, who had begun to really grow, would run to him and punch his older brother in the gut for fun. Manuel would buckle over, fall to the ground, and act like Paulo really hurt him, though I knew he couldn't. Just like my dad, Manuel was lean and sinewy and strong.

Manuel and I planted the guajillos and güeros and anchos, just like my dad did. We dug our hands in the dirt, the soil much richer outside of Reno along the Truckee than it ever was in southern Colorado. We prayed to the saints. We covered up the seeds. Then we sat and looked at the sun and talked about mom and dad. Manuel talked to me then under the spring sunlight, and then he told me that he blamed himself for letting our mom get out to help our dad. He was the oldest son, and he should have done it.

"I should be the dead one. Mama would still be on this earth with us. Maria wouldn't be gone. Paulo wouldn't have the wrong woman raise him to forget who we are," he'd say, over and over for years when we planted chiles. "I should be the dead one."

I didn't say anything to him. I just listened. I didn't want anyone to be the dead one.

We visited that chile patch even when we weren't planting or harvesting. Just to be brothers. We never took Paulo. If he meant to or not, he would spill the beans and tell our grandma—he was kind of a little shit. Our grandfather would surely then drive his tractor out to the patch and dig it all up. I know he would have.

That day, however, on our way back from the chilies, the postman caught us on the road.

"Hey, Cordova boys," he said. "Take this to your house for me, will ya. It'll save me some time. I'm hungry and ready to get home."

Manuel grabbed the mail from the postman. He scanned the letters, and then he held one out to me, and he said, "Look, your lover wrote you, sweet boy." He handed me a letter then he ran home with the rest of the mail, yelling, in earnest, "Don't let grandfather find that! I promise. It will lead to nothing good."

I saw Della's handwriting on the outside of the letter. My heart froze. She had written me back. My knees crumbled, so I grabbed onto a nearby fence post to brace myself. And then, with more fear than I thought existed in me, I opened the letter.

Dear John,

I miss you, and I think I love you.

Always,

Della

I held Della's letter in my hand. I ran my fingers over the letters, the words, the one sentence. Della wasn't the type to spray the letter with perfume, if she even owned any, and she wasn't the type to put on lipstick and kiss the letter. Her mom wouldn't even allow that stuff in the house. Wasted money, is what Señora Chavez would say. I could hear her saying it.

But I thought I could smell a hint of her on the page. It had to have taken the letter two weeks to get from Trinidad to Reno, but, somehow, I could smell apples when I opened it up. I believed that I could.

I knew then that I had to escape back to her.

Chapter Twenty-Three

Della
1935

It was the most beautiful morning. The sun shone so brightly that everyone seemed to have forgotten that just a few days earlier we had been hit by another dust storm. For the first time in a very long time, hope filled the air instead of dust. April 14, 1935.

We actually went to church that morning. My mom, like me, never really loved the idea of church, men standing on a pulpit and telling us how shitty we all were when we knew they were drinking and masturbating up a sandstorm of their own when they left the altar. Plus, she didn't grow up a Christian like my dad did. I think that stuff is transferred from generation to generation. Somehow trauma and grief and upheaval and migration moves from father to daughter and mother to son. It sticks in our blood and follows us. But we went to church that morning. The sun had been so bright and the sky so clear that my mom agreed to join everyone in our community for prayer. I think she really wanted to feel the hope too.

"With just a few rainstorms, we could be lifted out of this, let us pray," the priest said, and everyone prayed. It felt real that time, however. Birds flew by the stained-glass windows and sang. Little squirrels jumped from tree to tree. I know this sounds like some kind of scene from "Snow White" or some bullshit like that, but that's how it felt that day, hopeful and joyous.

After church, we changed out of our dress clothes and split up on the ranch. Dad did things he hadn't been able to do. He moved the pigs from one pen to another, cleaned out the original pen, and then moved them back. Ernie sat on the edge of the front porch and drew. I never really knew he had that in him, this need to draw, but he drew the horizon.

The little boys ran and played, and my mom took a well-used broom out and pushed all the dust off the windowsills and began to clean the outside of the house for the first time in years.

I walked through the crops. I let my hand graze the edges of the alfalfa plants and corn and beans. What I had done a year before made me so proud. Our crops were strong. We were making money again.

Three nights earlier, I couldn't sleep and heard my mother and father whisper at the kitchen table. Their voices drifted quietly back and forth to each other as if only their ears could catch them. That night too, I heard it again, which may be the reason that my mom went to church with us that morning. In the dead of night with only the coyotes calling out on the plains, they were nearly giddy.

"We're clear, Benita," my father said to her.

"Clear of what? Is this some kind of guessing game because I'm not a child and I'm not a goddamned mind reader," my mom replied.

"We have paid off all of our taxes this year. We are clear. We even made some money. It's a miracle," my father said. "It's a miracle. We sold enough pork and beef and alfalfa to other ranchers to pay it all off. We own the land. It's ours. We have been so blessed by God."

"Yes, Francisco, we have been blessed," she said. "But not by God. We haven't been blessed by the crop God or anything like that. We haven't been miraculously spared, Francisco. We were blessed with the smartest damned daughter in the whole county, hell, the whole state," she said. "That was our blessing. That smart-ass girl in the bedroom."

With this, these words that came from my mom's mouth, I fell backward onto my pillow and prayed. The praise felt like too much to handle. I didn't like it. I didn't like it at all. I wanted her to take it back. I wanted her to say something sarcastic and even demeaning. I prayed for her to follow it up with something like, "Only if that damned girl would clean up after herself or stop reading so much or learn how to talk to people without being so blunt." But she didn't; her praise hung in the air, and it was too much for me.

Three days later, I walked through the fields, proud. At that point, when all of Las Animas County believed we had made it through, my mom's words settled in nicely. I could handle it then. The praise. We had made it.

And then the air grew very cold, and I felt like the world had gotten darker and scarier in an instant. The winds came back, and with them a cold, cold air that ran across my body and literally, and I mean goddamned literally, sent shivers up and down my spine. Within minutes, the temperature dropped. It dropped thirty degrees in a matter of an hour from the Dakotas to Texas and to our little Las Animas County.

The wind carried something dark with it. Across the eastern plain of the valley, a mountain of a cloud stormed toward our home. Black and dark and opaque, thousands of feet tall and hundreds of miles wide, the massive dust storm raced toward us. It swallowed up the world, and if I believed in the wrath of God or the end of days, this cloud of moving dust that looked darker than the darkest pit would be what I would imagine. There was nothing behind it, nothing to the side of it, and nothing above it, only black.

Screams came from the fields.

My father ran from the distant bundle of cows that just stood there like the world was completely fine. He smacked them all on their big black and white asses and begged them to run with him. A bull followed him, and the rest came too. On his way to the barn, he scooped up both of my little brothers, ran with them toward the house, and handed them off to Ernie who grabbed them in each of his arms and ran toward the cellar door that led down below our home and into our smoker room and cold storage.

"Della, adelante!" my mom shouted to me from the kitchen window and then disappeared out of sight onto the porch and then into the cellar basement. The black wall of night that came in the middle of the sunniest, clearest day in months moved across the earth like the sky had fallen onto the ground. My father ran out of the barn, closed the doors, leaving a few cows still standing in the fields and waved to me to run with him.

We clasped hands one hundred feet from the cellar door and ran together toward our family, Ernie and my mom held one of the cellar doors each, the wind doing its best to rip the rusty, metal frames from their grasps. We jumped down into the cellar and locked the doors above us. Complete blackness blotted out the last bit of light that stretched through the cracks in the foundation and the cellar door seams. The wind howled, and I have never seen the dark so damned dark. It got cold down there. My little brothers cried until their tears ran out. My father held me, and Ernie held my mother who in turned held the little ones.

With their heads in their hands, the whole county sat in church and sang the praises of the Lord and believed the minister when he said the worst had come and gone. Just a few minutes earlier, I ran my hands across the stalks and down into the dirt and wore a proud smile on my face. We had made it through. We were all in the clear, just like my dad had told my mom a few nights earlier. As they say, just when the world seems darkest, the light will come through. But sometimes, just when the world seems brightest, the darkness descends.

We huddled in the belly of the house. The storm lasted longer than I could imagine a storm could ever last. I was scared.

Out of nowhere, without any warning, a small stream of light fell through a crack in the foundation. Then, following it, like an army of little specks of hope, more light came through, and the world outside became quiet. My dad pushed as hard as he could against the doors, but he needed Ernie and me to get the first one open.

Outside, the blue skies had come back, but the Black Sunday cloud had left a blanket of dust so thick that it felt like deep snowfalls, powdery and consuming. The cows and pigs called out from the barn. They lived through it, those that followed my father into the barn and stayed put. A few others lay dead under a mound of sand in the fields, their hooves sticking out from the piles, lifeless markers of a Dust Bowl that had changed our lives forever.

Men, trapped, and having given up hope, killed themselves with shotguns when they looked outside and the only thing they could see was black. A woman drowned her children in a bathtub because she thought it was the end of days and wanted them to go to heaven without suffering. Ernie said that our neighbor took one of his pigs for a wife and made love to it through the storm and then carved it up and ate it afterward.

And then there were the truths that came. Most everyone quit. They packed up and left Las Animas County. They left their ranches, all of their possessions, and even some livestock and walked away. The depression, the Dust Bowl, and Black Sunday had killed any lasting hope that they had. Like a mass exodus, they lined the roads with starving children and walked northwest to Denver or Colorado Springs to stand in line and hope for handouts.

My mom took the boys inside the house. Their faces were covered with dried creek beds of tears that cut through the dust on their cheeks and necks. My dad, Ernie, and I, walked toward the crops. At first, we could barely see them. The drifts had covered the outer edges of our alfalfa fields. The outer three rows of alfalfa had been covered and lost. We climbed above and through the graveyard of crops that circled the inner rows of corn and beans. When we got to the center of the first field, the dust had begun to thin. All the inner crops still poked out from the soil, and the beans were alive in the earth. On the outside, wild grass poked through the sand.

This time, we believed we had made it again. Most hadn't. We had. We owned our ranch, and no one, not even the US government could take it from us.

My father hugged us both.

Only if it would rain.

Chapter Twenty-Four

John
1935

I HAD PACKED UP A SACK FULL OF CLOTHES, SOME SCONES FROM my grandmother's pantry, wishing she made tortillas like my mother did, shoved my bag beneath the porch, and waited for nightfall. The plan was to sneak away in the middle of the night. Manuel would keep Paulo safe. He would take care of our younger brother. He would stay. I would run to the Chavezes. I would start work in the mines. I could. I was fifteen years old, and they would let me. They always needed young strong men in the mines. I would do what my father did. I was proud of how hard he worked, and I could convince Della to stay in Trinidad, and in a few years, we could get married and have children and live at the edge of the raggedy peaks of the mountains.

Night came. I woke Manuel to say goodbye.

"I'm leaving, Manuel," I said. "I'm running back to Trinidad."

Manuel pulled himself up from our bed and sat on the edge of it. He rubbed his eyes and ran his hand through his thick, black hair and then down over his face.

"Johnny," he said. "You don't have any money. How will you get there?"

"The trains," I said. "I'll hop the trains. It's easy. I'll go down to the rail yard tonight, hop a train to Ogden, Utah, and then hop a train to Denver. From there, I'll walk to Trinidad if I have to."

Manuel sat quiet for a long second. He closed his eyes, rubbed them with his palms, opened them, and then he put his hands on my shoulders and said, "Okay, hermano, but be safe. Give Della my love and Ernie a hug from me."

He stood up and gave me a big hug. Then he pushed me toward the door.

"And don't kiss too much. Your lips might fall off," he said. He was not funny. He never was, but I chuckled under my breath because he knew exactly what I wanted to do. I wanted to kiss Della. I didn't know what it felt like, but I wanted to do it over and over and over.

I slid out of the thin crack of the opened door and through the living room toward the back entrance of the house. It was hot outside. The middle of summer. My grandfather had left the back door open to capture the breeze rising up off the surface of the cool Truckee river just a few hundred feet away from the house.

"Goodbye, Paulo," I whispered into the night air. "Goodbye, grandma, and goodbye you fucking asshole."

I ran as fast as I could around to the front of the house and six miles to the train station. There, I crouched down and walked among the monstrous engines and flatbeds until I found an open door to a large cart filled with piles of stale hay. All of the farms in the Midwest and in Colorado were growing hay, selling it for nothing, and then dying under the weight of sand. This car held the remnants of a yield that no one wanted. It smelled sour like yeast and mold, but I climbed in anyway, threw my bag down, and lay against the thick, wet and clumpy pile of a wasted harvest

I FELL ASLEEP IN THE car. When it shifted and began to roll, I only wanted to make sure that it was heading east along the tracks. East would get me closer to Della. East would get me away from my grandfather. And East would take me home to Trinidad. To the mines and my new life.

I sat quiet with my head between my knees until the train began to move. I stood up and pulled the car door open. It creaked at its hinges and cried out along the track of metal at the bottom and top of it. I sat down, just like I had seen train hoppers sit, legs flailing in the wind and hands pressed down against the floor of the car. I was on my way. I looked down the train toward the engine, and like mine, ten or twelve other pairs of legs bounced along the railway.

With a mix of sleep and watching the landscape fly by—the terrible cliffs of the Rocky Mountains, the high fields of their summit valleys and the flattening out into the plains of Colorado that stretched all the way across the middle of the country—the train pulled into the Denver hub and stopped. I had picked the exact train I needed to pick. I knew, right then, that with this luck, I had made the right choice and that my life would go back to being one full of smiles, even though my parents and brothers and sister wouldn't be in it, not immediately, at least.

My life was going to be okay.

I imagined Della saying, "I miss you, and I think I love you." It would probably come out more like, "Damnit, John, I miss you. And I goddamned think I love you," so I imagined her saying it that way, and I smiled saying that over and over again on the train for miles and miles.

I hopped another train, made sure it pointed south, and got lucky again. A few hours later it pulled into Pueblo, Colorado, only eighty-five miles from home.

The train stopped, I ran across the tracks, hopped the security fence, and then ran toward the parking lot.

"Is anyone going to Trinidad? I could use a ride," I said aloud for two to three hours, both in Spanish and in English. I gave up hope and to started walking down the road toward Trinidad, when a man in his late thirties yelled, "Vamos, nino." He waved me over to his truck. Five other men sat in the bed.

"We're going to the mines for work," one of the men said. "It's the only place to get a job anywhere right now." The depression had hurt everyone. The mines, however, for men who were willing to work away from their families and risk their lives below the earth's skin, kept running. And someone was always dying in the mines, so jobs became available.

"Yo también," I said. Some men nodded. Others didn't.

The truck rumbled down the road, and within three hours, right when the sun fell behind the Rocky Mountains, we pulled into Trinidad. I walked along the road toward our home, climbed in the through the barn window and fell asleep on the sawdust. I would head to Della's the next day, rested and ready to kiss her and become a man.

I woke up with the rooster. The sun shone in from the morning. Dust had caked the windows since we'd left and found its way into the house, too. All of our old furniture had a thick layer of it on top. The house looked like it hadn't been lived in for a decade though we left less than two years earlier. Cobwebs fell all around like tinsel from trees, and my mouth was caked with mud, a mix of saliva and the detritus of dying fields.

I walked to the well and pulled up two buckets of water. Alone in the high plains that used to be covered with fertile wildflowers, I stripped down to nothing and washed myself, using the soap I had stolen from my grandfather's home. I wasn't going to be stinky when I saw Della. I was going to be fresh. I pulled fresh clothes from my bag, dressed, and began the walk back into town, where I hoped to find Della at school.

I ached for my mom and dad, but the thought that I could start life again in Trinidad with Della, the Garcias, and my job made me happy. At fifteen years old, I was becoming the man my father and mother would be proud of.

Trinidad was Trinidad. One- and two-story buildings. Two bars. One for miners. One for ranchers. Two diners. A town square. And that's about it.

I walked toward the window of the three-room schoolhouse where I knew Della would be. I grabbed an abandoned railroad tie and dragged it over to the base of the school and stood up on it. I peered in. And there she was. Ernie sat behind her. It was like seeing family. Warmth rose up from the base of my neck to my ears and then to my temples. The teacher talked in the front of the class. I knocked once. The teacher turned to me. She tilted her head and stared like she couldn't make out who I was through the blurry glass and daylight that shown through. She squinted.

Della and Ernie began to turn their heads toward me, and my heart raced with joy.

Everything went black.

With a sore head, and a gut-wrenching pain in my stomach, I woke up in the back of my grandfather's truck.

He leaned over the seat. "We got twenty more hours in this car together. I want you to remember one thing. You try this again, and I'll send Paulo to the orphanage. Got it, Johnny?"

Dried blood caked on my cheeks. And I could no longer imagine the good life that I had created in my head.

Chapter Twenty-Five

John
1938

"I MET A GIRL," MANUEL SAID. "I'M GOING TO MARRY HER."

He told me this the last time we ever harvested chiles. He had placed a long weed in his mouth and mumbled it to me with his teeth gritted together to hold the weed in place. He held a chile in his hand, ready to pluck it, but waited to do so until I said something.

I'd never felt more alone than I did at that moment. He was nineteen years old, I was barely seventeen, and it had been five years since we moved to Reno. Manuel was my only real family anymore who remembered it like it was.

There were small flashes of green against brown along the Truckee River that fall. Everything had begun to die except for the tall evergreens that seemed to stand and taunt the sage and grasses and the scrub oaks.

I slugged Manuel as hard as I could, right on the back of his neck. He fell forward. His face slid across the dirt and rocks. I stared down at him, wishing he would never get up, so he could never get married and could never leave me alone with my grandparents and Paulo.

But he got up. He placed his hands in the dirt, pulling them in from where they had braced him, the body's instinctual movement to protect the skull and face. He pushed up slowly like a prize fighter using every extra second within the countdown to gather himself before fighting again.

He twisted his body toward me once he got to his feet. And he slugged me hard. The jaw that my grandfather had broken wiggled and cracked on impact, but it did not break this time. I swung back, connecting with his nose. When he recovered and turned back toward me, I tackled him.

Our bodies rolled together from the edge of the chile garden to the banks of the Truckee River, and we tumbled in, floating downstream with the current, our elbows and knees and hands and ankles slamming into the rocks beneath the white-tipped current. Somehow, before we nearly drowned, we both landed two more solid slugs to each other. His fist barreled into my ribs, cracking two of them, and mine hit his testicles, a low blow I would have never meant to deliver but the shift of our bodies in the water moved his cajones right in front of my fist at the wrong time.

We both began to take in water, ending our fight. Our arms reached out, flailing to grab anything to stop our drifting, and we tried to dig our feet into the mud at the bottom of the river to stand up. Manuel threw his arms around a boulder and held on. I grabbed his legs on my pass by him. He held onto the rock. My feet searched for solid ground beneath me. My toes dug into the mud and the balls of my feet pressed hard against the rocks beneath them. Manuel did the same, and we both gained our footing and walked to the bank, nearly a quarter mile from our chile garden.

We lay there in the sun. Our clothes clung to us, heavy and wet and full of sediment. My ribs stabbed me with each breath, and Manuel coughed up way too much water to have taken in.

"Lo siento, John," Manuel said.

He rolled over in the mud and placed a hand on my shoulder.

"I didn't mean to meet her. We're getting married, and I've joined the Army."

That son of a bitch.

I wasn't surprised that I hadn't heard about any of this—the wife, the army. I was just angry, and so lonely, long before he even told me. I had been lonely since the day my parents died, and it wasn't Manuel's fault, not at all.

"Okay," I said. "What's her name."

I turned my aching body toward my older brother.

"It's Ida," he said. "Ida Luna Macias."

"That's a pretty name," I said.

"She's a pretty girl," Manuel said. And he smiled so big.

"The Army?" I asked.

"Yes, I have a wife to support," Manuel said. When he said wife, I could feel his excitement rise up out of him.

"Congratulations," I said. "You'll be a great husband."

Manuel and Ida got married one month later in the church. She was a year younger than me. I guess they met at church too, and her dad was happy to have his firstborn married off—fewer mouths to feed. That would be Manuel's job now.

Two weeks later, Manuel left for boot camp. After boot camp, I saw him for a little bit before he got shipped to school and then to somewhere in the Pacific Ocean to live on a big boat.

I was completely alone. My grandpa ignored me besides making sure I could never run away again by threatening to stop caring for Paulo if I tried, so I didn't. I only lived inside my own mind and dreamed of someday joining Manuel somewhere far away.

Chapter Twenty-Six

Della
1940

THE WAR IN EUROPE HAD BECOME NATIONAL NEWS. OUR PRESI-dent said we didn't have anything to do with it, so we would stay out of it, but, for some reason, recruitment had jumped in Colorado, posters splaying across windows. I guessed it had jumped all over the country. You know, just in case, right?

I did not cry that day. I told myself that if I cried, he would die. If I held it in, he would live. I'd always felt some strong form of intuition, and it always seemed to work the way I saw it, so when I gave Ernie a hug, I told him that I would see him soon enough and that if any of the little boys got in trouble, I would whip them with anything I could get my hands on. He laughed and gave me a hug.

My mom half hugged him and half shook him for signing up.

"You don't have to do this. They haven't called you yet. We're not even in this war, idioto," then she tapped his face again, this time holding her hand there in a caress. Ernie had grown tall. Some gene had passed its way down through the Chavez line and Ernie benefited from it. He stood a solid foot above my father and a foot and a half above my mother who was still able to give him two big slaps across the face when he told her that he had enlisted in the United States Army.

"You're only half American, pendejo," she said. Then she gave him one final slap across the face before he leaned down, lifted her little body off the floor, and hugged her until she cried, just a little. When he put her down, she wiped away the tears and said, "If you make it back here, I'm going to kick the living shit out of you, Ernesto. If you don't, I'm going to kick the living shit out of your father for not locking you up in the cellar."

She had somehow found a giggle in her voice. And then had somehow found a smile. She wrapped her arms around his waist and pushed him on the train that would take him east to some humid place in Missouri for boot camp.

My father just stood and watched. When Ernie boarded the train, he looked back and waved at all of us. The steam engine kicked into gear, and Ernie waved as the train drove off. Later that night, I found my father in the corner of our newly purchased store stacking piles of grain and salt so high that if one fell, it could knock him out cold.

I think he missed the fields since we sold our land, but I don't think he missed the worry of ranching, the stress of the yield, or the unpredictability of the weather or the random sickness that could kill a herd of cattle. I knew at that moment, however, that he would have walked the fields and dug his hands into the dirt. He cried in the corner, a soft whimper insulated by the large sacks of salt and grain.

I put my hand on his shoulder. He touched it with his. I was always his favorite child, I had thought, but in that moment, I realized something. A parent's favorite child will always be the one they might lose. He could lose Ernie, his oldest boy, and that made him love him the most.

"I can help in the store now, dad. I'm almost done with school. When I graduate, I can work here with you," I told him.

He lifted his eyes up to me and stood. He put his hands on my shoulders hard like he was trying to push me into the floor.

"This will never be your store, Della. Someday you will tell me about things that you have done, and I will be amazed, and I will believe it all," he said.

MY MOM WOULD TELL ME someday, maybe when her breast cancer came on strong, that my father was the best man she had ever met in her life. She would tell me that when she saw him, she fell in love with him immediately. It wasn't his dashing good looks, she would note. He had rough skin and somewhat of a pock-marked face that had gotten that way after he had suffered through a few years of large pimples, leaving his cheeks and his forehead rough with divots, scarred from those years of his life when his friends in the field would make fun of him and call him names like boil man or lumpy.

My mom was beautiful. She had coral-colored skin with black-as-night hair. She would tell you she was full Indian, but when asked what tribe, she would say, "We're long away from knowing that stuff. We're long away from that. My mother said we were Utes. My father said we were slave Indians. All I know is I'm full Indian from New Mexico and I don't know what I should know about all of that stuff."

She would tell me that when she saw my father for the first time, he was kneeling in the middle of the street as horses and shitty old Ford Model Ts zoomed by him. He called to a scraggly hound who had never been truly loved—matted hair melding together with bald spots falling on sharpened ribs that poked through his skin and coat could tell you that. He knelt and called to the mangy dog. People driving by harassed him. They honked. They told the stupid spic to get out of the road. He didn't. He stayed on his knees until the dog came to him. Then he scooped it up, ran off the road, and found water and scraps from the butcher for the dog.

She didn't see him in town for months after that but when she did, he was standing sweaty and covered in salt next to the driveway where farmers came and bought day help.

"Shovel pig shit. Who wants in?" the farmer said.

Some full white man, she would say, asked what the wages would be and when the farmer told him, he walked way. "I'm not shoveling pig shit for that little money."

"I'll do it," Francisco said. Before the man asked his name, he had jumped into the back of his trunk, sat down, and smiled.

She'd tell you that, at first, she didn't know what to think of him. She'd never seen a man like this before. Where she grew up, the men were beaten down so badly by the United States and liquor that standing up, at times, took too much effort.

That day she waited for him to get dropped off again. With her light skin and dark eyes, she told people she was Irish. This didn't help her case too much back then, but it helped her clear a few hoops. Sugar. Coffee. Milk. She held those things in her hands and waited for my dad to come back.

When he did, she walked up to him and said, "Shoveling shit is not a good job."

He smiled at her, and this is when she saw his dimples rise out from the pock marks and his eyes glow just from looking at her. She'd seen versions of that look that men gave her, but this one was kinder, softer, full of admiration.

"It's a job," he said. "I've shoveled enough shit now to buy land out there across the plains where its cheap and where the government is basically giving it away for nothing. Want to marry me and live there with me? We could have a family."

She would tell you that his brashness turned her off immediately, but that is a lie. She loved how brave he was, how honest, and how sincere.

"Okay, if I can have one cow for milk," she said. That cow would later become Ernie's cow. "And if you will always let the wild grasses grow."

Ernie rode away on the train. My father cried in the shop. And my mom stayed in the kitchen and cooked fried steak for the family. She made a plate for Ernie. No one touched it. We ate, praying that someday soon he would join us again.

Chapter Twenty-Seven

Della
1941

My mom sat on the porch and watched the road and looked toward the east every dawn and every dusk. The Colorado plains reached out toward the east. The few crops we still had came back. The wild grasses grew so tall that my mom and I could walk through them and disappear in the hair of the earth's scalp.

"I'm just watching watching the sky," she'd say.

"You're watching for the mailman, mama," I'd say.

"Callete tu boca, Della," she'd say over and over again. "Your mouth will only get you in trouble." Then she would go back to watching the long, dirt road that led to Ernie somehow.

I had been writing essays to get into schools back east. I'd find their addresses in a huge book at the library, send them a letter for information, wait two months for their responses, and then fill out any information they asked me to, send the letter back, and then wait again. I only had the option to apply to the oldest schools on the east coast because the book had been printed thirty years before I was born. There were hundreds of newer, easier to get into colleges that were scattered across the east coast and the rest of the country, but I had absolutely no clue about any of that.

A letter came that day. I jumped up, hoping that it would be from one of the universities. I thought about those letters every damned day. I dreamt about them. Once I had a dream that I *was* one of those letters. I began my journey on the shoreline, felt hot in the hands of the mail deliverer that picked me up from a desk in a college admissions office, though I pictured the office to look more like the interior of the local drug store, but what did I know? I traveled in cars and trains across the country until I hit Trinidad and was placed in Mr. Edmond's hand and delivered to our front door one hot afternoon. I had become that traveling letter of hope. That's what all of those letters had become to me.

That day though, Mr. Edmonds did not smile when he jumped out of his ratty old truck that doubled as his mail truck and feed truck. He held a letter in his hand and had seemed to slow down the closer he got to our porch. My mom, the quickest person I had ever met in my entire life, stood up, placed her hands on her hips, and yelled, "Turn around, Mr. Edmonds, turn around, and get the hell off our property. I don't want your goddamned letter. Turn around and walk away, or I will get Francisco's shotgun and I will shoot your hand straight off your arm."

"Sorry, Benita," Mr. Edmonds said. "Legally, I have to deliver this. I will just put it right here." He believed my mom's threat. He was smarter than I had ever given him credit to be. He placed the letter on a wooden post and ran back to his truck and drove away.

My mom couldn't do it, so I went and opened it. It was not a letter of hope that had traveled from colleges in the east. When I read it, which I would have had to do anyway for my family, for the first time in my life—like all those people who think they're so damned poetic say—part of me died too.

My mom never read that letter the day on the porch. She saw my face, and then she did something I never expected her to do. She walked slowly over to me, knelt down on the ground, wrapped her arms around me, and cried with me. She was silent, a skill very foreign to her, and when we finally moved, she grabbed the letter, walked with me to the house, placed the letter on the front table, took me to bed, and lay with me until our tears dried up the next morning. The most silent moments of my entire life were spent in her arms that night.

In the late afternoon, my father came inside. He saw the letter, and though his English wasn't perfect, he made out what it said. He howled into the night, and found us in bed, clutching my little brothers around his waist and then disappearing into the darkness of the house with them.

Chapter Twenty-Eight

Della
1941

I WENT TO SCHOOL, ALL THE WAY THROUGH HIGH SCHOOL, something very rare for a rural half Indian and half Spanish rancher's daughter to do back then, but I did, and then I left. I left in 1941, a twenty-year old girl on a train bound for the east coast.

I stood on the inside flap of The Pinon, the Trinidad High School Yearbook, in a photo parallel to the principal and equal to his photo in size. I stared off the page, toward the Atlantic, under the words: Most Likely to Succeed. It took me longer than I wanted. But raising enough money just to get myself out there, to have enough to pay for food for a few months before I could get a job at college—all that extra shit took time. But I did it.

Most of my classmates didn't. Most of them got stuck there, breaking their backs and dying young of liver disease or heart failure from the lard that made its way into every tortilla, into every batch of refried beans, and into the fry bread that always seemed to make it onto the table for every meal. The booze killed a lot of them. But goddamnit, I got my little ass out of Las Animas County.

I boarded a train at the station in the middle of Trinidad. I sat there, before the train began to move, before the whistle blew, before the fire had been lit, and before I really believed I was doing what I was doing. My mom and dad sat outside the window of the train and waved. My dad battled to hold back his tears, and my mom elbowed him in the belly. I could see her mouth move.

"Don't be a joto, Francisco," she said.

When the train started to move away from them, I saw her duck her head onto his chest. He wrapped one arm around her and led her into the station. I did not cry. I felt that I should, but I didn't feel sad. I would miss them, of course, but the only thing I felt was so much goddamned excitement to see the rest of the country and go to school and be around other girls who wanted to learn that I could barely keep my ass in my seat.

Trinidad's short buildings were so worn from the beating of the winds and the snow that sat wet and powerful on them for five long months each winter; they all looked so ancient already. The roads were cracked, and the cars were old too. There was so little money in that town.

"Adios," I said.

When the town got smaller—sitting like a tiny skin blotch in a valley of speckled flesh—I felt like I had boarded a train out of a town where time didn't exist and where it would never move forward, stuck in a future that would never change and stuck in a past that had never changed.

Everything in me knew that the turning wheels of the train would take me to a place where time moved forward. Where life didn't begin, live, and die at the bottom of a mine, or with hands under the belly of a cow, or with a rake on the top of the fickle fields. A smile rose up from my gut and stayed permanently on my face as I barreled toward Denver where I would board a much larger train and head east to Mount Holyoke College for Women. The east was a different world. It was the place where the stock market rose and fell and where the President lived.

WHEN I FINALLY GOT TO Mount Holyoke, I walked through a metal arch, twisting above me. Black metal flowers dropped down on both sides and were connected by two large pillars of handcrafted stone that shot up out of the earth like guards welcoming me in. The gates under the arch had been flung open as if they waited for me to join them.

Despite my excitement, there was a part of me that wanted to turn around. Me, Della Chavez, I did not deserve this welcoming. I had come from the stalks, stables, and land of the KKK. Hadn't some of that come with me, lining my dress or covering my shoes, or hanging on to my skin? Wouldn't everyone see that? I touched the gates. They felt hard, just as hard as the metal that had been molded and wrapped around our fences at home. This grounded me, like I stood on the same earth as I did thousands of miles away at home.

Once past the gate, autumn had painted the campus trees with brushes of red and yellow and orange. The river of color above me lined a sidewalk, and the fallen leaves of the trees covered the path that led to the largest building I had ever seen in my life. I walked up its concrete stairs and stood beneath the towering wooden doors at its entrance, no one else in sight. I could hear geese cackling along the edge of a large pond in the distance. I felt completely alone, but, at the same time, I felt as if the campus had wrapped its arms around me and given me a hug, like I had been there before, somehow.

AFTER BEING REGISTERED, TOURED, GREETED, and ushered, I was overwhelmed but happy when I stood in the doorway that opened up into my dorm room.

"YOU WILL BE IN ABBEY Hall, Ms. Chavez," Sister Mary May told me when I walked with her across campus. The nun's long black and white skirt seemed to be starched so stiffly that it would take a tornado for it to shift at all. "This hall was built specifically for young women like you, those who come from places in the country, for instance, that are unique, to create a community where you all can thrive together."

I was many things—abrasive, ornery—but I was not dense. I knew exactly what Sister May meant. I was a poor half Hispanic and half Indian girl who grew up in a place in the country that every single girl at Mount Holyoke had never heard of in their lifetimes. Most girls, though they did come from small towns that were scattered across the eastern coast, had no clue what it meant to grow up in the high valleys of the Rocky Mountains, and that was okay with me. I didn't mind at all. Damnit, I liked me. But damnit, don't beat around the goddamned bush, sister.

I didn't mind being unique. I didn't mind that no one knew where I came from. I didn't mind that I was poor. And I didn't mind that they put me in a dorm with other unique girls. The only thing that all this meant was that I got out of Trinidad, a city stuck in time, a town without my brother Ernie.

ABBEY HALL WAS BUILT ONLY a year or so before I walked in. It felt new. It smelled new. The paint on the large round pipes that snaked their way over the bed in the corner of the room—that was bigger than my family room at home in Colorado—still had driblets of paint that had dried unevenly. I sat on the bed and drowned happily in the moment. I would not have a roommate, not my first year, so I knew I would have to find comfort and a lot of friendship within myself and within my books. I felt okay with this, ya know. I trusted me. I trusted me a lot.

I lay there on the bed and thought about Ernie, how he too had left home just two years earlier. We didn't have to wait long for him to come back.

In my hands, I held books. Shakespeare. Biology. Latin. French. Geometry. I ran my fingers over their rough, used covers. My rough-skinned fingertips spelled out the subjects. And then, without a hint of feeling strange or awkward, I kissed those dammed books as if kissing a boy for the first time, soft and gentle and full of passion. I fell asleep with the books on my chest and didn't wake up until the next morning when the church bells rang for morning Mass and echoed across the green grass of campus that held the leaves of fall in its hands.

* * *

At Mass, I sat in the front row, clasped my hands in prayer, and asked the Lord to help make the two days before classes go faster, damnit. I couldn't wait to learn. I couldn't wait to raise my hand and share my thoughts about biology and Shakespeare and Latin.

Mass was different there. Sure, it followed the same structure. It had all the same readings. We prayed to the same Catholic God, but it was so quiet. While we rarely went to Mass in Trinidad, when we did go, the community swarmed in with rumblings and gossip and the sounds of children playing and then being disciplined by their parents to behave. Children hung onto their mothers. Fathers, some drunk, genuflected and fell asleep in the pews, only to have the priest yell toward them to wake up during his homily.

Me, personally, I liked the movement of it all. I liked the pattern of the Mass—the kneeling, standing, and sitting, choreographed with the readings and the songs—and I tried to count the seconds between when the priest would start a reading and when the first person would perform the sign of the cross and then when the crossing would end.

The whole thing was in Latin then, but we Chavezes had an advantage. We spoke Spanish, first, so most of the words made sense to us. I can't imagine what the English and German speakers did during Mass with their minds. They must have just thought they were along for the ride, hoping the priest had their best intentions in mind. He could have damned them all to hell on any given day, and they would have just nodded and raised their hands to God in appreciation. But us, nope, we would know if something like that happened.

At Mass at Mount Holyoke, silence dominated the hall. Long moments passed between the priest's words and our movements. It thrived on precision—all standing at the exact same time in some kind of crowd-like hypnotism. It was unnerving, to tell the truth.

When Mass ended, I followed the map Sister Mary May gave me to the library. When I walked inside, I felt I had stumbled upon heaven. Heaven didn't come to me in church. It came to me in the library where wooden arches stretched above me, and huge windows let in the dim light of the early fall morning where grey met the yellow and red and orange of the tree branches that waved outside the windows. And the books, all the books in the rich mahogany bookshelves, I could smell them. When no one was watching, I dipped my nose into an open book that I had torn from its shoulder-high shelf and pulled the aroma of knowledge into me before taking it and sitting under one of the arches that gave me both a view of the ornate library and the green campus that I would call home. Damn it all to hell. I was in my heaven. The library at Mount Holyoke could have been haunted, and I would have drunk beer with the ghosts.

I spent the next two full days in the library. There were get-togethers and socials and all that silly shit that schools make you do when you first arrive, but I didn't go. I could see girls playing icebreaker games on the lawn from my perch in the library, and holy hell, that was the last thing in the world that I wanted to do. I could see their giddy expressions as they tossed a ball to each other and said their names and where they were from and what they liked to do for fun.

I would rather be stuck in the fields with an unruly steer, knowing that the big bastard wouldn't move, than sit out there and tell other girls what I like to do for fun. In Trinidad, I worked, and I studied, and I read. If I did anything else for fun, I would not have been sitting in that library on that day in Massachusetts.

At night, I moved through the entrance of Abbey Hall like I had done something wrong and didn't want to get caught. I crept through the hallways and toward my dorm room and turned the key and cursed at the creak that echoed from the small turn of the knob needed to open the door.

I shut the door behind me and breathed out. I knew that someday I would have to interact with other girls, but I was doing my best to hold that someday back. For the moment, I just wanted to be alone, to live in the world of academia like in my own bubble.

"Who are you?" a girl said to me from beyond my door. "I know you're in there. I hear you breathing. You haven't joined us for all of the get-to-know-you charades. How did you get out of them? I want to get out of them. Holy God, they were the worst. One girl told us that for fun she likes to pretend she's married, cook for her husband to be, and then imagine what chores he'd like her to do when she was done. No kidding, I'm not kidding."

This person who stood on the other side of the door understood me, so I opened it up. I had never been shy. That wasn't why I avoided those activities. I had just always known how I wanted to spend my time and who I wanted to spend it with.

I cracked the door just a bit and did not expect to see who I saw standing on the other side of it. A tall, auburn-haired, absolutely gorgeous young woman carried a book in one hand and held her other hand up to the door, scrunched in a fist, ready to knock again—persistently until I answered.

I couldn't believe the sight of her. I know that men have always liked me—I'm not a dumb, falsely humble idiot who feigns modesty, dismissing every compliment thrown my way, but I also knew that this woman rose beyond men's tastes, their personal "types." She was prettier than all of that.

"Do you think you can avoid people forever?" she said.

"Excuse me?" I said. She was brash, strong, and full of confidence.

"Listen, I live here, down the hall. I'm Helen, and I saw you sneak through the front hallways. So, I followed you to your room to see why you're sneaking around so much. Everyone else is trying to fit in. The way some girls love to talk about themselves is enough to drive me crazy. They talk about their sweethearts, their moms, their dads, their place in The Hamptons. They talk about it all, as if someone gives a lily-white crap about any of it. So, how did you get out of all the icebreakers?"

Helen stood so tall and talked so fast that I didn't really know how the hell to answer her, but I knew I liked her immediately. I didn't want friends. I didn't really care if I made one friend in the years I would spend at Mount Holyoke. I wanted to get my rural, brown butt through college, absorb everything I could, and not waste a moment of any of it doing bullshit stuff.

"I just didn't go," I said. "I just went to the library. That was it. No one came looking for me, so I just ignored all of the invitations and the announcements."

Helen fell back against the wall behind her in hallway, placed her hands on her hips, and yelled, literally yelled, as if the hallway were her own goddamned recording studio or echo chamber, "Fucking brilliant."

There, right then, I knew that this tall, beautiful woman would be my savior at Mount Holyoke. Her and that beautiful library. I had fallen in love with both of them.

"Let's go," she said.

"Where?" I asked.

"Follow me, and this time you cannot just not show up because I will tie a rope around you and drag you with me. Any girl who would simply not show up to all the stuff that we are supposed to and treat it like she had just decided to not pee is coming with me. I don't care about their boyfriends or The Hamptons or their stuck-up mothers. You don't, and I don't, and I think we can not care about all of that stuff together. What do you say?"

"Della," I said. "Della Chavez, from Trinidad, Colorado."

"Okay, Della, from Trinidad, Colorado, follow me," she said.

She didn't ask where Trinidad was. She didn't ask about my family. Holy hell, though I love my family dearly, I didn't really want to talk about them, and she didn't offer up anything about her family either when we went to her room, when she pulled out two bottles of vodka, when we crossed the quad, when we drank until we were full and drunk, and when we didn't stop talking all night long.

What did we talk about? Nothing and everything. We talked about life, about love, about all the big things that people talk about when the details fall away. We talked about what it meant to be me and what it meant to be her.

I stood up, raised my glass to her, and clinked it against hers.

Chapter Twenty-Nine

John
1941

FOR THREE YEARS, I LIVED LIKE A GHOST IN THAT HOUSE. MARIA was gone, off to Elko, Nevada. Manuel was gone, off to war. Little Paulo was gone too, my grandpa sent him off to boarding school.

I worked from early morning to early afternoon, feeding the horses and milking the cows and carrying slop to the pigs. The winters were the hardest. The snow fell heavy and the winds came off Lake Tahoe's cold Pyramid lake, bone slicing and dry. After doing my work, I would hide in the barn. I had whittled down a stick to the size of a pencil, and in the open spaces between the animals, I would write letters to my mom and dad and Della in Spanish in the dirt, covering the whole barn with my words and then erasing it all with my feet when I finished and headed in for dinner, where I would sit quiet at one end of the table while grandfather talked and lectured about all the things I had done wrong. I missed the sound of my own voice. They did not.

The summers were much better. I finished all my work quickly and then headed to where Manuel and I used to grow our chiles. I tended to our plants every day, even if they didn't need any tending to. I spoke to them like my father did. I ran my fingers along their purple and red and orange and green skins. I tilled the dirt with my fingers and dug thin irrigation ditches along the edges of their roots that would fill with the water from the Truckee River and gulp it down when the sun covered the sky in the Nevada desert.

One summer in 1941, my fear came true in the form of a letter from the Navy, delivered to our home along the Truckee.

Manuel's boat had been sunk by the Japanese. My grandfather opened the letter, he handed it to me, and walked away. I read the words, and I let them sink in hard. They made their way through me like influenza attacking the body, slowly making my breath hot, my muscles weak, and my head fuzzy. I felt like a fever had taken me. My temples burned, and the back of my neck could have fried an egg. I was mad, madder than I've ever been. I wanted to kill the entire Japanese Navy, the entire damned country. I worried he would never come home, but I never believed it. Like the last blood-filled organ that my body relied on to live, the hope that Manuel would return safe, had been excised from my gut.

On that hot summer day, I shed all but my underwear and walked across the flood plain and into the Truckee River. Next to my chile plants, white rapids rushed all summer long. I waded into them. The fast, hard water pushed stiff against my ankles and then my calves and then my knees and then my waist, doing its best to yank my legs down into the current, but I would not let it. I placed my feet down on the rocks, each step precise until I stood in the center of the river. It was something about the water. It felt violent there, just like the rain that came down hard the night my mom and dad died. I screamed "CALLATE" over and over again. Then I sat down in the water. It smacked me on the back of the neck and head until I lifted my waist up to its surface and floated with it, the anger in it disappearing and turning to soft hands that carried me a mile down to where the river slowed and swirled.

I lay there, keeping my body afloat in the swirling waters of the Truckee, and looked up toward the sky. I dove down into the colder depths, ten or twelve feet down in the pool, and stayed there for as long as I could hold my breath. My father, if he were alive then, would have yelled at me to never swim in the weeds because they could have tangled me up, but he wasn't alive, and Maria was married to a used-to-be priest and Manuel was dead in the Pacific Ocean, and Paulo was at school where my grand-parents wouldn't allow me to go. I didn't really care if a weed were to wrap itself around my leg and tug me down.

But then I thought of the chance to see Della again. If I could escape my grandfather's home, I could see her again. I couldn't go directly to her. He'd find me there. He'd wrestle me back. Some-how, even at nearly twenty years old, he'd win. But if I could get away, far away where he couldn't wrestle me back, where he had no control of me, where someone else was in charge, I could escape.

I always had that fear, the one he planted in me so early on. If I did anything wrong, he would find a way to hurt Paulo. The crazy part was that I knew my grandfather loved Paulo, but I also knew that my grandpa's heart had a dark, black stain on it, and he would hurt the ones he loved to hurt the ones he didn't. If they Army made me go, he couldn't blame me, and Paulo too could escape soon enough, just a few years down the road.

After swimming for more than an hour, I made my way onto the beach and walked the mile up toward the chile plants, only wearing my underwear. I lay down in the rows between the sprouting guajillos and let the sun dry every last inch of my skin. I knew what I had to do.

I just had to survive another year.

Chapter Thirty

Della
1942

I LOVED SCHOOL SO MUCH. I LOVED CAMPUS AND THE BIRDS and biology and French and even calculus, which to me, was just another language like German or Latin or Dutch. Besides Helen, I was a loner. I wouldn't change those years or give up my time in the library for dances. I wouldn't have given up those mornings of sunlight where I sat and read under the gaze of only glass and giant trees while other girls ran off to the city or to meet their boyfriends by the water.

Helen would do everything on her own terms. She would go to the dance by herself even though she could have gotten a date just as easy as it was for her to breathe. Instead of dancing, she would sit in the corner with a flask and write down the tiniest details about dresses and coats and braids and nylons and fabric. She couldn't stop herself. Details are what made the world, she would tell me over and over and over again. She never made a judgment about how other girls pulled themselves together for an evening; she only noted what the details were and how they made the whole. She would scribble down words like "pinched, risen, flattened, dull," and "disheveled" or "classy" or "lovely." Math, to Helen, came to her like the boys would come to her if she let them within in ten feet. She didn't.

And she let me do my own thing, like not going to dances or to ceremonies or to socials. She knew that me making it to Mass three times a week had been like throwing handcuffs across my wrists, plugging me into a socket, and then scolding me for moving.

The summer came, and I dreaded it.

If I stayed, I would have to find a place to live and work. I didn't mind work at all. I'd grown up working, but the only options for me at the time lay in the service industry in Boston or Vermont. This meant I had to be around people all the time and on top of that, I had to pretend to be nice to them all damn day long.

Helen went to work in Boston. She didn't mind it all. She got tips just for showing up. She knew. She didn't care. She once told me that if old white men wanted to give her extra money for just standing there, she would take their money.

"They have money for a reason. We, as women, just barely got the right to vote. I figure they owe us for all the years of bullshit they've given us. The years, the decades, the centuries, the millennium of them dragging us around by the hair and fucking us when they want to. If I just have to give them coffee, I'll take their extra money. It's not my fault that they feel like giving me extra goddamned money because they think in the back of their mind, if they admit it or not to themselves, that I might just pull up my dress and say, 'open,' then I will rob them for their stupidity."

So she stuck around and robbed old men by just bringing them coffee and cakes.

It was 1942, and the war raged in the Pacific and across Europe, but the exodus of young men to the battlefront had yet to come, so jobs and places to stay were somewhat scarce outside the school in the rural part of the state. I did the only thing I could do that summer: I went home to see my family. I loved them. I liked being around them. Ernie wasn't there, and that weighed on me, but I knew my mom and dad would want to see me. The little boys, hell, they were in high school. They didn't give two shits if I came home or not.

Plus, I was dark, darker than the girls who worked the high-class clubs in Boston and Springfield. I always knew I was pretty, with long dark hair and the slightest upturn of my thin nose with a shrinking jawline and bright blue eyes that clashed against my brown skin, but I also knew that at that time, in the places where women weren't treated like complete objects, I couldn't get work. I wouldn't be treated like the men in my family treated me, like an intelligent, gifted peer, no matter the genitalia between my legs, so I jumped on the train home toward the high wheat and alfalfa plains of Colorado where the Dust Bowl had finally left.

When I walked through the door in early June of that summer, my mom held out her hands to me. In them, ten ears of early yield corn were wrapped in thick, thick husks. She wasted no time. The hug would come later that night when I stirred corn in the frying pan. She would walk up behind me, three or four times at least, and wrap her strong and wiry arms around my waist and kiss the back of my head, getting up on her tiptoes to do so.

I wasted no time with the corn. I walked out to the front porch, sat on the edge of our home, and tore the husks from the ears. The sun sat in the east in front of me. It hung there, far away, where I imagined summer on the lawns of Mount Holyoke. I could see and feel the dew of early morning on the blades of grass in the center of campus. I missed it. Mostly, though, I missed the library, the stacks of books that melded together like the clasped fingers of lovers within their wooden shelves, row after row after row like the corn and alfalfa fields of home.

My family laughed behind me, the stress of money and food all but gone away over the last few years. I felt like they had moved on without me during my year at school. I imagined that this was how my house sounded every night when I was gone, and I felt really goddamned good about it. Part of me came home that summer because I felt guilty for leaving in the first place. In one evening, I knew I shouldn't host that guilt, and it freed me.

Chapter Thirty-One

John
1942

On my twenty-first birthday, I walked into the recruitment office in Reno, and signed my selective service papers—all young men had to at age twenty-one.

My grandpa couldn't say a word two weeks later when I told him I had been drafted. I hadn't. I didn't wait for it, I volunteered. Fuck him. I had found my way out.

The man at the office looked at me and asked if I had a problem being under water for long periods at a time, and I told him the only thing I wanted to avoid was staying in my grandfather's house for any more "long periods of time." He nodded his head. I signed my papers, and three days later I was on a bus bound for New London, Connecticut, all the way across a country I had never seen. I wanted to kill the people who killed my brother. I wanted to use a big gun to do it. I wanted to make it through the war so that I could find and marry Della in Trinidad.

It had been six years since I saw her in the schoolhouse. The letters had been cut off. My grandfather threatened to pull Paulo from boarding school and make him miserable if I ever tried to go back to Colorado again.

But I had it all mapped out. I would go to boot camp. I would go to war. I would return to Colorado as a war hero, lean over and kiss Della in my uniform, and find a way to make a living in the rural high plains of Colorado with her. Even though it would take four years to get there, to see her, I didn't care.

In the meantime, I had a brother to avenge and a grandfather to escape. That too put me on the bus to boot camp with no hesitation lingering around me. Was I worried about Paulo?

About the threats my grandfather had made? Nope. Not anymore. Mandatory service was my shield from his hatred and cruelty.

Many times in those moments between being awake and asleep on the bus, I imagined Della sitting on her porch waiting for me to come home. In my mind, that's all she could do. I knew she loved me. That's what her last letter—six years earlier—said, so I knew that she would wait for me, passing the days by helping her mom cook, by tending to her smaller brothers, and by looking out at the sunset for me to come back. In my heart, I knew that's what she would be doing, and this gave me peace.

The bus dropped me and six other recruits at the entrance to the base. We stood, together, lost for a moment until a man yelled at us to grab our stuff and follow him through the open gate that led into the compound.

I could smell the ocean but not quite see it. Multiple two-story, wooden barracks stood between me and the waves of the Atlantic. I'd never been so close to open water before, but I felt like I was born to live in it, just like my swirling pool in the Truckee River. I knew, right then, that I had made the right choice, that the Navy—and a submarine—would be my home for the next four years of my life, even though I had yet to be assigned a ship or a mission. The sea called to me.

Chief Kelly told us to follow him, so we did. He led us past three rows of buildings until we hit the edges of the thick and wide Thames River. Compared to the Truckee, it looked like the ocean to me.

And then I saw them.

In the river, attached to docks that extended outward from the concrete covered shore, the submarines.

They lay on top of the river like long shotgun barrels. Their long, flat, grey tops kicked off no glare from the sun. Five or six men moved back and forth along the edges of a giant gun on the surface of one of the submarines, and one soldier sat in the metal seat at the back of the giant ten-foot-long barrel. He placed his eyes into scopes while two other soldiers practiced shoving three-foot-long shells into a chamber the size of three men. The gunman swiveled the gun around 180 degrees, slowly, resting it with the double barrels pointed across the harbor.

I wanted more than anything to learn how to shoot that gigantic gun, to spin it around and aim at an enemy ship, to be in control of so much power. I shook my head, dreaming of the day I would call a submarine my home, being afloat in an ocean so big that no one even knew I was there.

"This way, runts," Chief Kelly said to the four of us. "Stay with me."

"Yes, sir," I said.

He turned to me. He nodded.

He led us past a very tall spherical tower that had a spiraling staircase wrapped around it from its base to its summit. At the tower's base, soldiers walked in and out of a building that housed the entrance to the training facility. At its summit, an octagonal room with very few windows stuck out around the giant tube. Next to the tube, a square staircase, encased in wood and metal, mirrored the tube in height. From it, at three points in its ascent, enclosed bridges were connected to the tube. It shot up from the ground next to the submarines on the shores of the Thames River in Connecticut, a long way from my chile patches next to the Truckee outside of Reno, more than two thousand miles away.

Chief Kelly walked us into a large, sterile building at the end of the dock.

He told us to strip, right there at the entrance of the place. And I stood in line, in my underwear, shivering, for an hour until I got escorted behind a white curtain where a man, just as sterile and white as the walls of the room, gave me shot after shot after shot in the arm. He waved his hand for me to leave his curtained-off section. I followed, moved up one boy at a time until I got to the barber, and all of my black hair had been shorn and lay on the floor. I stood in another line, even colder it seemed without the hair on my head, until Chief Kelly walked across the line, assisted by a young soldier who dropped a uniform in my outstretched hands and into the hands of my fellow greenies.

"Get dressed," he said.

We did.

Then we waited, the shivers still shaking us from our bones outward. A boy next to me had to keep himself from crying. His eyes swelled. Sparkles of budding droplets hung on his lids. The sniffles that come with tears rose and fell quickly in his breath. And he wrapped his arms around his torso, embracing himself like his mother must have. He was tall and strong, but his knees seemed to barely hold him up.

I reached out to pat his back but got reprimanded.

"Cordova. Stand still. You're not this boy's wet nurse, understand? You move again, and this will be a horrible day for you," Chief Kelly said.

I pulled my arm back to my side and waited. That's when the boy's first tear hit the floor and when Chief Kelly laid into him so fiercely that I began to hurt inside. He yelled at the kid so hard that I felt bad for him and worried he might not make it through the screaming, but the kid pulled it together somehow, reining in his tears.

"Let's go, Boots," Chief Petty Officer Kelly said.

We followed Chief Kelly through a well-designed maze of barracks until he led us into our barracks that had no beds, only green Navy seabags that lay in rows on the barrack's floor. We turned toward the sailors in the room. Chief Kelly nodded his head, and the men, walking down the line of hundreds of Boots that must have come from other medical buildings, dropped our sleeping gear into our outstretched arms. A hammock. A mattress. Two fart sacks, mattress covers. One pillow. Two pillow covers. And two blankets.

"Boots, follow the leader," Chief Kelly said. A sailor walked up to us, pointed at the first ten Boots in the line and walked down the first row of seabags. The ten followed him down the row and intuitively stopped in front of each bag, except for one kid who kept walking after he passed his seabag and who got reamed in front of the entire group. Dumbass.

We all stood next to a seabag. There wasn't one extra seabag. They'd been counted and laid out for each of us, not one that didn't belong there even made it into the barracks that day.

I didn't move until I was told to move. My grandfather taught me that. But there are always a few in the group that hadn't learned to listen for orders.

Out of the hundred or so of us, twelve kids reached down to grab their seabags before Chief Kelly had told them to do so, and within ten seconds, twelve sailors had pulled them out of line and had them doing a thousand pushups while the rest of us stood there and watched. The dumb kids did push-ups. The rest of us waited in the cold barracks for thirty minutes until the dumbest of them finished. We all held the gear we were handed in our outstretched arms, angry. My shoulders burned. The liquid between muscle and bone had seemed to dry up, and pain replaced it. I feared to even crack my neck, worried I might look like I was moving out of turn. I learned really quick.

When the twelve Boots got back into line, Chief Kelly told us to place our gear onto the floor next to our seabags and stand back at attention.

He stood in the front of the room and talked as loud as a shout, but he did not shout, "I'm only going to show you this once. If you do not listen, if you do it wrong from now until you make it out of here, you will be sorry. Take your seabag…"

Chief Kelly listed, one-by-one, all of the gear that we had just put down on the ground. With each piece, including all of our bedding and the cot, he told us how the piece should be stored— rolled up or folded or laid flat—and in which order it should be shoved into the bag. Again, some dumb kid with his finger in his nose grabbed a piece out of order, even though Chief Kelly had told us all exactly which piece to grab next. The kid was pulled out and told to lap the group, hammering out forty laps around us while we all waited.

To me, the order of filling the bag made a lot of sense, so it worked its way into my memory before we finished the exercise. When we got done stuffing our bags, we stenciled our names on them. Like Chief Kelly instructed, we flung them over our shoulders while he spoke.

"Your seabag is your home. You have everything you need to be a sailor. Wherever your seabag falls, that is your home. Take care of your home because it's the only one you got," he said.

"Now, undo your seabags, set up your cot, and lights out," Chief Kelly said. "I want silence."

We would not eat that night.

The dormitory window framed the moon in the dark sky outside and snores echoed across and through the bunks. A bell rang loudly in the middle of the night. The light had disappeared from the window in the doorway. Two or three boys fell out of their hammocks at the sound of it, their bodies thudding hard on the concrete floor. A kid cried out in pain. Others shouted from being startled awake.

The roaming glow of flashlights bounced around the room like someone had released giant fireflies in the barracks. No lights had been turned on.

Chief Kelly's voice cut the darkness and the fear and the silence.

"Up and at 'em, drop and grab 'em, get it all in your seabag. Now, Boots!"

My eyes began to follow the flashlights and adapt to the darkness. Like me, most of us sat stunned at the end edge of our hammocks, hands rubbing through our hair and over eyes and bare-skinned chests—mostly bright white chests that moved up and down to catch some semblance of a calm breath.

"I ain't your mommy asking you. It's me. I'm telling you," Chief Kelly said.

The quicker of us jumped off our hammocks, folded them up, rolled our sleeping gear and mattress inside, stuffed our clothes and gear like they showed us how to do during our break down, tied the hammock to the seabag, and stood at attention. The less quick, following behind us, did their best to catch up, but their delinquency had already been noted by those sailors who walked up and down the rows with round lights from their flashlights leading them, as if they were sniffing dogs, to the stench of inadequacy.

Chief Kelly talked the whole time. His voice sunk into our skulls.

I stood, along with just a few others, at attention until the last Boot finished, sloppily, wrapping all his stuff up.

"Long, Davis, McCarthy, Cummings, Robbins, Cordova, Noakes, join me up front." Humping my seabag on my back, I followed the sound of Chief Kelly's voice to the front of the room and stood at attention in front of him, along with the other boys who had been called up.

"Do you boys think you're special?" Chief Kelly asked. "Do you think because you got your shit together that you're special, that you are better than the other Boots?"

No one said a word. Being the brightest of the group, I think we all knew that whatever we said would be turned against us, so no one answered, which, in turn, was turned against us.

"Again," Chief Kelly said.

Not dismissed, we stood there, a black kid named Noakes, his name stenciled on his seabag, stood next to me. I'd never seen a man stand so sturdy in my life, like his skin had been filled with bricks and concreted together. A rock of a man.

"You must think you're special," Chief Kelly said, "because you ain't moving."

With that, we ran to our spots in the rows, undid our sea-bags, undid our hammocks, laid everything out in order on the floor and packed it all up again, long before many of the other Boots had undone theirs.

I stood at attention. And, hell yes, I wanted to be special. I wanted to be the gunman who sat on top of the submarine and pointed that massive gun toward the people that brought us into that war, and if I had to be special to do so, if I had to be the best goddamned recruit there to get that job, I would be. I would earn it.

I made my first mistake three days into my time at New London.

That day, we put on our boots. We began to run in the very cold morning. The thick, humid air touched by the speckles of salt from the ocean, filled my lungs, and I could feel it; I could feel the rush of thick oxygen run through my legs, the legs that until then, had only been fueled by thin, dry air at four thousand feet above sea level. Like a balloon being unknotted and released, I flew out ahead of all the rest of the Boots, running around the hard track, finishing two minutes before any other Boot and grabbing my knees next to Chief Kelly, who, for the first time I had heard since getting off the bus a few days earlier, couldn't help himself by giving me a compliment, "God damn, private Cordova, that was the fastest first run I've seen in god-damn twenty years here. Don't disappoint me tomorrow."

For everything that we did in our ten-hour days—including our middle-of-the-night fire drills—at camp, he expected me to excel: the marching, the calisthenics, the rifle drills, the pulling of oars, the loading of heavy shells into the mammoth-sized guns, and even the clothes scrubbing. If I slipped away from the top, he hammered down my throat that I could do better, that I had disappointed him, that I needed to find my way back up before he shoved me straight back down to the bottom, and I did it all with hope that when our assignments came out, I would get the one I wanted—to be the man who held the gun to shoot at the Japanese, the people that killed Manuel.

He rode me hard. I rode me hard. He had his intentions. I had mine. And when we pulled the Mommsen lung over our heads and walked to the base of the tower and waited our turn in the loading shell before being thrown into the bottom of the one-hundred-feet deep tank, I wanted to go first, to prove that I was the best sailor who ever left New London.

When we entered the holding chamber at the bottom of the giant tank, we were, again, at the very bottom of the Navy totem pole, this time with one hundred feet to swim up. It was one of the major tests that either qualified us for sub duty or put us on top of a freighter or battleship. I wanted to be in a sub, to float in the depths of the ocean, just like I did in my pool in the Truckee. No one knew I lay there in the muddy weeds, ten feet deep below the surface, especially my grandfather. I had disappeared from the world, found my place between water and air. The sub would take me back, a home underwater for four years, only coming up to surprise and to kill. It sounds evil to say I wanted to kill the Japanese, but that's how we all felt. Every goddamned one of us. Mothers. Fathers. Sisters. Brothers.

We huddled together on our knees in the center of a fully metal room. Pipes and valves stuck out from walls and hung down from the round arch at the top of it, not the ceiling, just the top loading deck. At the front of the compartment, a small oval hatch led to the tank. The rounded walls of the tank expanded out to the side and upward.

I remember feeling wet, even though our bodies, only clothed in white swimming shorts that barely covered my cojones, were dry. The tank had been filled with water, and the moisture of a one-hundred-foot tank seeped out into our base chamber. For a brown kid from Reno, the humidity made it hard for me to breath. I started to gasp for air, doing my best pull in a full breath. Body odor mixed with thick, thick oxygen clogged my throat, so I lifted my head to get as clear as passageway to my lungs as I could.

"Cordova, move to the back of the line, Boot," Chief Kelly said to me. He must have thought I didn't want to swim. He must have thought I was scared. None of this was the truth. I just hadn't gotten used to such thick air. It was like trying to breathe soup.

I moved to the back of the line. I wanted to explain that I really thought I should be first, tell Chief Kelly that this had nothing to do with the tank, the water would be better than being in the tank, but I had learned to always keep my mouth shut when not asked a question.

"Noakes, you're up," Chief Kelly said.

Noakes pulled the heavy Mommsen lung over his head. He laid it over his neck. He shoved the mouthpiece into his lips, expanding them outward. Two tubes ran out of it and down into a pouch that lay across his dark, thick chest.

One instructor turned the large lever to open the hatch. He helped Noakes in. A hand reached out from inside the chamber, another instructor waiting to instruct Noakes once the outer hatch had been sealed—the first instructor sealing it immediately after Noakes stepped into the interior chamber. And then he was gone.

Seventeen other Boots entered the tank before me. Two of them, after being locked in the loading chamber, came back out a few minutes later. Their skin dripped with water up to their shoulders, but their hair remained dry. A steady tap on the hatch told the outside sailor to open it up. These two men would not be getting on any submarine. They didn't even make it into the tower.

Six or seven other Boots had to be pulled from the tank at the lower hatches in the tower. The sound of sailors unlocking the hatches thirty or fifty or eighty feet above us mixed with the slushing of water on metal told the story of soldiers who would have to stay topside on a massive carrier—again, the submarine would not be their home during the war; it was better to find out then, in a tank in New London than aboard a ship off the coast of Japan, hundreds of feet below the ocean's surface.

I finally walked up to the hatch and draped the Mommsen lung over my forearm, bending down to place the metal of the rounded edge of the hatch's hollow edge between my legs. Chief Kelly yelled out, "Don't waste our time if you ain't gonna do it, Cordova. Just climb back outta there if you're just gonna make these sailors waste their time. If they take you in there, if they flood the outer tank, and if you chicken out, you will pay to me. These men could be halfway to a shower and dinner by now. So, let me know, you wasting our time? You belong on a cruiser? No shame in that. But only submariners should enter the tank."

"I'm ready, sir," I said.

I took the hand of the sailor that stretched out from the interior of the tank and ducked in. Inside, two sailors stood in a small, rounded loading tank. They wore tight swimsuits like me and large swimming goggles that took up their entire face. One officer opened the vent by turning a small lever and then, speaking into a microphone, "Request permission to flood."

Time slowed down.

Earlier, some of the men had screamed, their voices barely audible through the thick metal that surrounded them. They were the two that never made it through the flooding tank.

Me, I couldn't wait to feel the pressure of the water on my shoulders, float in it like I did in the Truckee.

"Flood when ready," a voice echoed through a large, rectangular speaker at the top of the chamber. The instructor pulled a large lever from left to right along a semi-circle angle downward and then back up again, and water began to rush into the chamber at my feet and fill up the tank so quickly that it covered me up to my shoulders in just a few short minutes.

The air pressure in the tank, forced upward and condensed by the rising water, filled my inner ear and clouded my head with a hollow feeling of a dull pain.

"Stay ahead of the pressure. Plug your nose, put your tongue on the roof of your mouth, and blow against the pressure," the officer said, tilting his head back, placing his thumb and finger on his nose and demonstrating for me.

I placed my index finger and thumb over my nose and blew, releasing and popping the pressure in my ears. It still hurt like hell, but it worked. It relieved the pressure just enough to move forward toward the escape hatch that led to the hundred-foot tank that stretched up above me, where only about half of the men before me reached the surface of the pool.

The pool rose up around me. It settled on my shoulders and reached the top of the escape hatch that led out into the ascent tank. The instructor nodded at me again. I gave him a thumbs up.

He reached down into the water, unlocked the escape hatch, and opened it up, pushing it out away from the flooded tank and into the much larger, taller tank on the other side where two other instructors swam, this time in full SCUBA gear. Then he pulled the hatch all the way open and waved for me to enter.

It was time. I was excited. In the flooded tank, my body slowly became weightless with the water rising up around me. I felt freed from all the shit the world outside had put on, from Chief Kelly doubting me and from the way my grandfather looked at all of us like we were parasites. Just like I felt at the bottom of the Truckee or in the pool of water next to it where Manuel and I lay tired and happy after we had beat the shit out of each other, I felt relief.

The instructor in the tank with me tapped on my head, my

signal to drop down, place my right foot through the hatch and into the tall tank, and then slope my body down through the hatch and out the other side. I did it carefully and quickly, taking a giant breath, placing the mouth piece of my Mommsen lung into my mouth and breathing. I flipped my body around and faced the flooded tank. An instructor connected me to a cable that reached all the way to the top, and then, without warning, he let me go.

I exhaled. I placed my arms over my head and let go of the hatch. It felt like flying. My feet kicked me upward, pushing me to the surface as my lungs emptied. The feet markers on the wall passed by so fast, and then I popped out of the water at the top, breathless and dizzy and happy as a goddamned squirrel who had just found his nut.

The instructors at the top of the tank pulled the lung from me and swam me over to the ladder.

"Nice work, Cordova, the best today," Chief Kelly said. He had ascended the stairs while I prepped to swim and patted me on the back, nodding his head and then walking away. I had done exactly what I'd gone there to do.

Chapter Thirty-Two

Della
1942

I SPENT THE SUMMER HELPING AROUND THE HOUSE, MOSTLY. AT night, on the weekends, I would drive into town, the raggedy landscape of the west all around the city of less than ten thousand people, and I would buy vodka and lime juice to mix them together, the closest thing to a well-made drink in Trinidad. I'd sit in the park and watch cars drive by and men come in and out of the local tavern. They were all the same, really, miners and farmers. I admired their hands. My dad never chose to spend his nights at the bar after work, but I forgave them somehow when I watched them, tired and raggedy, nearly falling into their seats just inside the bar's door.

I tried to enter the bar once. I was run off by two prostitutes who owned the place, not in a business means but in a territorial claim.

I just felt like trying. There was no way I was going to drink vodka at home, not with my teetotaling mom and my overly proud father, so, instead, I sat in the park and imagined I was back at school, only one hundred miles from the ocean and Boston Harbor, where I had never been but knew I would see soon enough.

One night, before the sun fully set, a young man plopped his borracho ass right next to me on the bench as if I'd asked him to join me. He had deep blue eyes and wore a suit. He placed his hand on the wooden slats next to his legs and tapped his fingers again and again until I said, "Hello," just to stop his incessant need to get my attention. I had one week left until I jumped on the train back to Mount Holyoke. And I could barely wait. The time had drawn out so long that I felt, at times, like the spin of the earth had slowed.

"Hello," he said.

"Hi," I said. I sipped my vodka and flipped the pages of my book, the words just barely visible in the grey light between day and night. I shifted my body away from him. I hoped he would just leave me the hell alone and let me slide into my evening with my drink and my reading.

He slid closer to me. What a dipshit.

"You're beautiful," he said.

"You're sitting too close to me," I said.

"What are you reading?" he asked.

"Dostoyevsky," I said.

"A communist?" he said.

"An author," I said.

"A communist author?" he said.

"A brilliant thinker," I responded.

I placed my copy of *Notes From the Underground* between my hip and the bench.

His face wrinkled. He slid a bit closer to me, leaning over to see if he could read the book's spine. He wrapped his arm around my shoulders and lunged for the book, his hand pawing at it. The back of his hand brushing up against my thigh violently.

I stood up. And I slammed the hard-backed book across the man's face.

He clenched his fists, swinging one toward me.

I saw it all as if I had been there before—the fear in a man's eyes that I wasn't afraid of him. The same look I saw long ago when my father caught the blow meant for me from the KKK man. I ducked out of the way, and his weight carried him forward to the ground, his arms flailing with the momentum behind him, leaving his face to break his fall.

I grabbed my vodka and walked away from the park.

"Communist!" the man yelled. "Communist literature!"

Then men from the bar flooded out into the street. They too started calling me names like Red Bitch and Red Blood and Stalin Lover and Whore of the East.

Instead of running from the men, once I got a couple hundred feet away from them, I turned my body back in their direction and lifted my middle finger in the air, dropped down into my father's new car with my finger still raised to them, and shut the door. I split the crowd like the Red Sea as I drove, my middle finger like Moses' staff making it happen.

The next morning, I woke up, packed my clothes, gave all of my family long, full hugs, and I boarded the train to Massachusetts. I asked my father for a little loan, which he happily gave me, telling me that he would never accept repayment.

"Go do good things, Della," my father said.

My mother could only bring herself to nod. Age had softened her. Finally, goddamned, finally.

Chapter Thirty-Three

John
1942

WE WERE GIVEN A ONE-WEEK BREAK TO GO HOME. I GAVE Noakes a hug and caught my train west toward Reno, Nevada. It would take me two days to get home and two days to get back, so I would get three days in Reno. I planned to stop in Elko for one night to see Maria, and to stay one night in Reno visiting Paulo and showing my grandfather exactly who I had become: a sailor in the US Navy. It would be quick trip, and to be honest, I really believed it would be my last trip to Nevada, ever. Manuel would not be there. I was going, mostly, to say goodbye to him, to his memory, and to our childhood that I was glad to have survived and left.

DURING THE TWO-DAY JOURNEY WEST from boot camp, I moved from car to car, sitting with old people and young people and, many times, with other soldiers on their way home, sharing our first taste of booze since before the previous eight weeks of running and drills and nightly raids of our bunks. We talked about our chiefs. We talked about girls, though I had never really had any to speak about at that point, but we never talked about going to war to die.

I got a little homesick, staying silent for longer than I could handle. But what really, what was I homesick for?

In Reno, I walked out of the station, but instead of heading directly to the Truckee River and following it along its banks a few miles toward where I had spent the last eight or so years of my life, I wandered through the city I had never really known— not like the familiar, beat-down mining town of Trinidad.

I walked down Douglass Avenue. The bright neon signs read Harrah's Bingo and Reno Casino and Horse Booking and Cafe, thirty-five cent meals. With fresh money in my pocket, I stepped into a small cafe with a neon, rectangular sign that hung above its doorway and ordered steak and eggs, something I could have never done before joining the military. I sipped on my coffee until almost noon, accepting pats on my back from old men who walked by me. I managed to disregard a few comments like, "I'm proud of you. Even spics can have honor in this war." I let it go. Drank my coffee and stared at the beautiful young waitress who served me.

Her skin was creamy and smooth like milk and her eyes were as blue as new snow reflecting the skies above.

She brought me so much coffee that I had do everything I could to act like I could drink it all without running to the bathroom to take a leak. For some reason, that seemed like weakness to me, and to be honest, in that moment, I felt like if I left, the connection we had would disappear, go away, fall out the door when a customer opened it onto Douglass Avenue, or even worse, shift toward another soldier who came home and just got off the bus. She was beautiful.

When I couldn't take it anymore, when I had to go to the bathroom so bad, I stood up, walked up to her at the counter and I asked if I could come back later to take her to dinner.

"Yes," she said. "I'll be here at 6:00 p.m. and probably very hungry." Her voice melted me.

I told her thank you, touched her hand gently, gave her my best smile and walked out onto Douglass Avenue smoothly. Once I got out of her sight, I ran around the corner, dropped my seabag on the ground, and covered the wall with two gallons of coffee and water.

A Reno policeman walked around the corner right as I was zipping up and yelled, "You can't pee here. This is not a toilet." Then he stopped in his tracks, raised his hand to me, and said,

"Sailor, good luck out there." He pointed west toward the Pacific Ocean and then rolled his sleeve up. He was older, maybe in his fifties. Covered by his sleeve, on his arm, a large anchor tattoo shone black against his skin in the late-morning sun.

"Thank you," I said.

"Be safe," he said. "And don't piss on your dress blues."

I found the Truckee River and headed toward my grandfather's house. But something stopped me along the way.

The Catholic Church, rising up out of the ground, a stalagmite of rock and cross and brick, framed my grandpa's Cadillac that sat out in front. The car was as black and as clean and as shiny as the first day I saw it, a rolling symbol of my parent's death, the vehicle that stole us away from our home and my father's chile garden in Trinidad after we laid my parents to rest. There were no other cars in the lot. Just his. Alone like a devil that wasn't invited.

For a moment, I didn't know really what to do. Walk into the church? Or maybe walk home, steal away some time with Paulo and my grandma before the old man came home from praying to whatever sadistic god he prayed to. That sounded like the best idea, but the curious part of me really needed to see why his car was the only one there. The feeling of my dress blues gave me confidence, so I straightened my back to face the man I hated, strode up the stairs, pulled the large, ornately decorated wooden doors open, and walked in.

A toddler cried in the front pew.

My grandmother's head turned back toward me, her face covered in a flowing white veil.

My grandfather stood in front of the altar, just off center of it near the priest, staring at me from the red carpeted stairs where he perched himself in front of my brother Paulo and my sister-in-law, Ida, my older brother's widowed wife. Paulo turned and looked down the aisle. His mouth opened. His eyes widened. But he quickly reached for Ida's hands, pulled her toward him, and gave her the sealing kiss of marriage.

He was only a boy, eighteen years old, and he had just married his oldest brother's widow and become a father to her boy.

Part of me was proud of him. The other part of me wanted to slug him so hard in the gut that he would double over. But I didn't get the opportunity to sort through any of those feelings about my younger brother marrying my older brother's wife and raising his kid.

I stood there with my eyes and palms raised to the ornate ceiling, not in admiration but in a sign of pure wonder how this had all happened so quickly after I left, and my grandfather's open hand smacked my face like I was still a child that he could toss around. Blood spattered on my dress blues, and I brought my hands down from the sky and clenched them in tight fists in my grandfather's face.

"You soiled this day with your presence," he said. "No one invited you. All you are is a poor memory of Manuel, and we don't need his memory here anymore. You, your sister, and Manuel, you were all lost causes when I picked you out of that poor miner's house. When I was young, when I crossed into the states, I got beaten, spit on, and ignored. They called my wife a 'whore' and 'dirty.' Why, John, why? Because we couldn't speak English. Because we ate beans and tortillas and chilies. Because we were Mexican no matter if we built their railroads or cleaned their houses or dug their mines or fed their babies. We didn't speak a da English. Spics. So, when I saw your little brother, I thought I could give him the life I have now without him having to go through what your grandmother and me went through. You and Maria and Manuel, you were just stowaways. So get out of here before I hit you even harder."

I walked over to the holy water and cleaned the blood off my dress blues, moved slowly over to my grandfather, and swung a fast fist up and under his jaw, laying the old man out on the ground. My grandmother gasped. Paulo, like he had been born to do, fell into his new, older wife's arms, and stayed there.

"That was for Maria," I said. I turned toward Paulo. The pews, thick and shiny and mahogany, passed by me as I walked to my little brother. I pulled him away from his wife, threw my arms around him, and shook his hand. Then I gave Ida a small hug, turned and kissed my nephew on his forehead, patted my grandmother's veil, and walked out of the church and into a bar.

THE MORNING I LEFT, I sat in a bar in Reno and drank until my train pulled into the station. I remember this much.

"I think you've had enough," was not something bartenders said to you back then in Northern Nevada. They poured drinks and let you drink them as long as you had money, and if you wore the uniform, they didn't turn you away. I drank and I drank.

"Let me see your ticket," the bartender told me.

I slid my ticket across the bar to him. He placed his palm down on it and slid it toward his belly until he could easily wrap his thumb and index finger around it, turned it over, and scanned it.

"Okay, John, I'll make sure you get on that train," he said. Then he turned his back to me, scribbled on a piece of paper next to the cash register, swung back around, and refilled my whiskey and beer. "I'll make sure you get there."

I wanted to replay the sound of my fist hitting my grandfather's face, and smile. I wanted to feel like a long-lost hero that had come back and avenged his brother. I wanted to feel it all again and raise my fist in the air in victory. Instead, all I saw was my grandmother's face. Her tears. My little brother's shock that splashed across his eyes. My sister-in-law's disgust that I had ruined her wedding day. She had already lost my older bother to war, but she had found my little brother. It was their faces that I saw that day when I pulled the mug of beer off the edge of the bar and placed it on my lips. Their fear, sadness, and disgust, not my grandfather's face at the end of my fist.

The bartender never said that I had had enough, and I never said it either.

Chapter Thirty-Four

Della
1942

IN DENVER, I BOARDED THE TRAIN, FOUND A NICE EMPTY CAR, and closed the doors and shades to the hallway, and looked at my reflection in the mirror and the train station behind it and thought to myself, "Della, you're leaving. Yes, you're leaving." I smiled at my own smile in the reflection in the glass, hoped no one would enter, thinking the room full. This didn't work. First, a large wealthy family that had spent their holiday skiing in Northern California tried to budge in but there weren't enough seats for all of them, and I did not give them a welcoming expression, scowling at their youngest child who said, "I've never seen eyes like yours."

The mother moved them out and the father cursed me with barely opened lips, "Half breed." Hell, he was pretty observant, because he nailed it.

The train began to move, and a young man fell into my car, drunken. His body splayed across the seat on the opposite me, and he buried his face into the cushion, shielding me from taking a good look. He smelled of booze.

He could barely talk, and the seat cushion swallowed up his voice. He mumbled something about his little brother and his grandfather, but it didn't make any sense. He was a drunken sailor who couldn't lift his head up.

"My dad was a miner and my mother was a saint, until they died."

He wasn't making any damn sense, and to be honest, I wished he'd just shut his mouth and pass out. Drunks. I'd been around them before. At get-togethers. At parties. Just walking around town and running into them after school as they grasped at my skirt. I didn't want to be around this one, so I got up quickly, grabbed my things, and tried to move out the door.

I did what any smart woman would do. I left the car and found another one, the one with the ski family. They had heard the noise and let me in. I sat on the floor of their cabin until we hit Kansas City and they took another train.

The boy's snoring rambled through the train like a bear growling in the woods.

He really was a crazy asshole.

THE NEXT EVENING, I WENT to dinner in the dining car.

There he was. I could tell by the slick, oily black hair that fell across his arms. He sat there sheepishly with his forehead on the table and his arms wrapped around it like he was playing some sort of childhood who-done-it game; it reminded me of how my dad sat years earlier when he waited for my mother to cook steaks. The sailor wore a collared shirt, a brand-new one. I'd guessed he'd gotten his first paycheck from the military and spent some of his money on clothes. They all did, all the poor ones. He'd been crying, at least it looked like it, stains on his forearms. When he stood up from dinner, he accidentally dropped a photo that he had been looking at on the ground. I didn't want to have anything to do with him, first the drunk and then the quiet and sad man who could barely eat. Neither of these sides of him were attractive, but he just stared at the photo for a moment like some kind of idioto who had lost control of his hands.

With all the bad luck that could come my way, when he dropped the photo, I had already begun to walk back to my cabin and couldn't just let it lie there, so I reached down, picked it up, and placed it on the table. I did my best to not make eye contact with him.

Men are dumb, and many of them would take direct eye contact as a sign of flirtation. I placed the photo gently on the table in front of him. His awkward grasp toward it landed his hand on mine. I pulled my hand slowly away to not be too rude, and still did not make eye contact, lowering my hat down over my eyes and tilting my chin down toward the floor. I walked away, hoping that he didn't recognize me from the night before. I hoped I'd never have to deal with that young man again.

Later in my cabin, however, the photo came to mind, the one he had dropped on the floor. A family standing beside a new car with looming clouds behind it. A photo of a woman who must have been his mom, a poor beautiful woman with light skin and dark hair. And, somewhere inside me, a lightbulb went off and my heart broke for him—the little boy from Trinidad—the one that left for Nevada, the one I missed—John.

I stood up. I walked toward the door. I even opened it to go find him. I loved him. I missed him. He was there on the train with me. I stepped into the hallway to go save him. I understood why he cried. I understood why he felt such deep pain. I could make him smile. I could love him and give him love.

But then my life came back to me. I was on a train to go to school. I was on a train to get the hell away from Las Animas County. The boy who sat broken and hungover in the dining cart was everything I was leaving, even if I loved him. Hell, I loved my parents, but I left them to find whatever I needed to find out there, and they weren't some borracho who crashed into my cabin the night before and smelled like the underside of a big, pink pig on the ranch.

I closed the door. I sat down on my seat. And I decided to leave him be. I had to. For me.

Chapter Thirty-Five

John
1942

THE NEXT THING I KNEW, I WOKE ALONE, SMELLING OF BEER and sweat in my dress blues, in a train car somewhere in Wyoming. Like someone had slammed a mallet down hard on my forehead, everything hurt. My lips cracked, and my mouth clambered for water like the desert mountains where I was born. With each shift of my body, something else hurt. With each turn of my head, my brain slammed against my skull. I think I had drunk the liquid straight out of my brain, nothing left to capture the movement of soft tissue against hard bone. Everything hurt.

The light from the high-west morning screamed through the window shades.

I stood up, disgusted at everything in the world. I thought for the first time in my life that jumping from the train might be the best solution to everything, hurling my body onto the tracks, aiming my head toward the slick metal tied together by wooden ties and iron spikes. But I couldn't.

Noakes waited for me. My submarine waited for me. I believed I had earned my spot on the top of the ship to shoot down the motherfuckers that killed my older brother. I had to stay alive for that, but, to be honest, that was the only very thin thing that kept me from either leaping off the train or jumping off at the next town and drinking and going AWOL.

Somehow, I had carried my body to the dining hall. No one looked at me. I kept my head down, not knowing who I had run into the night before when I boarded the train, not knowing who saw me so drunk in my dress blues and thought, "What a disgrace to the uniform." I kept my head down, reached into my pocket to pull out the photos of my family the day the storm struck them down, and I stared at them, trying to do my best to bring some light into my life. And then I dropped them on the floor.

My body hurt so bad and my brain moved so slowly that it took me a minute to even realize what I had done, but someone else did. A kind woman bent down and picked them up. I didn't look up at her, shame still full in my belly. She smelled like lavender and vanilla. She placed them on the table gently, with all the kindness that I thought had dried up in the world.

I reached for the photos and accidentally placed my hand on hers. For a split second, a rush of warmth replaced all the pain in my head. She let me hold her hand for a second longer than I ever deserved, and then she walked away.

Somehow, that one kind gesture and that one gentle touch changed it all. Life was worth it. Kindness existed. My boat awaited.

I spent the next two days sober and thinking about Della. Something had brought her fully to me. It wasn't just the same fuzzy memories that I pleaded with my mind to resurrect. It wasn't just the daydreams of finding her after the war and praying that she hadn't met someone else and forgotten about me. Something fresher had taken me. Something more real had swept me up in my fantasies, like she was with me there on the train.

The smell of lavender caught me every once in a while, and the natural scent of it made me dizzy. There were a couple times that I thought about going to the dining cart for a drink, but to be honest, I felt so much shame for getting on the train so borracho that I ordered my meals in my cabin and watched the world go by through my window, thinking of Della.

The train slowed in Hartford, Connecticut. I had to get off and catch a train to New London. It seemed like the whole train emptied out too. I dragged my bag into the station and waited for my next train. The board flashed destination after destination: New London, Connecticut. New York, New York. Boston, Massachusetts. Springfield, Massachusetts.

I watched people from all over the country walk from platform to platform. They weaved around each other, oblivious to anyone else, and headed straight toward their gates. Trains pulled in and pulled out. And then the train that carried me there moved away from its platform. One last passenger walked out from the platform from where it departed.

The wind carried the smell of lavender. I took a long look at the woman. There was something eerily familiar about her. Her black hair down over her shoulders. The edge of her dress swung around her calves, and then she sprinted passed me.

"Della?" I yelled out.

I didn't even know where the yell came from. I hadn't fully realized that it was her when I said her name. Something from deep down yelled it out like I had no control of my own voice.

The woman slowed, she turned around. "Hi, John."

I stood up.

I didn't know what to do. It had been six years since I saw her through the window of the schoolhouse and more than eight years since we stood in the corn rows and nearly kissed. We were children. Now, as a man, I felt like that small child who ran with her to her apple tree and sat beneath it Sunday after Sunday and who looked at her in awe while she told me about science and agriculture.

"Shit, John," she said. "Well, shit." Della planted her fists into her waist just like her mother used to do when she got mad at us when we were children. She scowled at me like I had stolen her ticket from the train or taken her last bit of food after a long day of work. Her lips, however, gave her away. I wouldn't say they smiled. I would say that they moved around on her face like she didn't know if she should smile. Passengers rushed around her, but I felt like it was just us standing there in the train station.

"I miss you, and I think I love you," that's all I could say. I wasn't really quoting her letter to me as much as using her words from her letter to express my feelings. I didn't have words of my own.

"Goddamnit all to hell, John," she said.

Like she had been defeated, she dropped her fists from her waist, her shoulders dropping too, and put her head in her hands.

"I know you were on the train from Denver. I knew the whole time," she said.

"You picked up my photo, didn't you?" I said.

"Yes," she said. "I did."

"Why didn't you—" I asked. Heartbreak began to settle in, began to sink inside of me.

"Because I couldn't. You came into my cabin drunk the night before. I can't clean you up. I don't know if you need saving, but I can't save you."

"Manuel is dead," I said. "Paulo married his wife. Maria left with a priest."

None of this was a real response to what she had said.

"I came to Trinidad when you were still in school a year after I left. I saw you through the window, and my grandfather found me and took me back to Reno," I said. "I went back after boot camp and saw Paulo marry Manuel's wife and hit my grandfather in face and it felt so good. Then I got drunk."

She stared at me. These were the only words I had, so I just stared back. My hands gripped each other at my waist, and I could smell her perfume, like vanilla. She was a woman, and she was Della, and she was right there in front of me.

Chapter Thirty-Six

Della
1942

"I HAVE TO GO, JOHN," I SAID. "I'M TRULY SORRY. I HAVE TO GO to school."

His face dropped in front of me. The sadness that covered it resembled that of the boy who lost his mother and father, not the borracho from the train. It was the John I had always known. First, the quiet and happy boy who walked me home and then the weakened boy who looked lost when his mother and father died. The boy who almost smiled when I leaned in to kiss him before he left, and the frightened boy who looked back for us to help him when his grandfather pulled him from our home.

When I saw the borracho on the train, my decision to avoid him was easy. For the rest of the trip, I snuck between the dining cart and my cabin. I hid my face in a veil when I went to the bathroom. I even figured out where he slept just so I knew which routes he might take to get places on the train, and I avoided them like a spy moving through an enemy's castle.

That was easy. He was a broken boraccho who smelled like he'd just come out of a goddamned whorehouse.

That day on the platform though, it got hard to dismiss him. Real hard.

"I miss you, and I think I love you," he said. This hit me with some kind of damned emotion, but I couldn't say what it was, honestly, half anger and half love. "I came to Trinidad. I saw you in the window. I hit my grandfather in face and it felt so good. Then I got drunk."

I don't remember if I even responded to him during all of

this. I was numb and angry that my old world had come into my new world, even if it came in the form of a boy I loved.

"Manuel is dead," he said. "Paulo married his wife. Maria left with a priest."

And my heart sunk. I imagined Manuel leaving John. Maria leaving John. Paulo deserting him. It made me want to wrap my arms around him and squeeze so hard that he would crumble into me.

"Ernie is dead too," I said. I knew I shouldn't have opened up at all. I should have said, "I'm sorry," and walked away, but the goddamned words just fell out of my goddamned mouth. "Goddamnit, Della," I said out loud.

His face, again, changed. No longer did his eyes drift towards the ones he had lost. Instead, they focused on me. They stared so directly at me that it gave me a chill. He had lost his own sadness and fallen into mine.

"No," he said. "How is your mother?"

"She's a liar," I said. "She says she's okay, but she hasn't been the goddamned same since she found out. I think she'll get better, but right now I think she wishes the KKK would come back just so she could shoot somebody. The gun on her hip is always loaded. She's pissed off, John, really pissed off."

"How's your father?" he asked with that damn quiet sincerity that had always caught me off guard. Like we hadn't been apart for the last eight years, my shoulders fell from their defensive lift, and I answered.

"He's sad, but I was always my dad's favorite, so, you know, he's really happy that I'm heading to college to 'do something so special in this world,' like he always says. I give him hope, ya know?"

With that, with dad in my mind, my resolve came back again.

"So I have to get on a train to Mount Holyoke now," I said.

"Okay," John said. He didn't fight me. He sat back down. He

waved. He knew. He saw. He got it. The second that I told him that me getting on that train would save my father's hope, he backed down.

"Goddamnit, John, you son of a bitch," I said. "Fight, John, fight! Why don't you fight me? You fought your grandfather. It sounds like you won. Why won't you fight me?"

He looked up at me. His eyes fell on me again, "Because I love you."

Holy shit. Holy shit. Holy shit.

I hated him right then. Two minutes before he stopped me on the platform, the only thing I wanted to do was get to the university, find the library, and read, read, read until my goddamned eyes fell out.

"I think I love you too, John," I said.

And I realized, for John, by sitting back down and not asking me to stay, he was fighting for me too.

Chapter Thirty-Seven

John and Della
1942

THEY WERE ALMOST THE PEOPLE THEY WANTED TO END UP being during those days in Hartford, Connecticut. But they weren't there yet. They pretended though, knowing that they had to leave each other in two days, one of them jumping on a train to New London and the other to Mount Holyoke.

They changed their tickets to forty-eight hours later and walked down Main Street to find a hotel. They really didn't know what to say when the man at the front desk asked if they wanted one or two rooms. They asked for two rooms, but the hotel only had one left, one with two twin beds. In a shared glance, they nodded. Both sets of eyes hesitatingly blinked an okay to each other. The air felt thick with the decision, but they signed the agreement, paid the money, and walked together toward their two twin beds in their shared room.

They took bags up to their room, dropped them off, and sprinted out the door of the hotel. The room, together, scared them. The last time they had seen each other, they were practically children. Now, they had become adults with no one to chaperone them. They ran out onto Main Street and walked to the end of town.

On the other side of town, campers and tents and temporary housing formed slums. Men and women and children lived in them. Behind the slums, factories rose up, all making war-needed equipment and supplies. It reeked of garbage and sewage and body odor in the late summer, the smell drifting across the bridge to the edge of Main Street. They turned around.

"This is war," John said.

They walked back into town and found a cafe. When they walked through the front door, no one stared. They expected them too, but no one did. Instead, a kind woman seated them. She complimented their dark, shiny hair and caramel skin. She was darker than them.

They asked for something fancy. They were on the East Coast and had dreamed of living a life away from the dry fields of the high west and dirty faces of the mines.

"Something fancy?' she asked.

"Yes, something fancy," they said.

"You'll have to find it," she said. She handed them a menu.

They scanned it and found exactly what they were looking for. They ordered Manhattans and fancy finger sandwiches, but when the waitress gave them odd looks for their choices, they changed their orders to cheeseburgers. They faked as if they were just kidding around with the sandwiches and cocktails, both embarrassed. The waitress walked away. They smiled. The cheeseburgers were good, but the Manhattan tasted like sweet corn the moment it came off the stalk.

They had four more before they realized how much whiskey was in them.

"We should stop," Della said, and they walked out into Main Street to stand in front of the grand theater whose marquee hung over them like the mountains of their childhood.

They bought tickets that were more expensive than their hotel room, but they had money, enough to splurge, more than either of them had ever had before, and the liquor ran through them and made them brave.

They sat in the seventh row. The hall grew up, tall and elaborate, around them, like they were in a dream. School didn't exist. The Navy didn't exist. Only John and Della existed in the ornate world of the theater. They had never imagined they could sit there in the plush seats. Their hands intertwined. They thought, for a slight moment when they left the train station, that all that time apart would make this strange, but it didn't.

The lights dimmed. The man sang. His voice was like butter, smooth and rich and thick. They kissed for the first time in the dark at the edge of the singer's voice. Someone nudged their seat from behind Della and John and whispered, "This isn't the place for that."

But the man onstage felt differently. He waved the spotlight to fall down on them. Between songs, he asked, "Are you going to war, young man?"

They nodded, not knowing what to say, red and pink covering their faces. "Give her one more kiss, and then I'll sing again."

They did. The whole crowd clapped, and the person behind them stood up and left in frustration and his own embarrassment.

They stumbled out of the theater, drunk on love this time. Very slowly, they walked back to their hotel room. Decisions would have to be made there, ones they weren't quite sure how to make.

When the door closed behind them, they turned on the lights. They sat on one of the twin beds and leaned their backs against the wall. They shared stories of the last eight years and fears of the years to come. They kissed between the stories. They held hands. They fell asleep in their clothes and didn't wake up until midday.

"I love you," John said.

"Will you meet me back here?" Della asked.

"They're sending me to Hawaii. That's where I'll be stationed between my tours."

"I'll meet you there. I promise. When I'm done with school."

"I love you."

"I love you."

"Stay safe. Don't die."

Chapter Thirty-Eight

John
1943

AT THE TOP OF MY CLASS IN NEARLY EVERY CATEGORY, RISING up to receive my Sailor's Bible and the assignment that came with it, I stood in the front of the line of newly made sailors, expecting to have my pick of any job on the submarine, although I'd already put in my formal request.

Noakes stood next to me, his skin in even more contrast to mine against the whites of his Navy dress. He had done everything well. He even beat me at a few things along the way, and we had become friends, talking on the long runs in the front of the rest of the guys and whispering about our families and our homes before lights out. He too had put in a request. He wanted to be an engineman, to work on the diesel engines that drove the ship forward. We weren't officers. We knew we wouldn't be on deck, but enlisted sailors got to shoot the gun and run the engines. We put in for exactly what we thought we deserved.

Noakes and I stood in front of Chief Kelly right after the year had turned from 1942 to 1943, just six months after I had gotten to spend the most amazing weekend with the woman I planned to marry. Kelly nodded. He didn't speak. Then he placed his hand out to shake both of ours in turn. I remember how rough it felt, like he'd been rubbing it over sandpaper for days, the surface of his skin prickly and uneven, hardened blisters on his palm and fingers.

He led us in to receive our assignments. At New London, they had trained us for the duties we could do as non-commissioned officers. All the hard work. I wanted to sit in the gunner seat and shoot the five-inch-twenty-five-caliber gun, to watch it hit the Japanese men that killed my brother, to see the bullets pierce their skin, and to follow them as they fell into the monstrous depths of the Pacific Ocean.

"Good luck, sailor," Chief Kelly said when the door opened that led to a table of officers who would decide what I would be doing on the submarine for the next four years of my life.

The officers called Noakes and me in at the same time. We stood in front of a long table. They confirmed they had the right sailors in front of them by asking us to state our names. They read over their notes, all of our boot camp accomplishments and failures, and then they handed us two envelopes with our assignments tucked inside of them.

"Thank you, sir," we said in unison before saluting and turning and walking out the door, excited to find out where we would land in the next twenty-four hours, what boat we would climb aboard, and, very importantly, if we would be assigned to the same ship. We both walked with purpose and patience out the front door of the barracks. We stood in the morning sun, looked at each other, and in the restrained way we had been taught to move, we slid our dark hands into the crease and pulled our assignments out.

The first thing we saw was the name of our ship, the USS Snook.

"Que perfecto," I said.

"Snook?" Noakes asked.

"The blue fish," I said.

We hesitated to look down again. The next line would tell us our assignment.

"Cook."

"Cook."

Again, we both spoke together. This time, however, our voices rose together at the end of the word, a one-word question leaving out lips, "Cook?"

I turned to Noakes that day, and I saw his full blackness,

not the friend and perfect recruit that I had become so close to but a black man who had been assigned to cook for all the white officers and all the white enlisted men.

He looked down at me. And I could see it in his eyes too. He saw my dark brown skin that wrapped itself around me. We were no longer the two highest scoring Boots in our class. We were the spic and the black. We were everything we thought we escaped when we left Nevada and Chicago. We were cooks no matter how well we did at running, at packing our bags in the middle of the night, at ascending to the top of the water tank faster than any other sailor did. We weren't those men. To them, we were men who ate beans and picked cotton.

"Fuck this," Noakes said. It was the first time I had heard him swear in the year that I'd known him. He'd taken racial slurs from other Boots and let them slide right off his back because Chief Kelly always defended him, making the boys from Alabama and Mississippi run so hard after calling Noakes a "Negro" that they were scared to open their mouths to say anything at all. They called me wetback and spic and bean-eater, and I too just let it go and watched as Chief Kelly would throw those boys to the ground and wear their arms out with push-ups. It didn't happen much after that first week. Chief Kelly had our backs.

But this was different. This came from those in charge. The men that sat behind that table in the other room, even having read how high our marks were during camp, gave us an apron and hair net and some cigarettes to ease the burn.

"Pendejos," I said. "Pinche pendejos."

I hadn't spoken a lick of Spanish since leaving Reno. Hell, before that, my grandpa barely let me speak it without wrapping me across the face with the back of his knuckles, doing his best to make my tongue as light skinned as him, my grandma, and Paulo.

We had no choice but to report to duty. It was March 1943, the USS Snook waited for us in the New London dock, and if we didn't board the submarine at 8:00 a.m. the next morning, we would be AWOL, and we would be court martialed.

So that night, Noakes and I went to a bar in downtown New London to drink. We went there to fill our guts with whiskey and beer. We went there to hate the world. And we did it damned well.

Walking up to us and ribbing us for where we got placed on our boat was not a good idea after we had put down four shots of whiskey and four beers to chase them down our throats, but a young redneck from Arkansas felt the need to do so.

"Hey, cooks, why don't you whip me something up to soak up my drink. I'll take a steak and eggs, and, as a courtesy, don't sweat that dark, dirty sweat on my steak," he said. His words slurred out of his mouth. He leaned his elbow down on the bar and spoke to the bartender, "Get this Negro and this wetback a hair tie and give them a spatula. They might as well get started now."

Noakes turned and flattened him with one fast and hard punch to the nose and blood splattered the man's forehead when he hit the ground. The impact of his head hitting the back of the floor knocked him out cold.

His three friends were on us fast. They swung long, slow slugs toward us, but Noakes and I ducked, and simultaneously grabbed our beer glasses and broke them over two of their heads. The last one stood alone for a moment and then walked backward toward his chair and mumbled something about how black and brown shouldn't be on any naval ship that flew a red, white, and blue flag.

We both apologized to the bartender for breaking his beer glasses and offered to clean up the mess. The man leaned over the bar and placed his elbows on the shiny wood in front of us and said, "You'll have enough cleaning to do on the submarine."

He lifted his arm sleeve to reveal the same navy submarine tattoo I saw in Reno. He placed two beers down in front of us and walked away without taking our money.

The irony was that many nights, after we had gotten assigned to the Snook, they made us start cooking in the mess halls for practice cooking for so many men. When our shift ended, we would cook for each other. Noakes was a natural. He dipped his fingers in broth to test for texture or swirled a giant pot to eye the consistency of a rue. Me, I found the best peppers in the world in a market down the road from where we bunked. An old man who had a little garden had brought them to the flea market one day. Noakes and I lived at the flea market on Sundays, buying stuff for cheap, that to us, was something new. We'd never really bought anything in our lives, let alone be set free to wander and look.

The war was on. It was really on by that point. We knew where we were going. Soon enough, in the months to come, we would plunge into the depths of the Pacific and probably die, so we ate and drank. We had to live because we knew we could die.

We may have been assigned to be cooks against our will, but we were competitive, and if we were going to be cooks, we were going to be the best damned cooks in the Navy.

In March 1943, we took a transport bus to the Snook. She sat high in the water, the large gun on her metal back. I whispered *my boat* to myself over and over and over. My boat. And we set sail for Pearl Harbor.

Chapter Thirty-Nine

Della
1943

IN THE SUMMER AFTER WE GRADUATED, I SAT IN A RESTAURANT that overlooked the Boston Harbor. I had rented a place there with Helen by the water. The thought of going back to Colorado crossed my mind and then it quickly left. In my head, I had served my time there, and I dreamed of the day that I could earn enough money to bring my mom and dad out east. The east would really send my mom for a loop. She would shit her pants with happiness at the sight of the water and bars and the people. I could hear her say, "Holy goddamned hell, I like it here. I'm not a drinker, but give me one of the goddamned spicy martinis. Dirty? What do you mean dirty? Okay, give it to me dirty." My father, on the other hand, I don't think he'd like it much, but I would make him come anyway, and I would buy him a huge ribeye and some lobster. That's what I would do for him. He deserved a damn steak.

Graduation came and went. I graduated in the top one percent of my class, and missed out on being valedictorian by less than a percentile. Who got it? My bitch of a best friend Helen who rubbed it in my nose for days.

"If I didn't get in a fight with that chauvinistic bastard of an English teacher over the merits of Whitman's poetry, I would have won it, Helen. You know that," I told her the day she walked into my room with the news.

"If you didn't have a big, fat mouth, you mean?" she said. And she was right.

I got a job teaching high school freshman Latin, Spanish, and calculus at a boarding school for girls in the heart of Boston where I spent my weekends looking out at the harbor, drinking martinis, and avoiding the many, many men who tried to get my attention by buying me drinks or blatantly asking me to dinner from the boardwalk below. Sailors returning home for a short break were the worst. They crowded the docks. They cat-called us. They, without any shame, yelled up to us and asked for our hands in marriage. Being out on a boat or in a submarine with solely other men for months at a time made them animals. When they got back to shore, their young hormones boiled up inside of them and took the form of awful words that spewed out of their awful mouths. I wanted to slap the shit out of them, but, instead, I just ignored them, which hurt them more.

And for the men my age who stayed home from the war, I didn't want anything to do with those rich boys whose parents somehow got them off the draft list. They were the worst kind of men, in my eyes.

I went out alone to a bar by the water one late afternoon. Helen had stayed home with a cold for the day, one of those that hit you hard in the middle of the summer, make you feel like you're dying because it's hot outside, and you can't breathe.

Ships rolled in and out. Not too many Navy ships because they were docked a hundred miles north in New London, but freighters and a few smaller boats that were enlisted by the military and stamped with impermanent letters and numbers to signify their military consignment. The light was bright that day, damn bright. And though the war raged in the Atlantic and the Pacific, and there were supposedly U-boats somewhere out in the water in front of me, I couldn't help but bask in the sunlight. My skin had become so dark from my days in the sun that I looked nice in my long, white dress that made me feel as if I were flying when the breeze brushed the soft fabric against my calves.

"Excuse me," a man in a Navy uniform said to me. He was an officer. I could tell right away from his regalia.

"No thank you," I said. "I'm quite comfortable. And I have a good job, so I don't need anyone to buy me a drink." I had been there a hundred times before and found that being polite but just a little aloof seemed to do the trick to ward off oncoming hits.

I turned my body toward the sun again.

This persistent bastard walked around my back and stood in front of me. He took his hat off and held it at his belt line.

"I know," he said. "You're a teacher at a local boarding school and a graduate of Mount Holyoke. Your specialties are high math and language. You graduated in two and a half years from one of the most difficult schools in the nation with perfect marks. You never really had friends in school, besides a Ms. Helen Brigance, but you are as loyal as they come. Am I correct with all of this?"

I shook my head no. That was weird and shocking, and I needed to leave, immediately.

"I'm not sure what you're talking about, thank you," I said. "I think it's time for me to head to my next stop."

I placed my small purse around my shoulder and dropped down from the bar stool, moving the man out of my way with movement directly toward him.

"You're Della Chavez, born in Trinidad, Colorado, and savior of your father's farm during the Dust Bowl. If I am correct in these statements, I just ask for an hour of your time," the Navy officer said.

I froze. I placed my hands on my hips and stared up at him.

"Who are you?" I asked.

"I'm intelligence officer William Steadman, and the Navy would like to talk to you about a job. It will pay twice the money you earn as a teacher, and you will be able to live for free in Washington, DC, until the job is complete, if you're interested and if you pass the interview process, which is not a guarantee. Many very smart girls have not been able to complete the prerequisite tests, classes, and personality observations. Many just as smart or smarter than you."

I did not like the last comment he made. I did not like how

he called us "girls," as if we were pig-tailed babies taking his test. I did not like the idea that he said that I could not pass the test. That was bullshit. I could pass the test. I'd never failed a test. I was not a little girl.

I did like the idea of more money and moving to DC, so I dropped my guard and changed my tone.

"Well, I do have an hour," I said.

"Okay, I'll see you tomorrow," he said. He handed me the address to a downtown hotel. "And tell Ms. Brigance that I look forward to meeting with her too."

I flung the door open to our apartment. My hands pushed it open so hard that it cut a little divet in the wall. My legs shook, and my heart raced. Nervous sweat, the kind that smells worse than movement sweat, rung around the pits of my silk shirt, and beads of sweat ran over the top of my lip. And then I saw Helen, waiting for me like a dog waits for its owner to return.

She stood there with her eyes wide open. She was sick. I could see the swelling at the edges of her nose and the dry, crusty remnants of watering eyes on her cheeks, but she smiled so wide.

"Teaching? Who needs teaching?" she said. "When we can work for the Army!"

"Did he come here too? We don't even know what we would be doing. They probably just want smart secretaries. I'm not getting my hopes up too much for this. But it would be fun to go to DC for the summer," I said. I was excited too, but goddamnit, someone had to keep all four of our feet on the ground.

"They need us to take tests? We need to have degrees? We need to know more than one language? This is not for secretarial work, Della," she said. "Come on, now, you know this is more than that."

"Languages?" I asked. The officer was so brief with me that I didn't get any hints about what they actually needed from us. Obviously, Helen with her big smile, even covered in drying snot, was able to get the officer to open up a bit more than he did with me. I didn't doubt that for one damned minute. She could charm the panties off a nun.

"Yes, languages, sciences, calculus. Didn't he tell you all of this?" she asked.

"Well, we were in public, so he was pretty tight lipped," I said, hoping that was the reason he seemed to have tried to persuade Helen more than he did me.

"Of course, of course that's why," she said. She could read the worry on my face.

"Now, let's go shopping," she said. "We need dress suits."

I tried to say no. The 'nnnn' even made it to my lips, but she stopped me with a big tug on my arm, and we were out the door and heading to downtown Boston to find something professional and that "showed a little bit of curve too," according to Helen.

Chapter Forty

John
1943

THE SNOOK, JUST LIKE ITS NAME, MOVED SMOOTHLY OUT INTO open waters of the Atlantic. We sailed down the eastern seaboard. Sometimes we would surface, and we could see the skylines of the major cities that lined the edge of our country. Then we dove down into the dark of the Atlantic for days at a time before we resurfaced in the blue waters of the Caribbean. We got to take turns climbing up and out of the submarine and watching the land pass by. These moments were rare, but it was worth it to escape the stench of the hull below.

We headed toward the Pacific Ocean. I could feel the power of the engines, the push through the water, like we were in the middle of a bullet as it left the barrel of a gun. We stayed above water for the first three days. The entirety of the crew ran through drills and procedures and check offs to make sure the pollywogs, including Noakes and me, knew what they were doing. The engineers tested and tested and tested, carrying their clipboards around as if they were attached to their arms.

We found our bunks right away. They were placed right next to the kitchen. The anger in us had subsided a bit because once we got on the ship, we felt how important we were, not only to our fellow sailors but also to the captain and his officers. Food, on a submarine, was at the heart of keeping sailors happy, and we found out quickly that the Navy knew that being sent under water in a giant moving piece of metal with no fresh air for seventy-five days at a time was no trip to the brothel. They gave us the best food they could, the best food in the military.

That first trip of twenty-seven days from New London to Pearl Harbor was easy. We got to get out and walk along the edges of the Panama Canal. We were only underwater for a few days at a time. The time in the ship was almost cheerful. As cooks, we got nicer bunks than everyone else and everyone treated us good as we made our way through potato dish after potato dish, the order from our CO because potatoes took up so much room in our bunks, in the bathroom, and everywhere else.

When we pulled into Pearl Harbor, we were set free to shower and given the weekend to take busses into Waikiki. Since we had twelve days before we would have to venture out into the Pacific, we ended up getting two weekends in Hawaii. The first weekend was a blur. We quickly found a bunch of sailors who looked like us. It's crazy how easily that happened. And we joined a quick moving caravan toward Waikiki Beach and the ocean. I don't really remember that first weekend. Of the things that do come back to me, the crack of the first beer at the ocean's edge and the crack of the waves crashing next to us and a cheer. Borrachos, we jumped on a tour bus to the pineapple fields, plucked ripened pineapples and poured rum into them and chugged from the edges of the spikey skin, the blur coming on stronger with each drink and cheers. There's a glimpse of me dancing with a hula girl on a stage, and a few of our friends disappearing into Chinatown, one whipping out his dick and yelling, "They don't know what's going to hit them."

"Della," I remember saying to Noakes.

"My mom," Noakes said.

And we waved to our friends as they disappeared into the lights of Oahu's Chinatown. We wouldn't see them again until the next day on the beach, battered by drunkenness.

The next morning, Noakes and I woke up in a dingy hotel in the center of town.

"How'd we get here?" he asked me.

My face had become one with the pillow, and I could barely

breath from the thick, humid air of the Pacific island, something I had never breathed before.

"I don't know," I said.

Pain pounded between our eyes.

The place was small, made up of two twin beds lining the wall and a sink at the end of them. It wasn't much different than our barracks back in New London.

"Let's get some food," I said.

"Shower first," Noakes said. "Once we get on that sub..."

I knew what he meant.

"Yes, shower first, and coffee," I said.

We both showered and threw our dirty clothes back on.

"And clothes," he said.

"And food," I said.

"Yes, food and then clothes," he said.

I loved him. If it weren't for Noakes, I don't think I would have made it through. He had become my Manuel.

We walked down a small hallway and then down a small stairway and into the lobby of the hotel.

"Good morning, John and Edward," a small man with a thick waist and small shoulders said, "Did you sleep well?"

We both swayed our heads back and forth and closed our eyes.

"Yes," he said. "You were a bit under the weather when you came in last night."

"Were we kind?" Noakes asked.

Like me, he had no memory, but like me, he worried about the same thing I did. Were we assholes? I could handle getting drunk and blacking out, but I couldn't handle being unkind like so many men got when they got too drunk.

"Oh yes," he said. "Even though you could barely stand up, you did your best to ask about my family, how I got started in the hotel business, and if I needed anything carried for me."

The old, tiny man smiled at us.

"Oh good," I said. "Did we already pay?"

"Oh, yes," he said. "You actually paid double. You paid for two rooms, but I only needed to charge you for one. I tried to explain to you that you only need to pay a double occupancy for one room instead of for two rooms, but, you know, your logic wasn't completely with you."

"Did we, did we, umm, have girls with us?" Noakes asked.

"No, no. This one," he pointed to me, "wouldn't shut up about Della, and you, sir, wouldn't shut up about how you promised your mother that you would keep your dick clean. You said that she didn't say 'dick clean' and that you were translating for me."

He giggled a bit at the last part.

Noakes put his hands together in prayer and smiled.

"We need food. We need food bad," I said. "I would like something so spicy that I will sweat all of this out."

Noakes nodded.

"And a beer," he said.

"Yes, and a beer," I said. "Do you know a place that is open in the morning like this. We're cooks, remember, so we won't go for sideshow bacon and eggs."

"Oh, it's not morning, John. It's afternoon," he said. He smiled again and then pulled out a piece of paper and began to draw. His map wound us through streets away from the beach—that he drew by adding waves along a long thin line—and deep into the city. "Stay away from anything near the beach. I want to share a place I love with you."

He handed us the piece of paper. Then he traced the path with his finger.

"Follow this to a little home that sits between two buildings. You will see a tiny sign that reads Tim's Lo Mein. Tim is my brother-in-law. He's a real asshole, but he is an amazing cook. Ask for extra spicy with your Lo Mein, and you will feel better after. I promise. Will you be staying with me again tonight?"

"Yes, of course we will," I said. "Hopefully we won't be so borracho when we come in tonight."

"It's okay if you are, John, it's okay if you are. Two young men like you who love a woman and love their mother are always welcome here."

We took the map and walked out the front door of the hotel into a bustling side street of Waikiki. We had no idea where we were or how we found the hotel the night before, but we had a map, and we followed it through the streets to a little shack in the middle of two four-story buildings.

When we walked in, we said, "Nam sent us."

A tall Asian man greeted us and sat us at one of three tables next to a large, open interior window that looked into the kitchen.

"Nam's an asshole, but he's my sister's brother, and he only sends me respectable sailors like you. Spicy or not spicy? Chicken leg or chicken thigh or mixed?" he asked.

"Spicy with mixed," I said.

"Spicy with only leg," Noakes said.

"Spicy-spicy or pussy Kansas-boy spicy?" he asked and laughed.

"Do we look like we're from Kansas?"

"Spicy, spicy," he said. And then he started tossing things into a giant pan. We ate lo mein and drank a very cold beer—something that was hard to find the night before—that he placed in front of us, and after we chowed down and drank a few more beers, we felt like two roosters awake for another day.

That afternoon, we found clothes, including swim trunks. We sat on the beach, we drank beers, and we watched the ocean together. Like always, we talked about Della and Trinidad and Chicago and baseball. We got so drunk, again, and we saw our friends from the night before, briefly, before they headed back to Chinatown and its women.

We woke up the next morning, no memory from the night, except for a few more dances with hula girls, the moon, and sand between our toes. We went back to Tim's to eat again. Then we boarded our submarine for work until the next, last weekend before heading to war came.

The mood on the submarine that week was good. We worked during the day, ate dinner in the barracks at night, drank beer on base, woke up, and did it all over again. We practiced drills, learned even more of the intricacies of sea life, and went to briefings about what was happening above and below the water in the Pacific, in the theater of the ocean. We knew exactly what we had signed up for, we knew how the ocean might take us, and we knew that submarine life would be one of the hardest and trying lives on the ocean. We also learned what our job was: cut off shipping lines, wound the land-based armies by sinking the transports that carried all their necessary supplies, and torpedo their submarines and warships that aimed to sink our carriers and transports.

"I'm proud to be here," Noakes said, one night after dinner when we sat outside the cafeteria and looked up at the stars that hung so large and bright above the Pacific Ocean, "even if we are just cooks."

"Me too," I told him. "Let's cook the hell out of the food down there."

He nodded.

We had one final weekend before our first tour. This time, however, we didn't drink all day and all night. It seemed that we had gotten that out our systems the weekend before. Instead, we found a few hammocks on the beach where we could order beer and food and watch the girls in bikinis and easily charge to the ocean and jump in when we got too hot.

Instead of drowning out the weight of what was to come in a couple days, I sipped on a beer, took in as much sun as I could, and wrote Della a long letter. I would only write one or two sentences an hour. I would nap in the hammock and dream of her. We had tried to meet multiple times when we were only a couple hundred miles away from each other in Connecticut and Massachusetts during my training and her time at school, but it never worked out. My leave never matched her exam schedule.

I shared my fears with her, something I didn't even share with Noakes. I wrote how I used to think about her while I slept in my chile patches at home, staying away from my grandfather. I told her that I daydreamed how it would have gone if I just walked through that schoolhouse door instead of trying to find her in the window. If I had done that, she would have known that I had come, and she might have tried to come to see me or known how bad my life was in Reno. When I lay in the barracks in New London, I had wondered if she had seen me then, if she would have seen the bruises and the hanging, broken jaw, and if she would have seen my grandfather knock me out and drag me to his car. Maybe she would have stayed with me that night while I lay drunken in the train car instead of running away. We would have had a few more nights together that week on the train and in Hartford.

I wrote about how I had played these "what if's" over and over in my mind right before I thought about going to war and getting sunk and never seeing her again. I told her about how I prayed that she would still love me when this was all over. How, even though I had Noakes, I had always felt alone. The last five years since Maria left and Manuel left, I felt isolated, like the torn-apart carcass of the last of a herd—the vultures already picked away what they needed—left in the desert, with the rot and the smell consuming me. Until I found her again. Until I saw her walking through the train station. Until she smiled at me across the table and told me about all the things she was going to study. I wanted with everything in me to be her books, to be that thing that she wanted most. I felt full again. Not full in the belly. But full-bodied again. Whole. And I would be second place to books. I didn't care.

I told her all of this. All of it in a letter that took me two days to write on the beach.

Meet me here, Della. If I make it through this war. Meet me here, in Hawaii.

And pray for the USS Snook.

I love you,

John Garcia Cordova

Chapter Forty-One

Della
1943

"I'LL SEE YOU THERE, DELLA," HELEN SAID. "I HAVE TO PICK UP one more thing for my outfit before I go. Is that okay?"

"Yes, of course, I planned to take the bus. The time alone to think will do me well," I said. I hadn't really planned to take the bus. I had hoped that Helen would give me a ride in the car, but, honestly, I didn't give a damn any way, and the bus ride did calm my nerves a bit. Helen could be a bit talkative when I just wanted the whole world to shut the hell up at times.

Thirty minutes later, I sat in the lobby of a hotel in downtown Boston along with three other young women. Each of the women looked to be about my age. One had bright white hair and wore a pant suit, something so few women wore at the time. Another was short, wore a plaid heel-length dress and a conservative blue top. In her hand, she held what looked like an invitation that had been mailed to her, the US Mail stamp on the outside of the opened envelope. The third woman, instead of sitting on the chairs like me and the other two women, paced back and forth, acting as if she were admiring the paintings on the wall, but I knew that this was just a ruse. The woman's thumb touched her fingers in different sequences as she walked back and forth as if they were playing keys at the end of grand piano.

It was Helen, of course. She walked to the very corner of the room and then sneezed quietly, as if she were trying to just cool the tips of her fingertips with a small breath, and then she came back, sat down by me, and smiled. She placed her hand on my knee and then squeezed it tight, her way of telling me that she was so excited to be there and that she was doing her best to tamp down her excitement in the presence of other people.

"I went to the pharmacist to get something really strong for my cold, so I wouldn't sneeze all over everybody. Nothing like a big snot bubble to ruin an important interview." She giggled and held in a sneeze. "You see, that would have been huge if I didn't take that syrup he gave me. I don't know what it was, but it works, and I feel a little tipsy too. Don't worry, not the kind of tipsy that makes we want to dance around in my underwear, but the kind of tipsy that makes me feel confident enough to punch some handsy asshole in the mouth, that kind of tipsy."

I laughed a bit. The other women frowned at us both. *They can take their disapproving faces and shove them right up their asses*, I thought to myself.

"Della, did you know there are seventy-seven different patterns in these frames," Helen pointed at the wooden frames on the wall. "What the hell are we here for?"

Instead of answering Helen, I just shook my head, smiled, stood up, walked toward the paintings, shuffled back and forth in front of them and did my best to prove Helen wrong, but I couldn't. Helen had nailed it. There were exactly seventy-seven patterns in the nine frames—made up of swoops and crosses and slants and circles, all forming very specific and artful wholes.

"I have no idea what we are doing here. Or at least I have no idea what you are doing here. I'm here to pass a test." I had to tease her a bit. She would have been disappointed if I didn't.

With a nod of her head and her lips tightened together, Helen grabbed my hand and led me to the window of the hotel and nodded for me to look down into the street at the back of the building, opposite where I came in from. She had not only been counting patterns. She had been scoping the whole damned place out.

"What do you see?" Helen asked.

It took no time at all for me to catch her drift. Every single car parked on the northern street that lined the hotel had military license plates on them, and every single one of them were from Washington, DC.

I nodded at Helen.

"I'm here to pass a test too, Della, and you and I are going to DC," she said.

A woman exited a conference room door behind us. Her eyes were wide with excitement. Her hands made fists as she walked out toward the front door. In her purse, a large manila envelope stuck out. She didn't say one word to one woman before she left the hotel, making a b-line to the exit and not looking back.

"Helen Brigance, please join us," the Navy officer said.

With my thumb still in Helen's hand, I typed a message with it on Helen's fingers: good luck.

Helen returned the very quick message: thank you.

This exchange took longer than the officer had expected, so he coughed loudly to interrupt our brief moment. Helen dropped my hand, the last bit of her code tapping on my palm and walked into the room, her fingers crossed behind her back.

One hour later, she came out of the door. She too had a manila envelope in her hand. She too had eyes the size of quarter dollars. She too walked straight toward the door without saying a word to any other woman in the room, including me. But right as she made it to the exit, on her fingertips, with her thumb, and in Morse code, she signaled out, "Hell, yes." No one else in the room saw the fingers, but Helen knew I would be watching, and I beamed for a moment before letting the sliver of self-doubt that I may not get the yellow envelope or that I may not get to join my friend in DC slide into my mind for a long, fearful second.

They called the two other women into the room before they called my name. I sat there, more nervous than I had been before Helen went in.

I'd always been competitive, intellectually, aiming to be the smartest. I cursed the walls of my high school when they gave

my male classmate the valedictorian award instead of me because, as my favorite teacher put it, "The boy might be able to do
something with it and Della would not." The principal saddled
me with the salutatorian award instead, patting me on the lower
back so close to my ass that I almost told my father about it. I let
it go because I had two little brothers that needed to go to school
there, and my father's anger would jeopardize their time under
the principal's thumb. Plus, no one ever said anything about that
stuff back then, sure as hell not in rural Colorado where girls
were being married off in wink-wink fashion in exchange for
heads of cattle, like the tradition of dowries had never really "of-
ficially" gone away.

Instead, when the principal announced the awards at graduation, I waved from the audience and didn't get up to shake his
hand. I couldn't bear to touch his skin. I devoted the red painted
nail of my middle finger to my principal when I raised it to Trinidad High School on my way out of town on the train after high
school graduation. That was his special part of my "fuck off."

A short-haired woman went in and came out first. She did
not have an envelope, but she followed the same protocol as if
she had. She looked straight ahead. She did not smile. She remained silent. And she walked out the front door of the hotel.

The second woman, the one with the long, long dress, was
only in the room for five or six minutes. She exited and shook
her head no. Instead of walking out the front door slowly, she
galloped toward the exit as if someone had begun to chase her.
No one did.

"Della Chavez, please join us," the officer said with his hand
on the doorknob.

Chapter Forty-Two

John
1943

OUR FIRST PATROL.

INITIALLY, WHILE JUST GETTING OUR feet wet, we moved through the easy stuff to cook, the stuff we could just kick out in masses—beans, mashed potatoes, bacon, eggs. All of that good, comfort food that filled up bellies. But at the end of our shift, right when two other cooks took over, Noakes and I got to cook for ourselves, so we rummaged through the boxes in the kitchen and then the boxes in the showers and then boxes on the bunks and found a few golden items, those, I'm guessing, reserved for the captain's cook, the sailor who ran the show. There was nothing we did on that ship without asking him first. And everything was inventoried, so as soon we found a few spices and peppers and onions, and even thick bones covered in turkey meat, we asked if we could use them for our dinner after our second shift that ended just about supper time on the second day as we pushed out into the Pacific Ocean.

"As long as you cook for me and don't waste anything. I'm on shift, and I'll need some food," he told us. "The pantry and proteins are yours, boys."

"You cook something you like, and I'll cook something I like, and we'll share, sound good?" I asked Noakes.

"You're gonna love this," Noakes said. "See you back here in a bit."

Two other cooks stammered around the kitchen. They had never really cooked before, and cooking for the masses really confused them. In front of them on the counter, they had opened the large and barely together cooking handbook and procedures the Navy had given us right before getting on the submarine in Connecticut. Noakes and I had run our fingers through it and talked strategy, knowing that we would be cooking in a miniature kitchen with two of us in tight, tight quarters. The handbook that we shared had handwritten notes all through the margins. We had crossed out procedures we knew that were excess, and we added our ingredients to recipes. We knew what would work and what wouldn't. Noakes grew up cooking for his younger brothers and sisters, and I grew up cooking with my whole family and Della and her family until I lost my parents and had to move away from Trinidad and the Chavezes, so we both had a learned feel for the kitchen. The two new sailors who ran around the kitchen, pissing off the head cook by getting in his way while he prepped food for the Captain and lead crew, were such a mess that the head cook had to line them up three times and yell at them to "pull their square heads straight out of their round assholes."

Noakes and I stepped around each other, weaving and ducking like boxers in a stainless-steel covered ring, while we prepped and cooked food. There was a reason we scored the highest marks in our boot class. We were good.

"You'll like this too, if I can find the right stuff," I told him. We both went off in search of ingredients for our second supper on board the submarine.

I knew they were there. Somewhere. I saw them on the list. We'd spent a large part of our first days on the boat taking stock of all the available food items. Breads. Beans. Corn. Salt. Pepper. Potatoes. But we didn't come across the special ingredient items that I saw on the inventory list. The head cook said we could use anything we wanted, and I wasn't going to start cooking until I found them. I looked in the boxes in the shitter, praying they weren't in there. I looked in the showers that had been stuffed with tiny boxes. Three days into our mission, and no one had showered, so the boxes remained stacked under the sprayer.

And then I found them, hidden in a corner next to the captain's quarters. Ten or eleven little boxes all wrapped in cellophane.

"Thank you, Jesus," I said out loud. "Thank you, Jesus." I did the sign of the cross.

I worried that when the head cook said that we could use anything that he didn't mean we could use what was in those boxes. At that point, however, I had already pulled my pocketknife from my pocket and slid it along the top surface of cellophane and opened it up.

They weren't anything special, nothing my dad would have prayed about in his sweat-covered shirt in the middle of the Colorado plains, but they were something. Something that would add just enough kick to make the hunt worthwhile.

Dehydrated chile peppers. The box held only about five bags of dehydrated green and red chiles. From the look of them, they were just mild Anaheim peppers and pimientos, but I was so happy to see them that I said the prayer my dad used to say to the Lady of Guadalupe.

Bendícenos Señor, bendice estos alimentos que por tu bondad vamos a recibir, bendice las manos que los prepararon dale pan al que tiene hambre y hambre de ti al que tiene pan. Amén.

I don't believe too much in hoodoo voodoo stuff, but I felt my father with me then. I think he led me to those peppers. I felt his hand on my shoulders and his breath on my hair. I was in the middle of the Pacific Ocean, thousands of miles and a decade away from my father's chile garden on the plains, but I felt my old man out there at sea with me. The dry air of the desert was replaced by the humid, thick air of the hull of a submarine, but I felt like I had gone home with those peppers in my hands.

I dug my knife into another box and pulled out a brick of chocolate.

"Bendice me, la Señora de Guadalupe," I said.

Then, as if my father had become a real man, I heard a voice above me.

"Stand up," the captain said.

Chapter Forty-Three

Della
1943

I sat in front of five Navy officers and one Army officer. The Army officer looked out of place, his green uniform clashing with the beautiful Navy blue. They all placed their hands on the table in front of them as if it were a collected effort to hold it down. I crossed my legs. I sat up straight. I had planned to spend my evening watching the ships roll in and out of the harbor and drinking cheap vodka in even cheaper soda. If I would have known about the opportunity to sit in the lobby of a hotel with my legs crossed and my back straight before being displayed in front of five military officers without a table of my own to protect me, I would have pulled my long black hair up and worn a pant suit.

I smiled a courteous smile, one that barely moved my lips upward. I'd grown up around men much more intimidating than the ones who sat at the table in front of me, ranching men who, though very polite, were rough around the edges and full of machismo. These men didn't scare me.

Major Welker, the man in the center of the table who wore his name on a badge on his chest like all the other men, stood up and placed his hands on the table in front of him, a power stance meant to show he was in charge, not just of the committee but also in charge of me and my belonging in the room.

"Ms. Chavez, you're American Indian, correct?"

"Yes, I am. I am half American Indian," I said.

"How do you feel about manifest destiny?" he asked.

His fingers splayed out on the table, the tips of them starting to turn pink and white.

"I think the slaughter of innocent people, of innocent children especially, because of the color of their skin or the land that they own or the god or gods that they pray to should never happen. And if it happens, the best people should stop it, even it means they have to travel across oceans to do so," I said. Instead of remaining seated like they expected me to, I stood up and walked toward the table and stopped one foot in front of it.

"Don't you?" I asked Major Welker.

Major Welker shook his head one time—very, very slightly. It could have even been seen as a twitch, but I knew it wasn't. He was shaking away his surprise at my answer and my approach before he answered.

"Please sit down, Ms. Chavez," he asked politely.

So I did.

"I agree with you, Ms. Chavez, and this is why we are at war, well, one of the reasons," he said.

I had flipped the script on him.

"You are asking if I hold animosity against the people who slaughtered my mother's people and put them in reservations," I said. A statement. Not a question.

The Army officer at the end of the table coughed uncomfortably and said, "Yes, that is what we are asking."

I held my breath in and met each of their eyes. This made them shift in their seats a bit.

"I believe in our place in this war," I said.

"But that doesn't answer the question," another officer said.

"I believe that is the real question, isn't it? We forget the question of my mother and her tribe, if we skip the questions about my loyalty to this country, and if we ask the real question, do I believe in our place in this war and do I support *our* country, the answer is a resounding, yes," I said.

I placed my hand on my lap and did my best to shut the hell up.

* * *

ONE NAVY OFFICER HAD REMAINED quiet throughout the discussion. When he finally spoke, his voice was strong but not loud, gruff but not harsh, quiet but not a whisper.

"Della, beyond the loyalty question, can you remain quiet? Can you lie to your family? It seems that you don't hold true animosity against the government for what our ancestors believed to be manifest destiny. Hitler believes he should rid the world of the Jews, which we are over there to fight against, but can you lie to your father, to your mother, to your brothers for your country? Can you tell them that you are moving to Washington, DC, to solely work as a typist or a secretary after you left Colorado to become something more than the wife of a rancher or a miner? Can you swallow that?"

"My brother Ernie already died in this war. There is no secret I could tell that would bring him back. So, yes, I can lie."

The officer flipped through a manila folder that sat in front of him. He pulled out a stapled packet and thumbed through it until his eyes fell on what he wanted. He folded the previous pages back underneath that page and began to read, "A woman should not fall victim to the practices of tradition if those practices only create the perfection of stagnancy of cultural and feminist growth in society."

He looked up at me, "Do you believe this to be true?"

"Yes," I said. I straightened my back in the chair.

The third officer, the one that had snatched me from my tranquil afternoon, stood and asked with kindness, "We are here to give you a chance to break boundaries, to break tradition, to break the codes of our enemies and to save our men at sea from surprise attacks. To find enemy ships. To decipher the enemy's ciphers. You would be a very important link in our intelligence chain that will help us win this war. Is this what you would call breaking tradition and cultural and feminist growth, Della?"

I thought about it all. The idea of millions of puzzles, the image of breaking codes, the concept of reading other languages, translating them, and on top of that, working to open up the hidden meanings of codes within them. I felt happy.

"Yes," I said. My words came out, mirroring his tone, humble but also confident. The defensiveness that the other officer's question had built had been broken down by this officer's words and demeanor.

"Here's the hardest question of all for you, Della," he said. "When the war is over, will you be able to walk away and never utter the words cipher or analytics or speak of what you did there ever again? Can you stifle your desire to prove to the world that you broke from the tradition of just being a secretary or a runner or someone who just typed during the war?"

I sat quiet for a moment to think. All the other officers sat quietly too. This was a real question, one that had been laid out well, so the long silence, this time, felt appropriate, necessary. I wanted so badly to travel to DC to help break down the most important puzzles of my lifetime, but I understood exactly what the question was, and I understood why it had been asked. This would all be top secret, and the military was not joking about keeping it quiet. Then it came to me, the old concept about love that I had read in one hundred different forms in one hundred different stanzas from one hundred different poets from many, many different time periods. "It is better to have loved and lost than to have never loved." Shakespeare shared this. The Greeks shared this. Neruda shared this. Petrarch shared this. All the poets believed it to be true.

I accepted it when it came to breaking codes for the US Navy in a war to save lives and to win and to stop another genocide. "It is better to save lives and be quiet than to never save lives at all."

I stood up, I walked over to the officer who had all of my college work in the folder in front him with his annotations and notes and underlines on the pages, which made me feel even more necessary to the cause, and I shook his hand.

"Yes, yes, I can," I said. "And thank you for this opportunity, sir."

A WEEK LATER, I STOOD outside of Arlington Hall, waiting to be ushered inside. It felt like once I stepped into the halls of the old building that I would lose a part of me and gain another, and, God's honest truth, I didn't know which one I wanted more.

Helen had gotten the same orders, passed the same test, and left the next day after her interview.

"I have to get to DC early," she said. "I'll find you, Della. I'll see you at registration. I have to go see about some things." Then she was gone, gone to DC to do whatever the hell Helen wanted to do without giving me even the tiniest glimpse into what it was. Just like she said she had to buy something for her outfit and turned up with a quart of pharmaceuticals running through her bloodstream to not look sick during the test, "I have to go see about some things," could mean anything really, so I took care of my own stuff and headed to DC on the train.

The old building, a former dormitory, had been converted into a government operations building. Men in uniform walked in and out of the front door. Men with automatic weapons stood guard at every entrance, their hands wrapped firmly around the guns held at the waist and pointed toward the sky. Grey and white clouds drifted overhead, catching the jet stream toward the ocean just a few miles from where I stood.

I couldn't imagine what waited for me on the other side of those doors, and the officer who picked me up at the train station gave me no real time to ponder it either. He was cute with a firm jaw and strong shoulders, but he was way too honkie for my taste, a term I picked up one afternoon on my way from Trinidad to Massachusetts. One I liked to say, one I felt appropriate for people with too little pigment in their skin to like spicy foods or too much stick up their ass when they walked and talked. He was too damned honkie for me.

The man escorted me through the front doors. It was early morning, and I had yet to drop off my bags, so I had to carry them with me.

He led me to a check-in desk set up for people just like me, homeless young women who had no damned idea what they were doing. A man behind the desk handed me a clipboard to fill in all of my "necessary" information, which included more than I had ever been asked about myself in the past. But this didn't bother me—much. I knew one thing: I was there on the military's dime, and I expected them to want to know all about me.

I sat, I wrote, and then I handed the form back to the man behind the desk.

He scanned my form, checking the boxes with a pen.

And then his brow furrowed.

"You didn't fill out a local residence," he said. "This will need to be filled out before you can start work."

"Excuse me?" I said and then looked down at my luggage that sat next to my legs and then back at the man behind the desk. I wanted to say something like, "Umm, do you not see that I just got off the train, honkie?" Instead, I said, "I just got interviewed last week. They put me on a train this morning. I'm not sure how this whole thing works."

The man shook his head as if I had answered incorrectly; I would find out later that he was just a dick and didn't want to deal with another recruit who he would have to place in the makeshift dormitory for women about a mile from Arlington Hall, a place where hundreds of young women had been staying and would be staying until the end of their service, where three to four women shared a room and ten to twelve women shared a bathroom and showers. He was just a dick, and I was glad I held my tongue.

"We'll have to put you up in Arlington Fields," he said. He sighed and pulled out another set of forms that outlined how much I would have to pay, what the government would pay, and another form that said even though I would be living with other recruits, I could not discuss my work with any of them outside of Arlington Hall, even if we were working on the same project. I had signed form after form after form the day before that stated if I spoke to anyone outside of the US military about the work I would be doing, even though I didn't know what it would be, I could be tried for treason. I understood. And I loved the idea of it. Loved it.

"I won't tell a soul," I said out loud when I signed the paper. The dick behind the desk sighed as if I had disturbed his precious air.

Right before I signed the lease for my bed at the dormitory, which would cut deep into the pay the military would give me, a soft hand pulled the pen from my hand.

"She'll be staying with me and my cousin at our apartment downtown. She got recruited out of Virginia. She's nice— enough," Helen said. She asked the soldier if she could borrow my original form. He handed it to Helen, and she filled out the address.

"Is that okay with you…Della, isn't it?" Helen said, dipping her head down to pretend to read my name. "What is that name? Some kind of western name or something like that? Are you from the west, dear Della?"

I could have slugged Helen and hugged her at the same time.

I nodded my head instead and suppressed laughter that sergeant dickhead would have not approved of.

"You'll love the place, Della," Helen said. "It's small, and you'll have to sleep on the couch, but with the three of us there, the rent will be cheap, and we can save money, and we can avoid the dormitory."

The man at the desk nodded. He didn't give two shits what we did as long as it didn't add to his workday. He'd already become sick of our short banter.

"All privacy agreements must be upheld at your place of

residence," he said. He handed me a different form to fill out to ensure that I understood that even though I would work with the two women I lived with, the three of us could not talk about work outside of Arlington Hall. At the bottom of the form, there were six words that were strictly prohibited to be spoken at risk of treason: data, cipher, cryptanalysis, codes, cyber, and security.

Just seeing these words made me anxious and excited to get started. I wanted to drop my bags right there and find out what lay behind the security checkpoint.

The soldier made both of us take an oath of secrecy, even though Helen had already done it earlier that morning, and then he shooed us away, instructing us to report back to Arlington Hall at 7:00 a.m. the next day for "duty."

We took a bus downtown, the heat of summer in DC nearly unbearable; the sweat built up along the tops of our foreheads and leaked out through our blouses. It was palpable, grimy, and salty. At our stop, Helen helped me with my bags, swinging one of them over the top of her thin, sinewy muscled shoulders. We climbed the communal stairs of the townhouse, walked through the partially propped open door—a woman's shoe stuck between door and frame—and found Helen's cousin sitting in front of a fan, its blades spinning as fast as they could and still not able to beat off the humid blanket that fell over the room.

"I'm Debra," Helen's cousin said, reaching out her hand.

"I'm Della," I replied and shook Debra's hand.

The three of us shed our blouses, not caring about being modest, and stood around the fan.

Helen walked to the kitchen and came back with three cold vodka sodas that had been placed in the refrigerator before she left to fetch me, which she said had been her plan all along.

I preferred silence to talking for most of my adult life, succeeding in keeping a single-bed dormitory throughout my time at Mount Holyoke, not letting anyone else break into my space or my routine or my insurmountable need to read at all hours of the day and night.

"I think we're going to be breaking codes. You know Japanese codes and German codes. Since you know Japanese, I think you'll be jumping right into translating codes, dear Della," she said.

"You just broke the goddamned law, dear Helen," I said.

"Nope, nope, I did not," she said, "we don't know what we're doing yet. We don't know what they don't want us to talk about yet, so we are just guessing—conjecture—so we aren't breaking any laws."

This was true.

There, that night on the floor, our legs crossed, we laughed and we smiled and we conjectured like crazy. We were doing something together that was bigger than school, than study, than living on a campus, than even a teaching job. We, somehow, had been asked to do something special, and we got to do it together. That changed something, made our friendship deeper—immediately.

By the time we finished our drinks, Helen and I had begun a long, continually growing joke about the Navy officer who had checked us in earlier that morning, flashing our best impressions of his dull and annoyed facial expressions back and forth at each other and mimicking his flat, dumb voice, "Okay, sign here then," and, "Though you might work with some of your roommates—TREASON!" We laughed and touched each other's knees—and left Debra feeling like a third wheel.

It was one of those moments, one of those rare, rare moments when two people connect, when they fall into a line that seems to be placed there by the universe, and they are tugged by a string and pulled together to ride that line across the world. Those moments between people so rarely happen, but when they do, they are so profoundly recognizable that everyone else around can see them happening and feel as if they are the most alone person in the cosmos.

I think that's how Debra felt, at least.

She excused herself, leaving us to finish off the vodka and fall asleep next to each other on the floor in front of the fan that night.

This tightened grip on each other would stick with us over the next few grueling summer months. We spent our first days training alongside each other. We spent our nights drinking and then getting ready to go out into DC. That week when we still had no responsibility, before they let us into the war rooms, it was the best week of my life.

Chapter Forty-Four

John
1943

I STOOD UP AND FACED THE CAPTAIN. I PUT A BAG OF THE chiles in my left hand and saluted him immediately.

"Yes, sir," I said.

With hand still placed firmly on my forehead, I ran the smile off my face.

"Have you been given permission to go through my boxes?" he asked.

"Yes, sir," I said. "The head cook gave me permission to use any available item for our supper, sir."

He ran his fingers across his chin, thinking.

"Even these?" he asked.

His voice came out sternly with unmasked skepticism.

"I believe so, sir," I said. "I asked if I could use all available items, and he said I could, sir."

"I don't believe he was thinking of these boxes when he said yes, Cordova," the captain said.

He continued to run his hand along the scruff on his chin. It made a scratching noise that filled the small hallway at the edge of his quarters.

"I can put them back, sir. My mistake, sir," I said.

He didn't respond for a long, long minute.

"What do you plan to do with those, Cordova," he asked.

I took a welcome breath.

"I'm going to cook with them, sir, for me and Noakes and the head cook, sir," I said.

His hand went back to his chin and the scratching continued.

"What would you cook with chiles and chocolate?" he asked. His forehead scrunched, his brows went inward, and his lips seemed to meld together, all in a genuine expression of confusion.

"Sir, I plan to make a molé, sir," I said.

"A mole, Cordova?" he asked.

"Yes, sir, I will get the water back into the peppers. Then I will grind them into a paste. Then I will cook the peppers with the chocolate until the sauce becomes creamy. Then I will stew some potatoes and chicken in it, sir. Noakes is cooking something too, sir."

His eyebrows lifted, and a slight smile drew across his lips.

"Continue on, Cordova, but since this is my food, since this is my chocolate and chiles, I want to have a plate of this mole chicken," he pronounced mole like describing the rodent, "as soon as it is ready. Understand, Cordova."

"Yes, sir," I said. A bead of sweat ran from my back and into my underwear.

"What are you standing there for, Cordova? Don't you need to be cooking?" he asked, a hint of sarcasm on his voice.

"Yes, sir, but…" I began.

"But what, Cordova," he said. He was no longer smiling. I had already taken up five minutes of his time. His scrunched brow, his downturned lips, and his quiet glare returned before I had the chance to finish my question. I had lingered too long.

"I'll need another bag of each, sir," I said. I could hear the crack in my voice, nerves filling me from my feet to my larynx.

"Take what you need, Cordova, but don't waste an ounce. We can't restock until we hit the other side of the Pacific Ocean," he said. "Dismissed."

He walked past me. I saluted him again and ran to the kitchen.

Noakes stood above two small side burners that the other cooks had no use for in their prep. They didn't know how to cook in a delicate enough way that they would ever need a small burner. I filled Noakes in on what had happened with the captain. He nodded and ran out of the kitchen, coming back with more ingredients.

"If you get to cook for the captain, I'm going to cook for him too," he said. He smiled. He dropped a pile of ingredients on the one-foot-by-one-foot chopping block that I had managed to steal away from the cooks on duty. We both began cooking.

Our pits sweating and our brows warm from moving in the small kitchen, the head cook called us to attention. We turned to find him holding two seared steaks and two potatoes, each buddying up to each other on separate plates, the smell of the steak hanging in the moist, submarine air like he had spritzed the whole damn area with steak spray. A bit of drool ran to the corner of my mouth, but I swiped at it with my forearm before anyone noticed.

"I have a spot left on these plates for you two to fill with whatever you promised the captain. I expect these spots to be filled within the next minute, so his food gets to him warm like it should be, not cold like your lives will be if it doesn't." He said this with no hint of laughter or sarcasm.

"Yes, sir," I said.

My mole could have used another twenty minutes to stew, but I didn't have the time. I dug my finger into it and took a lick. It wasn't perfect, the swapping out of the rich anejos for the dull anaheims and pimientos left it a bit flat, but it tasted better than anything I'd eaten in the Navy so far. That sizzling steak, however, its juices beginning to run across the plate to the potato, would not be a disappointment to the captain, so the bar had been raised high.

"Sir," I said, dropping my head down toward the small bowl of mole I had filled. "I can carry this to the captain. Noakes can put his food in those spots."

I grabbed a couple slices of bread. We didn't have time to make tortillas or rellenos. The bread would have to do.

"He can put the mole on the bread, sir. Or his potato too," I said.

The head chef nodded. His lips started to purse with his growing impatience.

"Here you go, sir," Noakes said.

He walked toward the head cook with a big spoonful of shrimp and sausage and tomatoes and placed them in the open spots on the plates next to the steak and potatoes.

"Follow me," the head cook said.

I followed him with my bowl of mole.

Noakes stood still.

"You too, Noakes," he said. "If your food is bad, it's on your head, not mine."

We followed the cook through the narrow passageway toward the captain's quarters, up and over pipes and through the small oval doorways, until we stood outside of his door.

The head cooked knocked, rapping his knuckles exactly twice on the thin, fake mahogany door.

"Yes, come in," the captain said.

The head cook nudged the door open with his knee.

Inside, the captain sat with his XO, both of them already positioned on each end of the small, green table that sat in the center of the very small room. Hell, for some reason, I expected the door to open to a huge suite, maybe to another universe where all the creature comforts lay, but, no, it was a basic room lined with procedural books above the bed, a table, and a shitter. That was it. For some reason, the captain's room made me respect him more. Sure, he had more than we did with his own privacy and shitter and table, but not much more. He was down there in the barrel of the submarine just like the rest of us.

There wasn't enough room for all three of us to enter the room at the same time, so the head cook dropped his head down through the top of the door frame and walked over the bottom of it, not spilling an ounce of food from the plate. It was circus-like how he did it. He set the plates on the table in front of the men and then walked back out, grabbed my mole, and then repeated his movement back into the room with the same, genteel care.

"Is this the mole?" the Captain asked, again, saying it like he was talking about the rodent. Mole.

The head cook nodded to me to answer.

"Yes, sir," I said.

"And what's this," he said. He pointed to Noakes' dish that smelled just as good as mine but so completely different at the same time.

"That's shrimp and sausage like we make at home, sir," Noakes said.

The captain nodded and asked. "Noakes, now how is it that you came to cook for me as well?"

"Sir, Cordova and I, we do everything together. And, if I can be frank, sir, if he was going to get to cook for you, I was too, sir."

The captain let go of the slightest smile before grabbing his fork and first digging into Noakes' shrimp and sausage and to-matoes. The XO, on the other hand, dipped his bread into my mole.

The two chewed their food so quietly and slowly that I could hardly believe they actually had the food in their mouths.

"Dave?" the captain said to his XO, a familiarity in his voice that showed they had shared a lot of meals together.

"Captain?" the XO responded.

They both wiped their mouths at the same time, and I could swear I could see smiles on the side of their mouths that they had turned away from us, reserved solely for each other. Then they both took a bit of the opposite dishes, the captain eating my mole and the XO eating Noakes' dish.

"Captain?" the XO said.

"Dave?" the captain said.

The captain turned to Noakes and me, nodded, and waved us away with his fork, a nod of his head to us and then to his XO.

Chapter Forty-Five

Della
1943

HELEN AND I BECAME VERY GOOD, VERY FAST. BOTH OF US ROSE up the ranks within the training room. We winked at each other each time we solved something one of our male student peers could not. We walked out of the room together each night and took a taxi to downtown DC to eat dinner and have drinks and dance with soon-to-be-gone soldiers until our feet hurt. Then we awoke each morning, excited to do our jobs for our country.

"This is the best life, Helen," I said one night.

"It is, Della, it is," Helen said.

THE SECOND WE GOT OUT of training, however, things changed. The importance of breaking codes or my inability to break a code weighed on me more. I thought of those men out there fighting. I thought about them a lot. They carried their packs and their guns. They slept in huge metal tubes, one on top of another, crammed together for days beneath the ocean. I constantly thought about John. I thought about John in those metal tubes. I thought about his tiny ears. I worried about the pressure on them. I could imagine him sleeping in that canister of war, and I wished I could pluck him out of there and bring him home. I knew all the danger he was in. And I thought about loving him and not being able to tell him anything.

School was fun. Training was more fun. But once I sat down at a wooden desk in the hot, humid room in Arlington Hall, and once the four-digit numeric codes fell onto my desk, the responsibility hit me hard. I was there to win the war. I was there to save lives.

I shared a desk with four other women. Helen got sent to the Army code breaking unit. I got shipped to the Navy. I wished she was there with me. I wished we could work together, but we had no say in that. And we each had different jobs. I had been assigned to decipher the Japanese Navy's shipping codes. These codes told us everything. With the war in the Pacific raging, their troops needed supplies on the ground. Their ships needed oil. Their sailors needed food. If we could cut off a shipping lane or if we could sink a transport ship, we hurt them, and we hurt them where it hurt the most.

Luckily, before I got there, the team had figured out that a string of clusters of four numbers told us everything we needed to know. First, they told us where ships would originate. Then, they told us what they carried. Third, they told us where they were going. While this seems easy, the Japanese were always switching things up and changing the four-digit codes, so we spent our days breaking the ever-changing numbers.

Helen, on the other hand, worked strictly to decipher codes for the US ARMY and translate the Japanese verbal messages that got picked up over the airwaves. While the codes were delivered in Japanese, they were also garbled and reordered, so Helen's team did their best to break the terribly complicated messages that, even to those who knew Japanese fluently, wouldn't be able to understand. It came across more like scrambled eggs than hard boiled.

That summer, it got so damned hot in our room that I wanted to strip down and stand in front of the fan, and I didn't care who saw me. We broke codes for eight hours a day. If they needed us longer, we stayed longer. We were put on shifts. The code breaking went on every hour of the day. During the first week, they shifted us around so damned much. First, they would put us on the morning shift. Then, they would move us to the graveyard shift, and then the swing shift, and then the graveyard shift again. There was no pattern. They did it—I know now—to mess with us and to see who could handle it.

On the third day, Helen and I both started on the swing, and then, when I walked up to the desk to clock out, they said I had to stay for the graveyard. The officer just handed me a pile of codes to break and pointed me back to my desk without a word. There was no "please" or "thank you" that first week. The same thing happened to Helen. When I showed up at our apartment after two, full eight-hour shifts, she had just fallen down on the couch next to the fan and started yelling and bitching.

"They did it to you too?" she asked when I walked in.

"They sure as hell did," I said. "They sure as hell did."

She went to the fridge, pulled out a bottle of chilled vodka, poured it into a tumbler with ice, and handed it to me.

"Well, we know they can't call us back for at least another eight hours, so we might as well pass out hard," Helen said.

We clinked our glasses, sipped on the drinks for a while, and fell asleep, both of us smiling. Sure, we bitched and moaned, but goddamnit, we loved it. We were both cracking codes and trans-lating and using our brains to do something other than teach schoolchildren, and I'll tell you goddamned what, I would do it all over again for years at a time if I ever had the chance. My life had become a big puzzle with consequences, and I was the best at solving those puzzles.

As the first week went on, some girls either quit or were asked to vacate their post. One woman broke down after break-ing codes for more than ten hours. She stood up, pulled the bar-rettes out of her hair, and she started throwing them in the giant fans that circulated the hot, muggy air throughout the room. The barrettes shot out of the spinning blades like shrapnel, and by the time we all figured out that we needed to start ducking, one of them had lodged itself another woman's arm. The blade had cut it, making one end sharp enough to pierce skin, so when it came flying out of the fan at a hundred miles an hour, it dug into her arm, barely missing her main vein.

Another girl, who I really liked, but who could not keep her mouth shut, got kicked out on day four. She could handle the long hours, but she just couldn't stop gabbing about her family's ranch in Texas. Big steer this and beautiful horse that and the most beautiful creek that ran through the whole place, blah, blah, blah.

"What about the Dust Bowl," I asked her. "How were they able to keep it?"

She dropped her head down toward me and said, "Our hired hands, of course. They kept the horses fed, watered, and bathed. The steers had the best hay, shipped in for dirt cheap from places like Kansas and Colorado and Oklahoma. So cheap that we used it as bedding for the animals in their ranch house."

I wanted to smack her a couple times. They didn't own a ranch like we owned a ranch. They owned a dude ranch, where the horses were pets, not property, and where the steers were raised solely for prime cuts of meat. I didn't blame her though. It wasn't her fault she didn't know jack from shit. And she was smart too.

But she couldn't keep her mouth shut. They warned her once, and when she started talking about how she had taken a boat to Europe once, the local officer walked to her desk, picked up her codes, and escorted her out.

A fourth didn't make it through the week because she had to go to the bathroom and was told she would have to wait until break to go. She waited a few minutes, stood up, pulled her skirt up and her underwear down, and urinated in a fake bush next to her desk. She sat back down, smiled, and then went on code breaking. The officer led her out when the smell of urine started to ripen in the midday heat. It's too bad. She was good.

After the first week, Commander Edwards, the leader of the joint task force, asked the remaining women from both Helen's group and mine to join him in the auditorium. I had met him once before.

On my first day, he'd invited me and three other women to his office to welcome us. His desk was so clean. It shined in the afternoon sunlight that came through the tall windows that looked out toward the east, out toward the war. Beside three files—ours, I figured—that sat on his desk, the only other thing that he kept there was a picture of his family. In it, he stood in his dress uniform. His wife, tall and brunette and striking in a way, stood next to him and placed her hands on the shoulders of twin boys. They all smiled a military smile: pierced lips and tight eyes, like they had been trained to always look this way in front of a camera. Even the small twin boys looked in control.

He opened each of our files and perused them silently.

"Trinidad, Colorado," he said, kind of like a question but more like a judgment. "How did you get yourself way out here, Ms. Chavez?"

I placed my hands on my knees to steady my legs. They had begun to shake in the cold room.

"Mount Holyoke," I said. "They offered me a scholarship to study there, sir." I had never been around military officers in my entire life, but I picked up the "please," "thank you," and "yes, sirs" very quickly.

"Do you know anyone here?" he asked.

"Just my roommate Helen," I said. "We became friends at school. We are sharing a place in DC."

"DC?" he asked. "Isn't that difficult to get to and from every day?"

I tried to not smile. The thought of not living stuck in the expansive dormitory made me so happy inside that I wanted to scream, *It may take some time to get there and back, but holy shit, it's worth it, Commander.* I held this in, along with my smile, and gave him a more acceptable answer, "Yes, sir, it is, but the privacy is well worth it. I grew up on a ranch in the middle of nowhere. It's exciting to be in the city."

He didn't like that answer either. His frown and tossing of my file aside told me so.

In the huge auditorium I found out why.

"Please sit," he told all of us, about thirty in total. We began the week with nearly sixty, but day after day, the desks got emptier.

"Loose lips sink ships," he belted out from the podium at the center of the stage at the front of the auditorium. "In our case, loose lips sink the ships of our brave men in the middle of the Pacific Ocean. Any word of what we're doing here or how we're doing it could kill thousands of men that wake up every morning to the smell of an asshole sleeping less than a foot above them in the barrel of a submarine on the decks of a carrier. Loose lips sink ships.

"I know that a few of you have found a way to live in the city. You are lucky enough to have a car, or a friend that has a car to drive you back and forth and that you have your own living space, outside the caring and watchful eye of all of us here," he said.

He found me and Helen in the crowd, glanced our way, for just long enough to let us know that he was talking to us.

"I cannot forbid you from leaving your homes at night. I cannot legally even ask you to not leave, but I am sternly encouraging you to stay away from the city, from the restaurants, and from the night clubs. People are watching us. Ears are pinned open for any information the enemy can use against us. If you speak one word about what we are doing here to anyone, you will be tried for treason. Do you understand?" he asked, though no one dared answer him. We all just shook our heads in unison.

Then I heard a tiny giggle float through the auditorium. I recognized that giggle. Helen had let it go. I knew she didn't think what the commander said was funny, but I also knew that she couldn't handle anything too serious for too long because it made her nervous and uncomfortable. When she was nervous and uncomfortable, she giggled.

"Is this funny?" the commander walked around the podium and scanned the audience for the giggler. He locked eyes on Helen.

Then I spoke up, to save her, because if he were to stare right at her she might just explode in laughter. She didn't mean to be rude or disrespectful. Her body just couldn't handle it.

"That was me, sir," I said. "I had to sneeze. I tried to hold it in, but it came out like a giggle, sir."

He paced the stage until he stood in front of me and looked down at me.

"One more 'sneeze,'" he emphasized sneeze, knowing that my lie was bullshit, and said, "and you'll be sent back to that little hole in the wall you call home in Colorado. I will have a soldier escort you there myself. Understand, Ms. Chavez."

The words, "Yes, sir," came out of my mouth, luckily. I was praying that Helen didn't giggle again. She held it in and kept us both out of trouble. We were already the goddamned reason that he gave us all the lecture of loose lips and sinking ships. We didn't need another reason to be the focus of his anger.

"Also, no alcohol. I forbid alcohol while you are out in the city. Drunken lips not only sink ships, but they can also sink a whole operation," he said.

Please, Helen, don't giggle, I thought to myself. Helen thinking about drunken lips, just the sounds of the words, could send her into a fit.

"If any of you are caught out with alcohol on your lips, you will be tried for treason because women like yourselves are weak when it comes to keeping secrets when you're sober. You can never keep secrets when you're drunk, so we will assume that you shared secrets from your drunken lips," he bellowed.

First, I tell you right now, we were just as strong and just as secretive as any of those men who worked there. Hell, we were stronger and a hell of a lot more reserved, and I didn't see him line the men up and tell them the same thing. This whole lecture was asinine, but I let that all slide because I had to pray with everything in my soul that Helen had closed her ears and did not hear him repeat "drunken lips."

He turned his back to us and walked back to the podium. I took a quick glance back at Helen and saw that she had stuffed the end of her handkerchief in her mouth and bit down hard on it. Her eyes swelled, and I could see that she was just about to lose it when he changed the subject.

I found Helen outside the auditorium, her handkerchief still stuck in her mouth. I dragged her to the women's room. When we found a stall, I pulled the cloth from her mouth.

Immediately, she yelled with a shout of laughter that followed her words, "Super secrets and drunken lips. Holy God!" she screamed.

I placed my head on her shoulder and laughed so hard that I could barely breathe. "Drunken lips!"

We pulled ourselves together and came out of the bathroom to see Commander Edwards, with his arms folded across his chest, staring in at us.

He shook his head, put his index and middle finger to his eyes and said, "I'm watching you two."

Chapter Forty-Six

John
1943

WE KNEW IT WAS COMING. THE VETERAN SAILORS—THE SHELL-backs—had been on the rest of us for a week, calling us polly-wogs, kicking us in the ass when we walked down the hallway, pulling back the thin sheet that covered our bunks during our brief "quiet" and "private" times.

"Your time is coming," they'd say when they picked up their food from the line we had set up for them in the tiny mess hall. "Pollywog, give me another biscuit." We weren't supposed to, but both Noakes and I knew that if we didn't, our time during the Crossing the Line Ceremony would be worse, and to be hon-est, when we had two seconds alone we hoped, together, that if we cooked well and gave extra food to the sailors who we knew might be extra mean that we might escape some of the worst of the initiation ceremony when the submarine surfaced on the equator.

I think we hedged our bets well.

The sun was nice. I have to admit that. We hadn't had a chance to be in the sunlight for days. They lined all of us polly-wogs up. They stripped us down to nothing, they made us climb the ladder up to the top of the boat, and then they made us stand in the hot sun of the equator with our hands above our head as King Neptune, one of the higher ranking officers dressed in a toga sheet with a titan spear, paraded in front of us with a hose that was connected to a gas bucket that spat urine on our bodies.

The urine initiated us into the court of King Neptune. Our captain stood at the end of the line and smiled. Every single one of the shellbacks had done this before. It was our turn to take the punishment. After our initiation by urine, a shellback walked behind us and whipped our calves and asses with a hose. It stung like hell, real hell. I wanted to turn around and jack him in the face, and I could see Noakes doing everything he could to not retaliate.

We took our lashings, and then we dropped on all fours, formed a line—heads to asses—and crawled on the deck between shellbacks that kicked us in the ribs as hard as they could and sang songs to Neptune and navy chants we learned in boot camp.

I smelled shit. Real shit. Not the smell of shit that came out our pores after a few days without a shower, but real shit. I lifted my head in our crawling Tonga line and saw a shellback pull shit from the back of his pants and smear it on the back of the guy in front of me. That was the first time I was glad I was a cook. Another shellback did the same thing and aimed his hand at my back and face, but he was stopped immediately by my captain's voice, "Do not touch him with your shit, pollywog Cordova will be cooking for me and for us in less than two hours, and I don't want any of your excrement near him."

"Yes, sir," the shellback said. He let me and Noakes pass by him in our parade and smeared shit on the following guy.

Then I thought I saw someone die. There had been rumors that men had died during the ceremony, and all of us newbies somewhat believed them but didn't really want to. Right before they threw us overboard to clean us off, a shellback attached a long, frayed electrical wire of a generator to the end of broom. One sailor stood up, ready to jump overboard. When he leaned toward the edge of the boat, excited to clean the shit and urine off of his beaten ribs and legs, the shellback stuck the wired broom into his chest. The sailor convulsed and then fell into the water. The shock of the prod seemed to light up his eyes, and his fingertips shook like baby eels trying to escape the skin at the end of his palms.

I waited for him to surface in the water. It scared the shit out of me.

Then, after a long few seconds, his face rose out of the waves and smiled.

Everyone went through this, except, you guessed it, Noakes and me, the same command to save the hands of the boys who provided us food. We escaped the shit. And we escaped the shock torture because we could cook.

That morning, right after we jumped in the ocean to cleanse ourselves, a real baptism it felt like in the ocean on the equator, a pollywog got shocked, he fell to the water, and then he disappeared beneath the waves. The cavorting shellbacks didn't see it. The captain didn't see it. I don't know if I even saw it, to be honest. It could have been my paranoid imagination, but I don't think he ever came back up. A few minutes later, we were all called to board the ship again, dry off, sing new songs, receive our certificates and medals for crossing the equator, and then relax on top of the boat in the sun, joining the ranks of the shellbacks.

I watched for that boy in the water. I never saw him come up. I wished that it was my imagination that created his body in the water in the first place. But I felt, deep down, that it wasn't.

Chapter Forty-Seven

Della
1943

THE FIRST FEW MONTHS WERE TEDIOUS. I CONTINUED TO WORK on breaking codes for eight to ten-hour shifts. I would break a string of Japanese Codes, deciphering where a ship had left port, where it was headed, and, to the best of my ability, the route it planned to take, what it carried. I would hand these off to the runner. The runner would take them to another analyst who would put it all together, matching where vessels were in the area, and then, I believe, relay the message to a submarine, cruiser, or battleship. But I never heard anything from anyone once I handed my info off to the runner.

Helen dealt with the same thing. She would translate a message, unscramble it, and then send it off to a runner who would give it to an analyst—usually a jumbled mix of Japanese and a synthetic language they made up to throw us off—and she would never hear if she helped anyone, saved anything, or stopped something from happening.

At night, if we both worked the day shift, we would drive back to our place in the city, take showers to clean off the day's sweat, change, and then head out into town for dinner. We had more money than we had ever made teaching, and our apartment was fully funded by Helen's dad who thought we were making the world a better place by guiding youth in the inner city of Baltimore. We ate out every night and then hit the nice clubs.

I tried so much seafood. I never thought I would like it. My life had been filled with all things fried: beans, tortillas, corn, pork, beef (sometimes), and buñuelos. Seafood was fresh. It tasted like the ocean. It came out of the oven and sat clean and grease-less next to vegetables, green vegetables that were boiled or baked too. I fell in love with it all.

Helen and I drank Manhattans and Old Fashioneds, and we sat in the clubs and imagined what our broken codes did to help our men in the ocean. John and I had ordered Manhattans together back in Hartford, but felt so stupid doing so. Helen made me feel like I should never feel stupid about anything.

"I bet I saved four ships today," I would say.

"I bet I sank four ships today," Helen would say.

We imagined some general somewhere thanking us for what we had done.

"If it weren't for Helen and Della, we would have all perished today," he would say in our imaginations. We gave each other the recognition we felt we deserved for sitting in that hot office for eight hours a day and scanning numbers or listening to garbled messages in headphones. If no one else would thank us, then damnit, we would do the thanking.

And then, as it would always happen, men would come around. We sat in the corners and the shadows for a reason. We wanted to be left alone, but men are too stupid to figure this out. No wonder all the women were the best damned code breakers in Arlington. Men couldn't break one simple code: women, sitting alone, talking vehemently together, engaged in their own damned conversation, want to be left alone. Nope, they couldn't break that one.

Inevitably, two men would walk up to our little table in the corner of a club, sit down next to us, ask us what we wanted to drink, wave the waitstaff over, order our drinks, and then smile as the woman placed them down on the table in front of us.

"Thank you for these," I would say.

"Yes, thank you for these," Helen would respond.

"So, what are you two doing over here alone?" a man would say.

"Talking," I would say.

"Yeah, talking to each other," Helen would say.

We broke the code down for them, and they still couldn't decipher it. The message was very simple: we're sitting alone because we want to sit alone, and, of course, talk about stuff that could get us hung for treason, but the men didn't need to know the second part. They only needed to break the first part of the code—leave us alone. In their men's minds, they thought the message was: these women are just being coy, and they want us to join them because there is no way they could actually be at the club having an intriguing conversation and not be looking for husbands. Wrong. Wrong answer. They would be fired in a heartbeat if they had our jobs.

"David here, he is a stockbroker in the city, and I'm an attorney," Robert (it always seemed like it was David and Robert or equivalently pedestrian names like that), would say, dismissing our responses.

"Yep, I represent those who can't represent themselves," Robert would continue, easing back into his chair and smiling like he was some kind of goddamned hero.

"You mean you're an attorney. Isn't that what attorneys do? They represent people who can't represent themselves. Isn't that your job?" Helen would say.

As if he didn't hear her, he would continue on, "I make a good living in the courtroom, and David here, his courtroom is the stock market. The stock market is a system of publicly traded—"

"Yes, we know what the stock market is, Bob," I would say to our new, oblivious, friend. Again, as if I didn't speak, he would continue on, or David would break in and tell us something we already knew, leaning back in his chair and acting like a pompous wiener.

"Thanks for the drinks, gentlemen, but we would like to continue our conversation about makeup and our vaginas," I would say. The word "vaginas" would snap them out of their arrogant postures.

To them, a young woman saying "vaginas" in public like that was very, very un-lady like, so they would give each other a look of mortification, stand up on cue together, and walk away, leaving our martinis in fronts of us to drink.

We would delve right back into how we spent the day saving our men by breaking four-numbered codes and deciphering Japanese—purposeful—gibberish.

Treason be damned.

Chapter Forty-Eight

John
1943

TWO WEEKS LATER WE DOVE, QUE PADRE. WE DOVE DEEP.
The pressure in the barrel of the submarine grew up around us and squeezed tight. The moment the nose of the massive metal submarine dipped down and pushed through ocean into the darkness beneath, one guy lost his mind. He was a torpedo man. It was his job to load the torpedoes with the long ropes and levers and chains, pull them from their caskets in the torpedo room, hoist them up, shove them into the barrels of the biggest guns on earth, and then lock them in, all within minutes after another torpedo had been launched through the water and toward a Japanese ship.

Noakes and I were cooking. It was our shift.

We had just served up thirty sailors. We had gotten through quite a few boxes of food, so the hallways and the shitter and showers had been cleared. Fresh air hadn't come through the submarine in more than twenty days, and even when everyone showered, the body odor they washed off still hung in the air and in their clothes and all over the place.

THOSE DAYS IN THE SUBMARINE kitchen were some of my favorite, not just during those years, but some of favorite in my entire life.

Noakes told me all about his life. It was a pretty good one for the most part, except for one big glaring clusterfuck of an uncle who tried to ruin it all.

His uncle—his father's brother—had always been an asshole, I guess.

One day, as Noakes tells it, his dad and he went fishing. They climbed to the edge of lake Michigan with their rods in their hands and sat along the bank of a big pond where large-mouth bass begged for their bait. They had a great day. They caught ten fish, and they were going to cook them for dinner.

Noakes' dad, even way back then, was educated, the first in their family to go to college, and he had enough money to buy a nice house and get his kids to school. But his brother had none of that. He always wanted what Noakes' dad had. Especially Noakes' mom. That day when they came home from fishing, Noakes' uncle had pinned Noakes' mom down on the floor and had nearly ripped off her dress completely. Her eyes were wide open with fear when the door opened, and Noakes' dad, looking down at his scared wife and his brother on top of her, lost his mind and beat his brother up until he almost died. Then Noakes' dad dropped his brother off on the front door of the hospital and never picked him up. Noakes had never told anyone but me about that.

Somehow, down there in the belly of a metal monster in the middle of the Pacific Ocean, we found a way to laugh about the worst things that had happened to us before we got there, like they were only real above the water, like the hard earth was make believe.

THE MORNING OF THE DIVE, right before the boy lost his complete shit, the captain walked into the kitchen behind us. Noakes, out of the corner of his eye and with a pile of hash browns on his spatula, noticed the captain walk in, turned an about face with hash browns steadily in place, and saluted.

"Keep cooking while we talk," he said.

Noakes and I kept cooking, giving the captain enough attention to show him we were following orders.

"Was this your goal, sailors? To cook? Did you put in for this?"

"No, sir," Noakes said, his brashness surprising me.

But I followed suit.

"No, sir, we both put in for different positions, sir," I said. "Sir, can I expand, sir?"

"Please do, Cordova," he said.

The eggs and the hash browns were moved around the grill like we were trying to slide between girls.

"We scored the best in our boot class, sir, on all things, sir," I said. I worried that my confidence may get me humbled quickly, but Noakes began to talk.

"It's because I'm black, sir, and Cordova here is not so white himself, sir," Noakes said.

Then we both shut up. We knew we had already gotten away with a lot of free speaking. We didn't want to push it. We put our heads down and slung out ten more plates before the captain spoke again. "I'll wire back to New London to see if this is the truth, and—" An alarm sounded, red lights flashing throughout the submarine. We weren't under attack. A sailor had tried to break through and open the hatch to escape the submarine. The torpedo man.

The captain disappeared. The conversation ended. We finished our shift, both of us worried that we may have said too much, that our accusation of a racist Navy may have gone too far. We spent our sleep time talking about how we thought we may have fucked up.

We started our next shift with no sleep and anxious we might get some trouble for what we said. Beyond that, we worried that our extra ingredients might disappear and our privilege to use them for our meals might go with them. It was a long night that ended in a long day of cooking, both of us moving slowly across the kitchen.

"The captain wants mole and your sausage dish today," the head cook said behind us just as our shift had ended and we had begun to wipe the sweat from our brows.

With springs in our legs, we popped up, both of us finding an eager sailor to take our food as extras.

The head cook had already gotten us the last bit of chiles and shrimp and sausage and chocolate. We'd been at sea for nearly thirty days and had begun to run out of most anything that tasted good, so we had to make do with what we could find to add spice to our meals. We dug only for a few minutes because we knew the captain was waiting.

"Take your time," the head cook said. "This will be the last meal you cook because of what you blurted to the captain last time you spoke." He smiled a smile that I could see came from him being glad we wouldn't be taking his glory anymore. It's a big deal to make the captain happy on a daily basis, and we had somehow dimmed that light. He didn't like that one bit.

We took our time. This go round, I was able to let the chicken stew in the mole for more than an hour, and Noakes marinated his shrimp and sausages until the spices and oils saturated the meats so fully that I could taste the richness of the dish even before he let it all simmer in the tomatoes and sauce.

With the dishes plated, we followed the head cook to the captain's room, our heads hanging low at our arrival, and waited for our reprimand and demotion to some shitty job like cleaning the shitters and showers. We didn't want to be cooks, but we had come to love it and find out that it was one of the best damn gigs on the entire ship. We hated that we were stuck there because of the color of our skin, but we also didn't want to give it up now that we had it. It's one of those things in life that you can't see coming and you don't want to see going.

The captain stepped out from his cabin and met us in the shrunken hallway. His XO stood behind him with two sets of papers in his hands.

"I checked on you two, your boot records and scores," he said.

He waved his hand for the head cook to walk by him and

place the food on the small table in his quarters. Behind the table above his bed, he had hung large nautical maps and image after image of Japanese war and transport ships. You could see the stress on the man's face. There was no smile. We were getting close to the war, and it would be our duty to sink as many Japanese ships as possible before getting blown out of the water ourselves. We all knew that the second we asked to be assigned to a submarine.

"You've both been reassigned," he said. "We have one of the best gunners in the whole Navy, so I can't give you that job, but I can do better. You need to grab all of your stuff and move to the torpedo room. You are now torpedo men. Do me proud."

He saluted us. We saluted him back.

With no hoopla, we turned, walked quickly to our bunks, grabbed all of our gear, and walked to the torpedo room. On the way to the torpedo room, we passed sick bay and saw the boy. He lay unconscious on the bed with the medical officer over him. He had blood streaming down his face. The medical officer had begun to sew up his skin. Blood ran across his knuckles. Tears in his flesh bled so red that I couldn't believe that just a few days earlier he was on top of the ship with us smiling in the sun when we crossed the equator.

"What happened?" Noakes asked.

"Well, you can't leave the ship in the middle of the Pacific Ocean," the medical officer said. "We knocked his ass out, first with a fist to the back of the head and then with a sedative. We'll dump his ass off on some carrier somewhere out there, but until then, I'll dope his dumbass up until we get there."

We nodded and kept walking. We'd heard about it, people flipping out, but in the year-long training to even board the sub, we actually didn't expect to see it. They say the air pressure changes men. Even if they can pass all the tests, when we dive, the air pressure can fuck with the brain, they say.

We grabbed two bunks that lay above two giant torpedoes

and began following procedures. We had to learn fast. We had to learn smart. We did. We practiced loading the warheads into the canons for the two days it took to reach the middle of the Pacific theater. The torpedo problems—the misdirection, the misses, the duds—of the early war had been mostly solved, so Noakes and I had been put in charge of the most dangerous weapon in the Pacific Ocean that we knew of. We had no idea about what the scientists were cooking up in a laboratory a thousand miles away, and to be honest, I am glad we didn't.

We were torpedo men. We missed the kitchen, but we were exactly where we wanted to be—together, fighting in the war.

THE SMELL ALONE WOULD KILL ya, I swear. The armpits. The smell of body odor. It was a blessing to be put down in the torpedo room. On any given shift, there would only be two of us there with a couple of other guys sleeping in their bunks below the torpedo. Unless we were up and ready to fire. Then all six of us would jump up and place our hands on the long shafts of the Navy's muscle like laying our hands on an altar.

Our first patrol started off with a boom. We were lucky, I guess, or God or someone else was looking after our little boat in 1943 when we headed into the East China Sea. Our mission was solely to plant mines outside of Shanghai, but on our departure from the area we came across the Kinku Maru and the Daifuku Maru, two freighter ships. We fired on the Kinku, and she fired back, pushing us down into the depths. We hit her hard though, causing considerable damage. When we came back to the surface after hiding out in the depths for a bit, our captain ordered us to fire our torpedoes again, and we did. Noakes and I loaded and fired. At the end of the torpedoes' trails, hundreds of feet across the depths, we sunk the Daifuku Maru. Two days later, in the same deep waters, we sunk the four-thousand-ton Hosei Maru and crippled other ships before heading back to Midway for a rest. We kicked ass, is what we did.

On our second patrol, we were even better, even more precise. Somehow, again, the captain brought the Snook into firing range of two convoys, like we were ghosts or oracles. We came out of nowhere, and with just six torpedoes fired, Noakes and I sunk the Koki Maru and the Liverpool Maru. We were fucking brilliant.

The cheers roared throughout the submarine when torpedoes struck a ship's core and sank it. We felt like our flesh had been carried across the water on them like the skin on the farthest tip of powerful knuckles.

Our third and fourth patrols were just as successful, sinking tankers and war ships, but it wasn't until our fifth patrol that we realized our luck may have run out.

Chapter Forty-Nine

Della
1943

I ALWAYS LOVED THE NIGHT LIGHTS OF THE CITY. I LOVED THE blues and reds and hot white light that danced over the streets. Restaurants. Bars. Clubs. Stores. At times, I missed the wide-open western slope of the Rockies, but mostly, I knew that the time in my life in DC would come to end. That was the point, right, to end the war. And I didn't think I could go back to teaching after what I had done in the war room, so I embraced it every night that I could.

On New Year's Eve 1943, I sat alone at a club and waited for Helen. I had come a long way since running in the fields of corn and wheat and wild grasses on the Colorado plains, but every time I tried to cross my goddamned legs in a dress that girl came right back to me. I felt uncomfortable alone in the bar and hated men's eyes when they followed me. I wanted to slap their goddamned eyes right out of their shit-eating faces. But, as always, I found my strength in me. Like a movie, I replayed my journey in my mind, crossed my legs elegantly, and quietly said, "This is my world, and I will be comfortable in it, no matter what their eyes say when they look at me."

Helen had started her shift later than me and had to head back to the house to shower and dress for the night. I didn't mind being alone. That's for damned sure. I liked it, actually. I looked forward to 1944. Even though no one ever really told us so, we knew the war was coming to an end, and we knew that what we did in those rooms over the previous seven months played an important role in sinking the Japanese war efforts in the Pacific. We were happy, and we were proud.

I ended every night with a smile on my face. Many times, it was a tipsy smile, but it was there, except for those nights when I thought about Ernie. But even those nights I felt like I was avenging his death every day of my life. More than that, he would have been proud of me. I figured since I couldn't tell my mom and dad what I had been doing, since Ernie was in heaven or something, that he was the only one who could see what I had become. And I think he smiled too.

I sipped on a martini and watched people. Some smiled and danced. Others, I could tell, were there to be sad, to fall into their drinks like the mugs of beer were tiny swimming pools that could somehow insulate them from the problems of a war-torn world and the politics that consumed the city. Couples held hands. Couples fought. I never envied any of them. I loved John, but I never truly wanted to be coupled at all. My life was mine, and I wanted to keep it that way, at least as long as I could.

Smoke filled the room and drifted in the lights. I watched a man and a woman who sat on the other side of the bar in a dark corner. The woman leaned into him, placing her elbows on his knees, barely keeping her lips from touching his when she talked. He leaned back into the puffy vinyl chair and smiled. His long legs crossed in front of him, and her skirt fell off the pristinely pressed seam in the center of his pants.

"What are you staring at, Della?" Helen said.

She dropped down next to me and raised her hand for the bartender to bring her a Manhattan. Then she stood up and walked behind me, placed her head on my shoulder and followed my gaze with hers.

"Holy shit," Helen said.

"I know," I said, but I didn't really know why she said it. I figured she thought the same thing that I did, that the body language between the two people was captivating.

"That's Colonel Edwards," she said.

She dropped down behind me and pulled her seat around so her back faced them and her body blocked me from their sight.

"Oh shit," I said. "We got to get out of here."

"Yes, we do," Helen said.

He had told us we couldn't go out and especially that we couldn't drink in town, and he would see us doing both of those things—if he caught us that night—and we would lose our jobs for sure. "Loose lips sink ships. Drunk lips sink more ships."

Helen was not laughing.

I downed my martini and scooted to the edge of my seat, ready to run for it, but Helen grabbed my hand and held me still.

"What are they doing now?" she asked.

"They're still fawning over each other," I said.

The place wasn't that big. There was maybe twenty-five feet between us.

"If we both get up and rush out of here, I'm sure he'll see us. We have to be covert," Helen said.

"Okay, I'll go first," I said. "I'll walk with my back to them toward the bar and then just slide out the door. You follow."

Helen nodded her head and pulled her collar up around her neck as if that would save him from seeing her there.

I shifted my weight, stood up, and then walked as casually as I could toward the bar. I placed my hand on the railing that lined the wooden top and then slid my body along it toward the exit. When I turned to walk out the front door, Colonel Edwards stood in my way.

"Ms. Chavez, why don't you join me with your roommate for a moment. I think we need to talk," he said and then led me back to where Helen sat with her collar up around her neck and her eyes as wide as our two empty glasses.

Helen stood up. Then she sat back down. Then she stood up again. She didn't know what to do. I think she wanted to run, to be honest. I could see it in her eyes. It was his word against ours. If we ran, could he prove it? I think Helen thought no.

Then she sat down again and pretended to take a leisurely sip from her empty glass. She fooled no one.

Colonel Edwards pulled a seat out for me and motioned for me to sit. He did not waste time. That would not have been his way. Instead, he leaned on the table, crossed the fingers of his hands, and said, "Loose lips sink ships. Drunk lips sink more ships. Your drunk lips. Our sunken ships. Do you remember me saying this, ladies?"

And that was it. That was the last straw. Helen lost it. She blurted out in a fit of laughter that she couldn't control. "Drunk lips" sealed her fate. She would never be able to regain her composure, so I thought.

"Ms. Brigance, I don't expect you to be completely quiet, but I do expect some level of respect from you, even if we are away from the war room," he said. In his entire military career, I don't think anyone had ever laughed at him the way Helen did.

"Sir, it's not her fault," I said. "She laughs when she's uncomfortable. She can't control it. I promise. It's not disrespectful. It's just her body's natural reaction to awkward or uncomfortable situations."

Helen placed her hand over her mouth to hold in the laughter and nodded her head at Edwards.

"It's true," she said, the words muffled behind her hand. "I don't mean any disrespect."

He nodded and then continued, "I have to suspect that if you are out tonight that this is not the first time, and, therefore, I have to suspect that your drunken lips have put our ships and our mission in danger."

Helen turned to the wall to avoid eye contact with Edwards and to do her best to hold in her laughter. She did pretty good.

"No, sir," I said. "First, we never drink to get drunk, and we never talk about work."

Helen nodded, her hand still over her mouth.

"I don't believe you. I'm not in a position to take you at your word or give you the benefit of the doubt. I can't. You will both be asked to vacate." He got interrupted by a soft voice from behind him.

"Karl, are you going to join me again, or would you rather spend the evening with these two beautiful women?"

The woman who had been sitting with him, placed her hand on his shoulder, and then leaned down and whispered in his ear.

I stared at her in the light. She was tall, brunette, and beautiful, just like his wife in the photo on his desk, but here's the kicker, she was not Colonel Edwards' wife.

Colonel Edwards looked at both Helen and me. He was assessing the situation, trying to figure out if we had put two and two together. And that's when I winked at him, that's when I let him know from the slight twitch of my eyelid that yes, in fact, I knew that he was out that night with a woman who was not his wife and that by the way they touched, this was not the first time. They were close, intimate.

I said, "What were you saying about vacating?"

He looked at me. He looked up at the woman. He looked at Helen.

"So, you're telling me that you have never spoken to anyone about your mission?" he asked.

Helen finally found her voice, "No sir, we have never spoken a word, and we never will." Then she too winked at him.

He stood up, put his arm around the woman, and returned to the corner booth across the room.

Chapter Fifty

John
1943-1944

We headed back to Pearl Harbor for some rest before our fifth patrol. I climbed up out of the submarine, headed to the shower, and found a letter from Della in the mail cube with my name on it. My heart jumped up. I hadn't heard from her since a phone exhchange before I left port. I called her to say goodbye, ringing her apartment.

"Hi, Della, it's John, I just wanted to call to say hello and that I will write you when I can. I leave for Pearl Harbor tomorrow. I love you," I said.

"Hi, John," she said. "Don't be an asshole and get killed, okay?"

And then she hung up the phone. That was it. That was all she said, but I knew her, and it didn't hurt me. Honestly, it was the most real Della I knew.

The letter, however, hurt bad.

Dear John,

I just wanted to write you to let you know that I have moved to Washington, DC. I got your letter. Thank you for it. I hope you are safe. I have a new job. It pays good money. I am a secretary for a nice man. I believe he is a contractor for the military, but he doesn't tell me much about his business. Like I said, it's good pay.

As of right now, I hope to keep this job indefinitely, so I am not quite certain I can meet you in Hawaii after your tour.

All my best,
Della

Where were the goddamnits and holly hells and the sons of bitches and, most importantly, the *I love you too*. The letter, though not cruel, broke my heart. It felt the same as getting my parents swiped out from my life by the hating rains of the high plains. It felt like watching Maria drive away in the priest's car, my jaw broken and hanging from my face. It felt like finding out that Manuel had been killed at sea. It felt like all of them wrapped up together.

When I lay there in my tiny bunk, when I swam back to the boat after the initiation rights, when I sweated in the kitchen and then in the torpedo room, I dreamt of Della, I relived our time together in Hartford, and I hung onto the richness of the few words, "I think I love you too, John."

"Motherfucker," I said.

"John?" Noakes asked.

"Let's go get drunk. Let's go get laid," I said.

Noakes shook his head.

"How about we spend the weekend on the beach. We can hula dance. We can flirt with girls. We can go surfing. We can drink beer and eat lo mein. What do you think, John?"

"I'm getting laid," I said. "And I'm sure as hell not going to Washington, DC, to find Della so she can keep a secretary job. First, I can't believe the way she coolly dismissed me. Second, she's smarter than that, smarter than falling in love with a secretary job. She found a man. That's the only reason she would be content with a brainless job like that. And tonight, I am going to find a woman."

Noakes shook his head and just followed me out into the night.

With my mind set to erase Della by finding another woman, Noakes and I stood at a bar in downtown Waikiki. Other sailors stood around us. We looked like a bunch of Popeyes throwing back cans of spinach as fast as we could. Our spinach, however, was liquor. As his forearms would grow, so did our egos and aggressions. Fights always broke out, and now that Noakes and I had survived four patrols across the deadly Pacific Ocean, we too had heads the size of pineapples. Add that to the fact that Della had coldly told me that she would rather be a secretary in DC than meet me in Hawaii after the war, and I wanted to hurt someone.

"She could be a secretary in Hawaii," I said to Noakes after my fifth beer and same number of shots of rum. "She could be a fucking secretary anywhere in the world. She could be a secretary in fucking Trinidad, Colorado. She didn't have to get a fancy degree to be a secretary. I can't believe it, Noakes. I can't believe the whole thing. And I think she loved me. I really do. Not just in Hartford but for all those years when we were kids. I think she loved me while I was gone. I could see it in her face, Noakes. I could see it in her face."

"Who? Your Indian girl?" Indian came out "engine" from a sailor who sat next to us. "Why don't you shut the fuck up about her? Or just fuck and move on? Jesus Christ."

I turned my body around to slug the guy in the face, but Noakes beat me to it. His big fist slammed hard against the sailor's face, right across the temple, and the sailor fell backward and onto the floor—out cold. The sailor's friends backed up and found seats behind them without looking away.

"Thanks, Noakes. You're a great friend and even a better person," I said.

"I don't like to hit people, John. My mother frowns on violence," he said. "So let's get you to bed so I don't have to do that anymore."

"I want to get laid," I said.

"Okay," Noakes said. "I'll take you to the district. Then we'll see."

I stumbled out of the bar. We walked down the road toward our hotel in Chinatown.

"Let's check in first, so we have a place to come back to after the night," Noakes said.

"Good plan," I said.

The streets of Waikiki were crowded with sailors. Just like us, they had come off a boat—a freighter or transport or cruiser or sub—and their sea legs, mixed with alcohol, made the whole bunch of them look like a warbling crowd of sloths moving through the street.

We walked into our hotel.

Nam greeted us both with a hug.

"John here wants to get laid," Noakes told Nam.

"So you do, John. Sit down first. Let me get you some coffee," Nam said.

"Beer," I said.

"Fine, fine, let me get you a beer," he said. "Noakes, would you like a beer too?"

"Yes, please," Noakes said.

"Have a seat here in my office," Nam said. He pointed behind the reception desk of his small hotel and waived us through.

We walked in and sat down on the most comfortable couch I had ever sat on. Noakes seemed to think so too because he kept pushing down on it with the palms of his hands to test how soft it was.

Nam came back with three beers, one for each of us. He sat in a rotating chair next to a desk covered in neatly stacked receipts.

"The couch isn't so comfortable," he said. "But I suppose you've just been living in a metal tube since I last saw you two boys."

"I love it," I said. I did. I loved that couch right then.

"John, how's Della?" Nam asked. The way he said it made me only want to share everything with him.

I told Nam about the letter, about how cold it was, and about how I suspected another man, and Nam leaned back in his chair and took a long sip of his beer.

"So now you want to go have sex with a prostitute in the district just like every other sailor that just gets off the boat, eh John?" Nam asked.

Noakes shook his head next to me.

"Can I ask you something, John?"

"Of course, Nam," I said. I could feel the calmness take me again, the way I felt when I cooked chilies or harvested them in the in garden, first with my family, then with Manuel, and then with Noakes beneath the water.

"Do you think sticking your little dick in some Polynesian girl is going to make Della come to Hawaii? Or is it going to make you feel better or worse? Take a drink of beer, let it flow coolly into your stomach, and then take a big breath before you answer me."

At first, I felt the rage come back, the rage that came with hating my grandfather, but Nam was not my grandfather, so I did what he said. I took a long sip of beer, let it flow down my throat, and let it sit there for a moment. Then I took a big, deep breath. By the time I finished this little ritual, my head felt warm and a little dizzy, but it also felt a little clear. I didn't answer him. I thought about sleeping with a woman. I thought about how I would feel afterward. I imagined it. And the only thing that flooded through me was a feeling of guilt and shame.

"No," I said. "No, it wouldn't make me feel better."

"That's what I thought," Nam said.

We sat there that night with Nam. We drank beer. We helped him with soldiers who came in too drunk to stand.

The next night was New Year's Eve, 1943. We stayed with Nam again. We cooked for him. He told us the wildest story about how he came from Vietnam to Hawaii and how he lost his young wife to tuberculosis right after they moved to Oahu.

"I wish I could just kiss Della again before we head out to sea," I told them both after midnight.

"I wish I could give my mom a hug," Noakes said.

"I wish I could give my wife a hug," Nam said. "And I've never gone to the district to replace her because I knew I never could."

We clinked our beers.

We hugged.

We stayed in Waikiki at Nam's for the next week. Noakes and I would head to the beach during the day and just lay on the sand.

On January 5th, the day before we were to ship out on our fifth patrol, Nam gave us both a hug and said, "Thank you, boys. Be safe."

He handed us both a tiny conch as gifts.

And we said goodbye to our old friend.

Chapter Fifty-One

Della
1944

THE NEXT WEEK AT WORK WAS WORRISOME, TO SAY THE LEAST. I expected Edwards to walk in, push my stuff off my desk into the trash can, and have me escorted out and tried for treason. I kept my head down. I deciphered codes. I handed them off. I went home to an empty house and watched the people walk by outside.

They scheduled Helen and me on alternating shifts, so I only saw her for a moment on the third day after our encounter with Edwards. I gave her a hug, and she squeezed me back. We could have been in big trouble. They could have been building their case against us. We did share information with each other outside of the office, and this alone was a punishable offense.

"We could run to Mexico," Helen said that morning when we hugged.

"I know the language," I said. "Or we could just go to Trinidad. They'd never find us there either. No one wants to go there." She smiled. I smiled. We let each other go and hoped we wouldn't soon feel the cold, hard metal of handcuffs wrapped our wrists.

"We could go to Norway," she said.

"I don't have a passport," I said.

"Oh yeah, but we could pay our way there in sex," she said.

"But that would take a whole lot of effort on our backs, and I don't think we have that kind of time," I said.

"Men don't need much time, at least the ones I've been with," Helen laughed.

"Me too," I said, though I had never slept with a man before.

We shifted gears. The jokes ended. I headed off to work, and she walked toward her room to change her clothes and wait. We didn't leave the house, except to go to work during those three days. We didn't want to push it.

I drove her car into Arlington, walked through security, nervous they would stop me, and then found my old, wooden desk in the cold office on the second floor of the naval decoding branch of the fort. Codes had been placed there in my "in" basket, and I began to break them down, looking for any correspondence between what the Japanese ships had to transport and where they transported it to. I searched for a battleship's coordinates and where it headed. The numbers had become so garbled to slow down our attempts to reorder them by the near end of the war in 1943 that it took more effort and time to put it all together.

"Ms. Chavez," a man's voice rang out over the heads of the code breakers.

I looked up to see Colonel Edwards staring at me from the doorway.

"Yes, sir," I said. I stood up and walked around to the front of my desk.

"Come with me," he said. Without another word, he walked through the office door and down the hallway to his office at the corner of the building. Like time had slowed, I walked like a child ready to be whipped by her parents, knowing that once she entered the room, the punishment would come, but if she were able to walk really slowly, she could hold it off long enough to live another life in those moments.

Helen stood next to Edwards' desk.

"Hi, Della," she said. "An officer picked me up just a few minutes after you left this morning."

"That's enough," Colonel Edwards said. "Both of you, please have a seat. As you can see, we have something very serious to discuss this morning. Sit, and we'll get started with the logistics of all of this."

In that office where I deciphered codes, that home where I lived with Helen, and in those clubs at night in downtown DC, I had never been happier in my adult life. Coronal Edwards was about to take all of that away in a short time, and I nearly began to cry, but Helen shook her head at me and pursed her lips.

We both sat down in front of the frowning man. He pulled out both of our work files, histories of what we had done before we got there, and what we had done since. He flipped through the pages slowly. I wanted to reach across the desk and slap him. "Get it over with, you bastard!" I wanted to scream.

He took his time, sighing with the turn of each page. He pulled out another folder, flipped through it, and then turned it toward us. Hundreds of four-digit numbers, thousands of paragraphs in Japanese, all mixed together in a what looked like a tossed salad of codes that had been thrown into a pile.

"You two are the best we have," he said. "And we need you to take care of this immediately. We have a boat, the USS Snook, that we believe is sitting below the water near one of the biggest Japanese shipments that we have seen in months. If we were to be able to get the submarine in the right shipping lane, we could severely handicap their war efforts. We could damage their whole Pacific fleet along with the ground troops that are waiting for the supplies."

He stood up, walked around the desk, and sat his ass crack right on the corner of the wooden frame. I never understood how men did this. It seemed painful to me.

"We've set up a dedicated room for the two of you to work over the next twenty-four hours," he said. "We need this done now."

Helen burst out laughing. Her roar shook my seat. Her worries had broken, and her relief left her in outward shout of happiness.

Me, on the other hand, my adrenaline had released, and I

felt my body sink back into my chair like a popsicle melting in the sun.

Edwards looked at Helen, shook his head, and then called in another officer.

"Show them to the room," he said.

We were assigned to one ship, the USS Snook. It had left Pearl Harbor on January 6th, 1944 and headed out toward the coast of the third biggest Japanese island, Kyushu. It was loaded with torpedoes armed to cripple some of the remaining Japanese armada, a blow that, if successful, could be one that could push us close to the end of the war in the Pacific Ocean. We had one responsibility: find the Japanese ships and sink them.

I deciphered the numbered codes and Helen scanned and translated what came across the airways. We worked twelve hours a day for the next twenty-three days while the USS Snook crossed the Pacific toward Japan. We sifted through code after code and found that a Japanese gunship had planned to move across the Pacific Ocean off the coast of the Bonin Islands.

With each ship that the Snook sunk, Colonel Edwards came into our office, poured us a glass of champagne, and sat with us, only speaking to list the ships names that the Snook had sunk. He didn't say we sunk them. He didn't reveal what happened. He sat down. He said names of ships. He toasted us. Then he left. He gave us no information that would put his career or ours in danger.

By January 23rd, we were exhausted. It had been nearly three weeks since we started plotting the path of the USS Snook. We had taken her across the Pacific and into the theater, and on the 23rd, we led her to the coast of the Bonin Islands. She sat there waiting, just like we radioed the captain for her to do. We gave him the coordinates of the Magane Maru, a 3,120-ton gunboat.

30°06′N 141°19′E

That was where we found her. We worked on breaking her code for two of those three weeks with no real goddamned guarantee that we could, at all. We would lose the entire god-damned thread of numbers and letters. Then start the damn thing again.

We followed the Japanese lines. Once we were able to record a set of transmissions after standing and twisting and turning knobs over and over again and again, we got the codes, found the "begin here" code that the US had cracked earlier that year and then the "end here" code. The room was hotter than the crack between a baboon's ass, and our faces looked just as red.

30°06′N 141°19′E

We sent the code to the USS Snook. Then we waited.

By the end of the day, we got the news. It sunk the Magane Maru. The gun boat heading out to kill more of our men.

When we got home that night, right before I took a shower, I pulled out John's letter, and I kissed the words. I thought about him out there in the Snook, floating next to that gunship, sitting under the water cooking for the captain. I wanted to hug him. I wanted to show him love. I ached to meet him in Hawaii. I'd never been anywhere tropical. The humid air of Washington, DC, didn't fucking count. But who knew when this would all be over. I couldn't tell him that I would meet him. I didn't want to give him hope. I had signed away any freedom until the war was over. I could be in Arlington breaking codes long after his deployment ended.

I loved him.

I read the letter in the bathroom and cried that night for the first time since I found out that Ernie had been killed in the war. I got in the shower to wash away layers of dried and wet and dried-again sweat, the salt stinging my eyes, and to wash away the tears.

When I got out, Helen sat on the toilet. I didn't hear her come in. I didn't see her come in, the palms of my hands covering my eyes to push back the tears and worry. She handed me a towel. She let me dry off, and then she said.

"Della, goddamnit!"

"What?" I said.

I moved the towel across my face to dry my eyes and then wrapped it around my body.

"John is on the Snook. Damnit, Della, you should have told me," she said. "We need to get off this assignment. You need to tell Edwards. We can't do this. What if we fuck up, Della? Can you live with that?"

She was serious. Really serious.

I dried my body, and with one slick move, I grabbed the letter that she had lifted from the counter and obviously read.

"I can't live with someone else trying to save John's life. Not now. I was able to do it before we were assigned to the goddamned Snook, rationalizing that they weren't in danger, but now that I know where they are, I can't leave it up to anyone else," I said.

I wanted to slap her for reading my letter, but, instead, I knelt down next to her, placed my head on her knees and said, "And I need you too, Helen."

She placed her hands on my wet hair.

"Vodka. Vodka is what we need," she said.

Chapter Fifty-Two

John
1944

NOAKES AND I AND A FEW OTHER GUYS LOADED THE TORPE-does into the barrel using those damn ropes and pulleys. I'd never sweated so much in my life. Noakes locked them in tight because he was the tallest and strongest, but I could clinch the barrels closed faster than anyone else.

We wanted more control like the gunner had, but we were happy to be doing a real part in breaking apart the Japanese fleet. When we heard the sound of the torpedo speed out of the barrel, the cheers of our shipmates above us, and the announcement that we sunk another ship, it felt amazing, like we had somehow reached out a long arm, tapped the Japanese Navy on the shoulder, and slugged it hard in the face. That's what we were doing out there, crippling the Japanese Army by taking away its supplies.

It was all scary, being out there in the middle of the Pacific Ocean with a whole navy of ships looking to sink you because your submarine had sliced and diced them in the open water.

By this time, talks about ending the war had already begun. The allies had started marching on Berlin, and Hitler had retreated, so there were already places in the open sea that had been deemed demilitarized, places we weren't supposed to be. But we were there, sitting off the coast of Japan in early January, as deep as we could be under the ocean's current. The moon sat two worlds above us. There was the underworld where we lived most our days, and the upper world where we got to stand in the ocean breeze, a place where our feet had nearly forgotten how the steady earth felt beneath them. And then there was the night sky. Sometimes we would surface and get to climb up on the long flat top of the submarine and look at the stars in the middle of the ocean. To me, it felt like those nights back in Trinidad with my dad and Manuel and Maria picking chiles and praying. After my parents died, it would be nearly ten years before I felt that warmth again. I felt moments of it before Maria left and before Manuel went to war, but those moments were fleeting and broken up by my grandfather's rages. I finally felt that warmth again when Della and I spent that night together, but that too was ripped away from me, so when I looked at the stars in the middle of the ocean, I had to forget so much loss to remember glimpses of love.

On February 23rd, we hit a goldmine. The captain led us into the deep water of the Pacific, and we dove until the dark of the water eclipsed the light of the sun. We dove under an eleven-ship convoy. We knew that if we could knock out this convoy that we would win a major battle at sea. The captain, somehow, knew exactly where the convoy was. He led us through and around them all.

Noakes and I fired three torpedoes early on. They sunk three ships out of the thirteen. We celebrated quietly in our metal home, a wall of cold, dark sea around us. We had gotten damn good at our job. We loved to cook. We loved to make people happy, but we sure loved sinking ships too. There were rumors that some really smart men had been hired to decode the Japanese naval codes and those men had been relaying coordinates to our captains out at sea.

Someday, I said to Noakes, if we ever get to meet those men, I was going to hug them and thank them for helping us out. There was a rumor that they had hired women to decode the messages, but all we could do was laugh at that notion. They would crack under the pressure.

We shot those three torpedoes, sank three ships, and then we dove to hide for a while and attack the rest.

"Women breaking codes. Hah!" everyone laughed, from the cooks to the enginemen to us.

Chapter Fifty-Three

Della
1944

I HAD NEVER BEEN SO EXCITED AND SCARED AND WORRIED IN my whole goddamned life. We barely slept. When we got to go home at night, we didn't go out. We opened beers and sat by the heater and watched the people walk by outside our window. We clinked our bottles and never said a word about what we had done that day. We didn't have to. We lived it together.

I felt like I was the USS Snook, angling through the waters.

31°05′N, 127°37′E

On February 23rd we led the sub under the bellies of an eleven-ship Japanese convoy and screamed with joy when we heard the Snook had downed three of those ships with quick hits from only three tornado shots to the metal ribs of the boat's torso.

"Della, Helen, get in here," Captain Edwards screamed to us from his office. We'd huddled around the bombe machine, twisting and turning knobs to decode even more codes, to hopefully set up the Snook to win the goddamned Medal of Honor.

"Yes, sir," I said.

"The Snook lost its engine," Captain Edwards said. "If they can get it going again, we need to point them away from the convoy. If they can't, they will die out there, either by surfacing and releasing their air and getting shot by gunships or by staying put and getting blown out of the water by…"

"The three Japanese submarines that joined the convoy yesterday," Helen said. She had broken that code the night before when we had headed home.

I couldn't goddamned speak. I couldn't do anything.

"Della?" the captain said. "Are you alright? If we lose the

Snook, it won't be your fault. It's an engine problem not an intelligence problem. You will not be blamed. We will assign you another ship."

"Della, let's go to work. All we can do is plot a course for them to get out of there if they do get the engine going," Helen said.

Chapter Fifty-Four

John
1944

THE SHIP SAT QUIET UNDER THE WATER. WE WERE THERE SOLELY for reconnaissance. The captain, again, had known exactly where to be, but we were sitting blind and motionless because we couldn't power up without being detected. We waited for twenty-six hours, just watching the coming and going of Japanese ships.

After sitting for so long, our barrels loaded, the captain, his sixth sense piquing, turned the ship and moved us slowly back out to sea behind a Japanese war gun boat that headed east toward the United States western coast and Hawaii. We followed the war sub for forty miles into the deep water. We locked the torpedoes in and then we fired them, missing the submarine completely. We loaded more torpedoes.

We tried again. And we missed again. At that point, the submarine had to know exactly where we were. It had to be either sprinting away from us or turning around to return fire. Our engine fired up to move, but then, as if a giant switch had been turned, the submarine engine fell silent except for giant thud that reverberated through the tiny hallways. The metal tube creaked in the water. We stopped moving completely. The engine had failed.

Noakes stared at me. And I stared back at him. We both knew that this might be the end of it all.

"I wish I could have seen Della one more time," I whispered, making the entire possibility that we might die any second real, our bodies exploding and floating out into the ocean like fleshy shrapnel for the fish to eat.

"We're not dead yet," Noakes said. He gave me a hug. "We're still breathing, John."

We could hear the engine of the other submarine through the thick metal casing of our own. The water vibrated around us.

I shook Noake's hand. He squeezed mine tightly.

"Could go for some mole with hot chiles right now," he said.

"I could really go for some shrimp and rice," I said.

The whizzing sound of torpedoes zooming past the boat sent a chill down the sweat of my back.

"Fire two torpedoes," the captain said over the intercom. "Fire now! At twelve o'clock."

We went to work. Noakes lifted a torpedo with the pulley and shoved it in the giant barrel. He lifted the second one while I cinched down the metal door behind it. Then we let them fly. If we missed, there was no way we were going home. An explosive crash of the torpedoes slamming against metal reverberated back and shook the Snook hard. Another crash shook us again. We took the brunt of the aftershocks, but cheers rang from above us.

"Get to the engine room, Noakes and Cordova. Fix the engine!" the captain shouted. There was no time for us to celebrate. We sat under three other ships. They could sink us easily. We ran.

Chapter Fifty-Five

Della
1944

LIKE UNRAVELLING A MAZE FROM THE INNER LINE, WE WORKED backward through codes to find a way out for the Snook, if they ever got their engine started again. We looked at the last few days of codes for all the ships we knew were in the Japanese convoy and broke down where they came from, when they arrived, and where they might be at the exact moment we found out that the USS Snook sat in the middle of the ocean, lifeless with a target on them.

There were hundreds of codes. Helen laid out all the ones she had deciphered over the last twenty-four hours, and I laid out all the ones that I had broken. We listed the names of thirteen ships, consisting of passenger ships, cruises, submarines, and gunners.

"Son of a bitch," I whispered.

Helen rolled out the map of the area in front of me. She placed her hand on my back.

"If this were me, what would you tell me to do, Della?" Helen asked.

"I'd tell you to plot your goddamned ships because if you didn't, there would be slim to no chance that they'd make it out of there alive," I said.

"Yep, now plot your goddamned ships," she said.

I picked up my marker, and I began to plot, starting with the Lima Maru at 31°05′N, 127°37′E.

Chapter Fifty-Six

John
1944

We left our post, ran through the narrow corridors, and dropped down the ladder into the engine room. It felt like we had dropped into hell, the heat of the place searing our skin.

Noakes opened the door to a wave of scorching air, and the smell of gasoline smacked hard against our faces. The whole room had been clouded with steam and smoke. We could barely see. I grabbed Noakes' hand. He grabbed mine. We led each other through the winding pipes and gears that created a maze of hot, hot metal. The whole engine had overheated and came to the grinding halt that left us marooned in the ocean among ten Japanese boats that still looked for us in the depths.

An engineman lay across the ground. Another lay on an exposed duct, barely conscious.

"One of the piston rings broke and stopped removing exhaust," the man groaned. "We need to get a new ring on and get the crankshaft moving again before we suffocate." He pointed toward the trunk-style crankshaft and pistons behind Noakes. We had spent a year learning every part of the boat. Every submarine man had to. But it had been a while.

The engineman passed out. I turned to Noakes. We ran to the closet in the engine room. We found the reserve piston rings. That would be the easy part. We had to get the shell that wrapped the crankshaft off, replace the ring, and start it all up again before we inhaled too much exhaust or got blown out of the water.

We both wrapped our arms around the shell, squeezing and tugging at it together. When we got it open, we found that the piston ring had broken on the farthest ring from us. Normally, we could easily slide across the top of the whole thing, replace the ring with a wrench the size of an arm, and then get on our way. It was protocol to do so every time we left shore, but everything in that room had gotten so damn hot that the path to the piston was lit up red like the Devil's altar.

"I'll go," I said. "I'm smaller than you. Less surface contact."

"That doesn't make any damn sense, John," Noakes said.

I jumped up on the top of the cylinder and slid across the top of it on my gut. I lay down, and with a big tug, I ripped the piston ring off. I could smell the sear of my skin while I felt it melt the flesh around my belly.

"Give me the ring," I said to Noakes.

He handed it to me.

I cranked it back on.

"Pull me back," I said.

Noakes grabbed my legs and pulled me back across the hot metal.

He steadied me on my feet next to the engine, and I looked down to see my shirt had melted into my skin. On the top of the cylinder, a long thin piece of shirt and flesh sizzled on the top of the engine. Pain ran through me like I had never felt before. A button had lodged itself inside my burnt flesh and then melted.

There was a time that I wished I never surfaced from the bottom of the Truckee River. I had lain there and waited for the water to flow into my lungs and for my world to end so that I didn't have to live in a world without my family or Della or the Chavezes or live in a world with my grandfather. But death never came. I always floated to the top and took a deep breath.

Down there in the Snook, under the water, I did not want to die in the depths of the ocean. I didn't want to let others die. I wanted to float up to the top and eventually take a deep breath and live in a world where I knew Della was happy somewhere, in a world where I had shed my grandfather's hatred of me, and in a world where I could breathe deep, fresh air again, so I ignored the searing of my belly that ran from my waste to my nipple and waved to Noakes to fire it up.

Noakes looked at me and shook his head. Then he hit the button to start the whole crankshaft up. It worked. The room began to clear of exhaust, and the purr of the engine woke the ship up from its deep sleep.

We carried the other two men out of the engine room. The flesh from the left side of my belly sizzled and smoked on the engine behind us.

Chapter Fifty-Seven

Della
1944

TWO COOKS.

Two cooks saved the ship. That's the news we heard from Edwards. Two cooks put the engine back together and saved the ship.

I knew one cook on the USS Snook. I knew it was John. I could see him there. Quiet. Brave. Withstanding the pressure. That would be John. Standing up to what came his way. That would be John.

I was proud of him.

"Now, let's get them the coordinates to get out of there," Edwards said.

We handed them to him.

"And, on the way out, they could hit the Lima Maru," I said, doing my best to deliver the message without sounding like the Snook was any different from any other ship we delivered coordinates and information to.

"Yes, yes, good, thank you, Della and Helen," he said.

We were dismissed. We went back to our desks and acted like it we had just broken any code from any general assignment, and we waited, again, to hear about the fate of the Snook. The information I had handed to Captain Edwards put John in danger again. I knew that. But it was my job, the one that I swore and would goddamned swear again to do. And I had to goddamned do it.

I also had to live with not knowing if I sent John on a mission that he would not come back from, but to be honest, I knew that if anyone saved him, I saved him.

Chapter Fifty-Eight

John
1944

"Noakes, Cordova, back to your post," the XO said. We received pat after pat after pat on the back and cheers from every sailor we passed on the way back to our post, but we were still in deep, deep shit. Now, two submarines flanked us. They knew exactly where we were.

Out of nowhere, our captain announced that we were going to dive. The submarine dove deeper than it had ever been asked to dive before. We could feel the whole boat rattle and turn.

We sat in the water, our ship quiet in the water, the sweat dry on our clothes and the air stiff from so much time without us moving through it. We waited. It's crazy down there. Everyone remained completely quiet, as if the boats could hear us talking. At any moment, a submarine could approach from any angle and blow us out of the water. Our sweat evaporated in the heat by the torpedoes. Some boys prayed. Some kissed the charms they had brought with them. We were somewhere our government would never admit to us being if we sunk. We were in the middle of a dying war.

"Fire, Noakes," the captain told us over the intercom. Once we fired, the enemy would know exactly where we were and would fire back. We had to hit our target. Though Noakes and I had no control over the guidance of the torpedoes, it was our duty to load them correctly. If we didn't, their projection and aim would falter. It was all on us. We knew it.

We fired a torpedo, one aimed to go almost directly up. From the silence, the rush of the torpedo sounded like a hurricane when it cut through the water. We waited. We prayed.

The explosion above us shook our submarine. But it wasn't over. There were four boats up there, and we would not know what we hit until we surfaced.

We loaded another torpedo, our arms shaking from exhaustion.

Another explosion.

At any moment, we could be blown out of the water, but we shoved a third torpedo into the hole, and we fired again. Then two more times.

Two more hits.

Another hit, this time directly east.

The captain moved the boat back and forth. We did this four more times, and then we surfaced.

There it was, the Lima Maru. It was split in two, sinking. Men jumped overboard and tried to swim, but the carrier drowned, and its three thousand soldiers drowned with it, the eleventh largest ship to be sunk in the entire war, a slice of metal in the even bigger ocean. I thought about those men for a minute, but then realized it was a soldier like one of them that killed Ernie and Manuel.

The whole submarine cheered. We opened the hatch and stood on the top of the boat. The Japanese convoy had been reduced to giant pieces of metal that littered the sea.

Though I knew the war was not done with me, I was done with the war.

Chapter Fifty-Nine

Della
1944

EDWARDS WALKED INTO OUR WORKROOM THAT AFTERNOON and held out a telegram. The message had come from the Snook's captain over the wire.

Helen and I read the letter from the captain, confirming the Snook's safety and conveying his thanks. That day, we watched the clock until our shift ended, exhausted from our brains to our toes, and when our time was done, we packed up our things and headed back to our apartment.

I had sweated through the armpits of my shirt so goddamned bad that I just tossed it in the garbage can next to the toilet when I took off my clothes to shower. I stood in the water for ten minutes, letting the warmth of it encircle me. I cried. Something had broken inside of me, and, this time, I let it all out.

The Snook was safe, and I was overwhelmingly relieved, but I wanted to so badly to know if John was safe, too.

I got out of the shower and dressed. Helen had opened the bottle of vodka. We would not be called back to work for three days on Colonel Edwards's assurance, and we got drunk and laughed and sang, "We are heroes too."

AND THEN, WITHIN JUST A few short months, the military complex didn't need us anymore. It was 1945, the seas of codes had dried up, and the Allies were winning on all fronts. The Japanese had all but surrendered the Pacific.

Colonel Edwards called all of the coders into the auditorium to release them from their duty. Overall, it was a shitty day that everyone knew was coming. His assistant asked Helen and me to wait outside the auditorium until we were called, so we did, sitting in our desks across from each other and only half smiling.

When his assistant finally called for me and Helen to enter the auditorium, we walked in, sat down in two creaky, wooden chairs at the front of the auditorium. The air stood still but a mix of sweat and ten different kinds of perfumes lingered around us, the mist of hundreds of women's presence still floating in the musty air of the empty auditorium.

Edwards stood up from a table on the stage, straightened his jacket, and then walked down the short flight of stairs to the auditorium floor. He stopped in the middle of the wooden edge in front us, leaned back on it, and wrapped his arms across his chest.

"You two are troublemakers," he said. "Loose lips still sink ships. Remember that you will remain under oath until instructed by the United States of America that you are no longer under oath." His lips tightened up and his arms squeezed his chest even tighter like he wanted to put himself in a goddamned straight jacket.

We stood, thinking that was it. He wanted to lecture us one more time. I wanted to tell him to shove his lecture straight up his adulterous ass, but when I began to open my mouth, he gave us the universal sign to sit down, waving his hand palm down toward the seats.

"Thank you for your service. The USS Snook will dock in Honolulu in three days," he said. I wanted to ask him how he knew. How did he know that the boy that I grew up with, the boy I had fallen in love with, the boy I had ignored for two years because I had to was on that ship? But before I could, he stood up, walked away, and repeated, "Loose lips, sink ships."

We stood up, tried one last time to not laugh at Edwards and his loose lips, and we walked out of the auditorium, through the stuffy, hot hallways, through the doors and building and out into Arlington.

Helen and I decided to treat the evening like a big event. We started the evening in out apartment with martinis and Manhattans. The sun dropped down early, hiding behind the apartment buildings to the west of us, but remnants of natural light shone through the window, breaking through the creases of the buildings, and highlighting the dust in the air. It felt magical to sit there and watch the dust, as if we were watching the world breathe.

"I miss the tall buildings. DC is nice, but it's no New York City. Want to come with me, Della?" she'd asked so many times. "We could rent an apartment together and teach."

"That sounds nice," I'd say, but I wanted to see something different. I wanted to see the waters we protected. I wanted to see the Pacific Ocean. With Helen's father paying for our rent over the last two years, I had saved up a lot of cash, and I dreamed of visiting the ocean. I dreamed of John there too. I knew the USS Snook was docking. I knew that I had to go see him, even if he didn't forgive me for my cold, cruel letter.

That night, we found the nicest seafood restaurant in DC. I ordered the lobster. Helen ordered a steak, and we drank champagne.

"I'll miss you, Helen," I told her.

"I'll miss you too, Della," she said.

We drank and laughed. This part of our lives had ended, and another would begin. Just like the special moment in her apartment a couple years back—when we drank beer and sat without our blouses next to the fan—I knew that our last night in DC was special too, that we would never be able to relive it, to relive our lives the way we lived then. I would never have another friend like her.

By that time, I have to be honest, I was ready to be done with work. No more sweaty rooms. No more silence. No more keeping Edwards' secrets. I had helped win the war. I had saved John's submarine, and I was ready to see the Pacific. Instead of using my one ticket the military promised me to go back to Colorado, I used it to take me to Hawaii. Helen packed her bags and went home to New York City. We hugged a thousand more times, and then we said goodbye, promising that we would find a way to see each other every year of our lives until we died.

Two days later, after my flight across the Pacific, I stood and waited for the busses to come to the city. Waikiki beach was alive. It breathed in and out, so different from Colorado. Colorado's breath is quiet and crisp and thin in the high mountains, but its taste on the tongue before it hits the lungs is full from the earth's high crust and the animals that wander it. The breath of Waikiki and Honolulu moves thick and moist through the city, inhaling the sea air into the city and exhaling back out into the ocean. Sailors flow into alleyways and do not come back out. Locals walk among them like fish circling freely at the edges of a current that doesn't know they are there. The ocean runs right up to the city, and sandy edges of the island, the link between a world that grows upward and world that lays out flat forever.

I waited for the busses. I had my favorite white dress on. It was linen and light. It moved with me when I turned to look at the waves for a moment, and then back with my body when I swayed to see if the busses had come. When the breezes from the water blew by me, my hair, like my dress flowed along the edges of my skin, and I wished I could save that moment forever because right then I believed that John would get off the bus there instead of getting off a bus at the airport miles away on his way back to Nevada. I prayed that he would do what he said he would, that he would wait for me in Hawaii, even though I told him I would not come. He would listen to why I decided to cut him off and that he would forgive me. I wanted to capture that moment of hope in the breath of the sea.

Two busses pulled up. Green and ugly and worn down like every other military bus I saw driving around Arlington and Hawaii. Young sailors, salivating at the goddamn chance to get drunk and laid, fell out of the bus like trash being emptied from a bin. I looked for John, but when the first bus' door closed, my hope was cut in half because he did not get off. I imagined him getting off another bus, one miles away at the airport, his gear over his shoulder and his face painted with that infuriatingly quiet sincerity that always covered it. Lips straight. Brows cinched. Eyes forward. Like he couldn't smile just to goddamned smile.

The doubt and the worry got to me. I didn't want to be that woman who stood and waited alone for a man to never come, to keep standing there and staring at the last bus as it drove away like some idiota in love with a man who never loved her back. No one I knew would see me standing there and think this, but someone would. Someone, even if it were the damned bus driver who had probably seen hundreds of pregnant, young Hawaiian girls waiting there for men to return, standing there crying because they didn't, either because they died at sea or boarded the other bus to fly home to their white high-school sweethearts. I looked at my dark skin, my black hair, the contrast between it and my white dress. I could easily pass for one of those poor girls, heartbroken and lost, and this memory would beat the living hell out of me, so before the second bus opened its door, I ran fifty feet away and sat down on a bench near the edge of the beach, crossed my legs, placed my hands in my lap, and acted like I was just enjoying the breath of Waikiki.

A second bus drove up, and a short, dark man with John's exact build exited first. He walked down the stairs, placing each foot down with purpose, and then turned and saluted a bunch of sailors as they rushed out and on toward the city. He stood there as the bus pulled away. He brought his hand down to his side and shoved it up under his shirt and just stood there rubbing his belly. And his goddamned face wore that goddamned sincerity. This time, however, I didn't want to slap it. This time, I cried tears of relief and happiness and hope. He pulled his hand out of his shirt and turned to walk away, and for the first time in our lives, I followed him down the road instead of him following me.

Chapter Sixty

John
1945

IN 1945, I STEPPED OFF THE USS SNOOK, AFTER WHAT WOULD become one of the most famous submarine tours in World War II history. We landed in Pearl Harbor, and my time was up. I carried my seabag on my back, walked toward the busses that were taking many of us from Pearl Harbor to the airport to fly home. Noakes told me I was always welcome in Chicago. He gave me a slug on the arm and walked away and took the bus to Waikiki with all the soldiers on leave, just like I had done with Noakes on those brief weekends we had away from the Snook over the previous three years.

The bus was full of giddy young men. The war was over, and even though they would no longer have to fight in the Pacific, they would have to return to the boats and head back out on patrol beneath the water or on the large decks of giant war ships. I could smell their excitement to get drunk and get laid. Their freedom wafted through the air in mists of cologne and deodorant starch that all could have been rung out from their clothes and their skin and their slicked-back hair.

The bus stopped in Waikiki, and I got off first. I saluted them all as they ran past me on their way to the bars, and I said goodbye to the USS Snook, the war, and my youth, forgiving everyone in that long moment that no one was a part of but me.

I touched the large, scorched scar on my belly and knew that I had no reason to be angry anymore, and I thanked my God, the God of my mother's prayers for saving me out in the middle of the ocean so that I could stand there and wave goodbye to my life on the boat and, even more than that, to my childhood, to the loss of my family, and to my broken heart.

Running my hand up and down the leathery swaths of skin, my forever trophy for what Noakes and I did that day to save our submarine, I forgave my father for buying the car that drove them to their deaths. I never knew I was so angry with him for this until that day next to the bus. I forgave Maria for leaving me and Manuel for dying. I forgave my grandfather for the pain he gave me, filling my life of up with loneliness and fear, for the broken bones and for stealing me away from Della in Trinidad when I ran to her. I didn't need the anger anymore. The burn from the engine had given me a second life.

And then I forgave Della for saying no, for being cold and forgave her for how it broke my heart into something that I no longer recognized, and I realized that what she gave me—hope—throughout all those years at my grandfather's home along the Truckee River had saved me from even more pain, and while I walked the rows of my chile garden, it was her face that made me smile. Her face when we were children. Her face when we grew to into our early teens. Her face that I saw in the window when I ran to her. And it was her face, placed so close to mine in my memory from our one night together, that gave me the hope and courage to pull my searing skin across the engine and live to walk out again into the fresh air. I loved her still, but I forgave her. I moved my hand from my deep, wavy scar to my heart, and I thanked her for my life.

With the war behind me and my honorable discharge papers in my seabag, I no longer wanted—or more honestly—needed what these sailors needed. I was not going back under the water in the tunnel of a large piece of metal. I didn't really know what I needed that day, so when I got off the bus in Waikiki, I got a room, threw my bags on the bed, went shopping for some new clothes, and found a bar on the beach that served fresh seafood for cheap. The whole Pacific lay out there in front of me. I'd spent nearly four years living in it, and I never wanted to go back down under again. I was done. Done with cramped rooms. Done with the smell of the latrine. Done with being bossed around every second of my day. Done.

I sat in the sun and ate seafood and watched the ocean. The waves lapped up against the land. In the boat, we really never felt the water around us. We could only feel the slight sensation of being pulled through when our engines turned on. There on my stool next to the water, I watched every wave, the swell of each one and then the crest and then the break and crash. I had given up on ever seeing Della again, her long, black hair and smile that had always been made up of half laughter and half deviousness. I ached for her in a way that felt full and empty at the same time.

I turned to wave at the bartender for another drink, the taste of beer and salt on my lips. Beyond the bar, a dark, beautiful woman walked up the beach, asked for a table, and sat down only ten or so feet from me and ordered a martini.

"All we have is beer and rum," the bartender said.

"I'll have a beer, thank you," she said.

She turned toward me, walked over to my table, placed her hands on mine, shook her head at me. "Goddammit, John," she said. She raised her glass. "To Manuel and Ernie."

She was beautiful. She had come.

Chapter Sixty-One

Della and John
1946

AT ONE POINT IN THE NIGHT HER FEET TOUCHED HIS. SHE pulled her body close to his chest and whispered in his ear. He lay still except for the up and down of his chest. Then she rubbed her hand slowly across the scar that ran from his chest to his waist, a swath of chewed flesh.

They had spent a year in Waikiki. They didn't leave each other's arms—not by the beach, not in their tiny apartment that looked out over the water from the hillside Della ran up after their first and only argument. Who knows what they fought about, but when she ran back down the hill, her silhouette framed in the green flash of the Hawaiian sunset, the fight had died, and they laughed about her running up there with all of the lizards. They didn't leave each other's arms, and, at night, when they lay in bed, exhausted from a day at the edges of the ocean, they told each other everything, except for the one thing Della had promised the US military that she would never tell a soul, and this secret ate at her every single, goddamned day.

That one night when her feet touched his, when she ran her hand up and down the scar that John had so proudly earned and displayed on the beach, young children pointing at it and embarrassing their parents, she leaned into him in, the moonlight shining on his young, dark face. She whispered, "I wasn't a secretary, John. I was a code breaker. I saved the USS Snook. I was the one who broke the codes, who guided the ship through the ocean."

John turned his head to her and kissed her black hair and moved it across her forehead and kissed her skin. She moved closer to him, wrapping her body around his, and he squeezed her in his arms. The moon moved across the sky. They lay there awake together until the sun rose in the window frame.

Epilogue

JOHN STOOD ON THE SIDE OF THE ROAD WHERE HIS PARENTS had been killed by the angry rain. A small boy held his hand. The mountains stretched out in front of them, the shallow basin rising slowly into the face of the Sangre de Christo whose rocky cliffs climbed into Colorado's blue sky. The boy squeezed John's hand when his father began to walk the both of them down into the gully that ran along the edge of the road. The wetted grasses of late spring smelled so rich that the boy plugged his nose with his other hand.

"It always smells like asshole around here this time of year," Della yelled. She followed the two of them down into the gully. Her black hair had been pulled back into a ponytail, just like her mother's had always been, and blended into her black dress. Della's lips were painted a pale red, and her eyes matched them, the remnants of a day of crying.

"I hate the smell of wet grass in the spring," she said to her son who held his father's hand and to her daughter who ran off into the field around them. She carried a shovel and three clay pots in her hand. John was quiet, as usual, not saying much, and his little boy mimicked his father, half smiling in the sunlight.

The boy let go of his father's hand and waved his mother and sister down toward them.

John knelt down and dug his hands deep into the wet dirt in the bottom of the gully.

"This is where they died, Ernie and Manuela," he said. "They were so kind. You would have loved them, and they would have loved you. If I have one great sadness, it's that they never got to meet you both. You would have made your grandpa laugh and your grandma smile and place her hand on your head and pray for your well-being every other minute because I know she would have loved you so very much. That is my one great sadness."

Della walked down into the gully and knelt next to John and the children.

"Shovel," she said. "Let's get this done. I hate the smell of wet grass in the spring. Assholes. It smells like assholes."

He took it from her hands and dug up three pots full of dirt, soil melded together by the roots of the grasses that began at the road's edge and stretched across the valley of the Sangre de Cristo.

"It's big," Ernie said. "The mountain is so big." He pointed to the glowing face of the mountainside. Trees ran up it until the bald summit above the tree line touched the sky.

"Sangre de Cristo," John said.

"Sangre," Manuela repeated.

On the other side of the valley, alone in a cemetery made for two outside Della's childhood home, the little family stood next to a freshly made mound of dirt. Della placed the pots of dirt and grasses on the ground next to her mother's freshly dug and filled grave.

"Shovel," she said. "Let's get this done. We don't have all day to sit out her and cry and feel bad for ourselves and all that crap."

John shoveled a hole in the dirt mound. He leaned down and kissed his children's heads one at a time while Della placed the wild grasses from the foot of Sangre de Cristo into the hole. Her black dress had become covered in the wet detritus of the earth where John's parents had died when she knelt down in dirt earlier that day to say goodbye to them. There, at her own parent's gravesite, she fell to her knees and said a quiet goodbye to her mother and father.

"Shovel, goddamnit," she said.

John used the shovel to smooth the dirt around the mounds of soil and grass they added to the gravesite. He patted the earth down to make sure the roots would survive the wind and rain of early spring along the high plains. When he was done, Della grabbed Manuela's hand. John grabbed Ernie's, and they turned them away from Benita and Francisco's grave to let the wild grasses grow.

Acknowledgments

I am profoundly grateful for the people who helped bring *Let the Wild Grasses Grow* to the page. This book would not exist without the belief, labor, and editorial vision of my agent, and friend, Elizabeth Copps: thank you for the long discussions about plot, character, and theme, but, mostly, thank you for believing in it from the very first—and very different—draft and helping me mine out the real heart of the story. I'm grateful to all the people at Torrey House Press who brought such love and engagement to the birth of this book: Kirsten Johanna Allen, Anne Terashima, Kathleen Metcalf, Michelle Wentling, and Rachel Buck-Cockayne.

Thank you to Liza Mundy, whose book *Code Girls* served as such a wonderful reference to the lives and careers of such brave and intelligent women during WWII.

To my dad: thank you for the endless stories about life in the US Navy and aboard submarines. They inspired me to bring them to life on the page as a mix of your anecdotes and research. All my love to you.

And thank you to my wife and son for always putting up with me. Love you.

Author's Note

To my grandma and grandpa Cordova, the inspiration for Della and John. I wish you were here to see this book come to be. I think you would have "goddamned" loved it. Thank you for everything you gave to me: wit, laughter, and love (and the freshest tortillas known to humanity). In the epilogue, John says this to his son about his parents, and they are the exact words I say to my son when he asks about you: "They were so kind. You would have loved them, and they would have loved you (they would think you are so funny and smart). If I have one great sadness, it's that they never got to meet you."

About the Author

Kase Johnstun lives and writes in Ogden, Utah. Author of *Beyond the Grip of Craniosynostosis* and coeditor of *Utah Reflections: Stories from the Wasatch Front*, his essay collections have been named finalist for the Autumn House Press Awards (2013, 2020) and the C&R Press Awards (2020). His essays can be found in literary journals, trade magazines, and online zines, nationally and internationally. He is the host of The LITerally Podcast, a podcast devoted to sharing the successes of other writers. Johnstun is a graduate of Weber State University, Kansas State University, and Pacific University, where he received his MFA in Creative Writing. A Utah native, Johnstun can be found running the trails along of the Wasatch Front.

Torrey House Press is supported by Back of Beyond Books, the King's English Bookshop, Maria's Bookshop, the Jeffrey S. and Helen H. Cardon Foundation, the Sam and Diane Stewart Family Foundation, the Barker Foundation, Diana Allison, Klaus Bielefeldt, Laurie Hilyer, Shelby Tisdale, Kirtly Parker Jones, Robert Aagard and Camille Bailey Aagard, Kif Augustine Adams and Stirling Adams, Rose Chilcoat and Mark Franklin, Jerome Cooney and Laura Storjohann, Linc Cornell and Lois Cornell, Susan Cushman and Charlie Quimby, the Utah Division of Arts & Museums, Utah Humanities, the National Endowment for the Humanities, the National Endowment for the Arts, and Salt Lake County Zoo, Arts & Parks. Our thanks to individual donors, members, and the Torrey House Press board of directors for their valued support.

JOIN THE TORREY HOUSE PRESS family and give today at www.torreyhouse.org/give.